MURDER

Some of us were starting on our second lobsters when Ted stood, spilling his plate of food onto the beach. Another toast? But he wasn't holding his glass. He tried to say something, but he sputtered. He couldn't talk.

We all stopped. What was wrong? He pointed at his lips, and throat. Then his face and one of his arms started twitching. Jeremy and Abbie jumped up. Abbie put her arm around her father, and Jeremy held his arm.

"Are you choking? Do you need something to drink?"

Ted kept trying to talk, but only gurgles came out of his mouth.

"Who has a phone? Call 911!" I shouted.

Books by Lea Wait

TWISTED THREADS

THREADS OF EVIDENCE

THREAD AND GONE

DANGLING BY A THREAD

TIGHTENING THE THREADS

Published by Kensington Publishing Corporation

TIGHTENING THE THREADS

Lea Wait

KENSINGTON PUBLISHING CORP.
http://www.kensingtonbooks.com

KENSINGTON BOOKS are published by

Kensington Publishing Corp.
119 West 40th Street
New York, NY 10018

All Kensington Titles, Imprints, and Distributed Lines are
available at special quantity discounts for bulk purchases
for sales promotions, premiums, fund-raising, and educational or institutional use. Special book excerpts or cus-
tomized printings can also be created to fit specific needs.
For details, write or phone the office of the Kensington
special sales manager: Kensington Publishing Corp.,
119 West 40th Street, New York, NY 10018, attn: Special
Sales Department, Phone: 1-800-221-2647.

Kensington and the K logo Reg. U.S. Pat & TM Off.

ISBN-13: 978-1-4967-0628-7
ISBN-10: 1-4967-0628-5
First Kensington Mass Market Edition: April 2017

eISBN-13: 978-1-4967-0629-4
eISBN-10: 1-4967-0629-3
First Kensington Electronic Edition: April 2017

10 9 8 7 6 5 4 3 2 1

Printed in the United States of America

33614080187254

Chapter One

"Jesus permit thy gracious name to stand.
As the first efforts of an infant's hand
And while her fingers o'er this canvas move
Engage her tender heart to seek thy love."

—"Wrought" by Lucy Ann Babcock, age
    eleven, in 1831. Lucy lived in Augusta,
    Maine. Her sampler is now in the
    Maine State Museum.

Haven Harbor's streets and yards were littered with green leaves that had fallen too soon.

During the ten years I'd lived in the almost perpetually neutral shades of Arizona I'd missed seeing Maine hills glowing with gold and scarlet and orange in late September.

But the only bright color in Haven Harbor this late afternoon was a blood-red sumac bush near the patisserie. I paused, admiring its brilliance. Was it poison sumac? I should ask Dave Percy. He was the Mainely

Needlepointer who knew poisons. Poison or not, the bush was gorgeous.

And right now Dave was busy, teaching at the high school during the day and resting his leg at home in the evening. Arrow wounds don't heal quickly.

Besides, I was looking forward to a "girls' night." Just Sarah Byrne and me and a little needlepointing. She was an expert. I wasn't, but I was learning.

I stepped around puddles and cracks in the uneven pavement. ("Step on a crack! Break your mother's back!") Memories of skipping rope and drawing patterns for hopscotch on these pavements took me back twenty years, to serious competitions between friends for neighborhood rope competition bragging rights. I'd practiced hours in my driveway, determined to be the best. In private, I hardly ever missed. In public, I'd been good—but never the best. Never the prettiest. Never the smartest.

After a while I'd given up trying.

I hadn't skipped rope since sixth grade. Now I was twenty-seven. All grown up. Or so I kept telling myself.

I had no desire to relive my childhood, although, like now, memories haunted me.

Sarah's apartment on Main Street above her antiques store wasn't far from my home. She'd promised homemade pizza and time to talk. My contribution was a cold six-pack of Sam Adams. We hadn't had a quiet evening together in weeks. Summers in Maine were busy.

Twilight shaded the harbor as I knocked on Sarah's door.

"Come on in!" she called.

I opened her door and caught my breath. "Where did that come from?" I blurted, as I handed Sarah the six-pack. I stared at her wall.

"It was a gift," she said quietly, putting four of the beer bottles in her refrigerator and handing me one.

The painting was immense—or seemed so in Sarah's small apartment. The canvas was four or five feet long and maybe four feet high. I don't know much about art, but this seascape of pounding surf below the lighthouse standing guard over our harbor was special. I moved closer, drawn to the scene. An un-expected spot of red, a lobsterman's buoy, was barely visible, caught in the waves.

"When? Who?" I asked. "It's amazing." I looked around. "And how did you get it up the stairs and into the apartment?"

Sarah laughed. The streaks of blue and pink in her white hair glinted in the overhead spotlight focused on the painting.

"Practical Angie! You're right. Getting it in here wasn't easy. Jeremy Quill and Patrick West helped me. Jeremy installed the spot, too. Said no painting should be hung without proper lighting." She grinned, and added lines from an Emily Dickinson poem. "'Edifice of Ocean Thy tumultuous Rooms Suit me at a venture Better than the Tombs,'" Sarah might be Australian, but she was also a big Emily fan.

Poetry wasn't my thing. "Who's Jeremy Quill?" I asked. I knew Patrick West, the artist son of actress Skye West. The guy I was—sort of—dating. "And how did Patrick get involved?"

"Jeremy works for Ted Lawrence, over at the gallery. Has for years. Patrick's working there now, too."

Why hadn't Patrick told me he'd taken a job?

Sarah saw my expression. "Patrick's only been at the gallery since Labor Day. Ted suggested it would be good for him to get out of his house a couple of days a week and work with art, since his burned hands aren't ready to paint yet. He's helping out Fridays and Saturdays, when they're busiest."

I'd met Ted Lawrence. Tall, elegant, owner of a high-end art gallery down the street here in Haven Harbor, and another at his home outside of town. I'd heard about the prices of his art and been too intimidated to venture into the gallery. Sarah had become friends with him over the past months. He was more than twice her age, and she'd sworn it wasn't a romantic relationship, but she'd been spending a lot of time with him, at the gallery and at his home. I figured sometime she'd explain. So far she hadn't.

"It's spectacular," I said, turning to face the painting. "Mesmerizing. I can almost smell the sea and feel the winds. Did Ted paint it?"

Sarah hesitated. "No. His father did. Robert Lawrence."

That stopped me. Even I'd heard about Robert Lawrence. *The* Robert Lawrence. One of the finest painters of the twentieth century. People came to Haven Harbor just to see where he'd lived. His work was in collections and museums all over the United States. Maybe the world.

"I love it," Sarah continued, looking at the painting. "It's too big for my apartment, but maybe someday I'll have a better space for it. In the meantime I'll admire it up close."

"But a Robert Lawrence—it must be worth thousands!" I looked from Sarah to the painting and back again.

"Hundreds of thousands," she said softly. "Or maybe millions. His work has been going high in auctions recently."

I sank into Sarah's flowered couch. Her apartment was furnished comfortably with secondhand furniture she'd bought at Maine auctions while she was looking for antiques for her shop, From Here and There. The Lawrence painting was from a totally different world.

"It was a gift?" I asked again, incredulously.

"From Ted. He gave it to me a couple of weeks ago. I've been dying to show it to you, but we've both been busy."

"He gave you a painting that might be worth a million dollars?" Ted Lawrence was an artist himself. I could have understood his giving one of his own paintings to a friend. But this one? "Why?"

"Because I liked it," said Sarah.

"Just because you liked it?" I said incredulously.

"And because Robert Lawrence was my grandfather."

Chapter Two

"Honor blest the Maid whom circling years improve
Her God the object of her warmest love
Whose useful hours successive as they glide
The book, the needle and the pen divide."

—Worked in 1805 by Ruth Sewall, age eight,
in York, Maine, in silk thread over linen.
Ruth was the youngest of six sisters. Her
mother died the year she completed this
work. When Ruth was nineteen she married
Captain Brown Thornton of Saco, Maine,
who was forty-seven. After he died she
married Dr. Jeremiah Putnam of York;
they had two children.

"Robert Lawrence was your grandfather? Haven
Harbor's Robert Lawrence?" I couldn't get my head
around my Australian friend now claiming Maine
roots.

She nodded, flushing.

"But . . . how?" And then I realized. "Then Ted Lawrence is your—uncle?"

"Yes."

I started laughing. "If you knew how many people in town wondered about your relationship, about why you two've been spending so much time together. Everyone's assumed you two were . . . an item."

Sarah smiled self-consciously and looked down. "We are, I guess. Just not the sort of item people imagined."

"Why haven't you told anyone? Why didn't you tell me?"

"I'm telling you now," she said, looking straight at me. "I'll tell you everything. But you have to keep it a secret. Don't even tell Charlotte."

Not tell my own grandmother? "Why is it a secret?"

"Because Ted hasn't told his children yet. They should know first."

My mind was still confused. "How can Ted Lawrence be your uncle?"

"It's a long story."

"Then put that pizza in the oven, and start talking, Sarah."

She grinned. "Will do."

I followed her to the small kitchen connected to her living room, glancing every few minutes at the painting that dominated the space. "I've always wondered how you happened to end up here in Maine."

Sarah sprinkled her dough with several cheeses and seasonings and added artichoke hearts, black olives, sliced scallions, and crumbled bacon. "These toppings okay?" she asked.

"Better than fine," I said, peeking over her shoulder at the pizza-in-progress. "Of course, we're going to die because of that bacon."

"Then we'll die happy," she pronounced. "I have enough dough for another pie if we finish this one. The second will be cheeses and wild mushrooms." She slid the pizza into her oven. "About fifteen minutes, I'd say. Let's sit."

I'd seen spectacular sunsets from Sarah's windows on other evenings. But today's gray day had turned to night. The only bright colors I could see were in the Robert Lawrence painting. "So, talk."

She settled into the blue-cushioned armchair across from me and sipped her beer. "You knew your mother. You have your grandmother. Your Haven Harbor roots are deep. Roots that can hold you strong when storms hit. That's what I've longed for all my life. Roots."

I let her talk.

"I've heard you, and others here in Maine, talk about your families in terms of generations. I grew up knowing almost nothing about anyone related to me, at least on my father's side."

"You didn't ask him?"

"He didn't know anything about his family. The not knowing haunted him." Sarah took another sip.

"He must have at least known who his parents were," I pointed out. Although, I immediately thought, I didn't know who *my* father was. I didn't even know if my mother had known who he was. Without thinking, I reached up and touched the gold angel I wore on a chain around my neck. The angel Mama had bought me for my first communion. The last gift she'd given me.

Sarah got up to check the oven. "I told you, it's a long story." She sliced the pizza and put it on a platter on the low table between us.

For a few minutes we ate in silence. Then I took the

needlepoint canvas of a great cormorant I'd been working on out of my bag. Might as well stitch as I listened.

She began again. "My father was born in the UK. He thought probably he was from England, not Scotland or Ireland or Wales, because older people teased him and the others about their accents."

"'The others'?"

"When he was about seven—he didn't know his exact age—he and dozens of other children were put on a ship and sent to Australia."

"'Sent'? By whom?"

Sarah put up her hand. "Just listen. My father didn't live long enough to tell me his story. But he told my mother's mum, and she told me, when I was old enough to understand. All the children were told they were orphans. That there was no place for them in the UK, so they were being sent to a place where they'd be welcome, where it would be warm, where they'd go to school and have loving new families." Sarah paused to put down her beer. "It was a lie from the start. No adults paid attention to them, even on the ship. They took care of themselves. When they arrived in Australia they were divided into groups. My dad went with several other boys to a place in West Australia run by an order of monks. Grandmum said whenever he told that part of the story his voice hardened. There was no school there, and no love. The boys, those who came before him, and his group, and others later, were forced to build a monastery, stone by stone. They were flogged and abused in despicable ways, and never had enough to eat." She paused, staring at the painting. "Some died."

"That's horrible! No one did anything about it?"

Sarah shook her head. "If anyone knew, they didn't

interfere. Dad left that place when he was seventeen. But he never really escaped. He did marry my mother, and for a while, I was told, he was happy. But she died—breast cancer, it was—when I was still in nappies. Dad got very depressed, and drank too much— I guess he'd always done that. When I was two he hung himself." Sarah's voice was steady, but her hands were shaking.

I sat, listening in horror. Should I hug Sarah, or scream? "That's awful," I said, knowing words were totally inadequate. "What happened to you?"

"I was lucky," she said. "My mum's mother, my grandmum, took me in and raised me. She's the one taught me needlepoint." She pointed at a framed needlepoint map of Australia hung over her television. "She gave that to me on my eighteenth birthday. Told me I should be proud to be an Aussie. Taught me about her side of my family. They'd left Ireland during the potato famine in the 1840s, and opened a small used clothing and furniture store in Australia. More than a hundred years later, Grandmum was still running the family business, but it had changed over the years. She was an antiques dealer. I grew up learning how to value what our ancestors had treasured in the past, doing my sums in back of the counter, and learning how to be polite to customers."

No wonder Sarah now ran a small antiques business here in Haven Harbor.

"When I was six, in 1987, the whole story broke. Dad had died before then, of course. I grew up knowing at least a little about the scandal."

"The scandal?"

"Between 1938 and 1970 social welfare people in the UK sent about ten thousand children abroad. The foster system in the UK was overburdened, and the children were sent to former British colonies like Canada and Rhodesia and New Zealand—and Australia. The idea was that those countries could use cheap labor and, some said, wanted to increase their white populations. Some of the children—they called them the child migrants—had been abandoned in Britain. Some had been born out of wedlock. Many had one or even two parents who couldn't care for them temporarily. Some were as young as three; most, like my dad, were between the ages of seven and ten. Still young enough not to remember a lot, or to question that they were orphans. But most of them had living relatives."

"Didn't those relatives ask questions?"

"That's one of the saddest parts. They were told their children had died in foster care."

I put my needlepoint down and took a sip of beer. "That's awful! And no one knew?"

"Not until several child migrants who'd been sent to Australia went back to Britain as adults to try to find out who they were. In 1987 Margaret Humphreys, a social worker in Nottinghamshire, met with them and started putting the pieces together. Her search ended up as an international investigation."

"She was able to prove what happened?"

"She was. I was still a child when it all broke, but Grandmum, bless her, knew it was important. She registered me as the child of one of the migrants. The idea was to try to connect the children, now grown, of course, or their children, with family members who might still be alive in the UK. A trust was set up to help make that happen. A few years ago the British government finally apologized for the program."

"A little late for that," I pointed out. "So what did you do?"

"When I was growing up I knew my dad had been one of the child migrants, but I didn't think much about it, and I didn't want Grandmum to think I didn't appreciate her bringing me up. I was happy, helping her with the store. Then when I was twenty-five Grandmum died."

I shuddered. What would my life be like without Gram? I didn't want to think about it.

"I decided I wanted to know about my father's background. Find out whether I had family in the UK. So I applied to the Family Restoration Fund." She paused. "It took two years before they were able to help me."

"And did they find your family?"

Sarah nodded. "They found Dad's mother. Of course, she was an old woman by that time. Grandmum had left me a little money, and I sold her store and its contents, so I could afford to do whatever I needed to do. The Fund helped me get to England to see my other grandmother."

We'd stopped drinking or eating. I focused on Sarah.

What if I'd been separated from Gram? She'd raised me after Mama disappeared, the way Sarah's grandmum had raised her. But what if there'd been another woman I'd been related to? A woman in another country? Would I have traveled around the world to find her?

Sarah's voice was taut. "Meeting my English grandmother wasn't easy. She was almost ninety, and she'd had a hard life. Her sight and hearing were going. She was living in a home for the destitute elderly. At first she didn't understand who I was. After all, she'd been told her son had died years and years before." Sarah picked up her beer and took several swallows. "She had a picture of him, though. He was with her at a park, on a swing. Dad would have treasured that. He didn't have any pictures of his mother, or of himself as a child." Sarah got up. "Would you like to see it?"

"I'd love to."

When she returned from her bedroom she handed me a small framed black and white photograph. It was out of focus, but the smiles on the little boy and his mother were clear.

"I couldn't change my grandmother's life, but I wanted to know more about her, and about how my dad ended up in the foster system."

"It must have been very hard. Being in a new country, talking to an old woman about events seventy years ago."

"I kept thinking my dad would have wanted me to be there, with his mom. Getting to know her a little."

"Did she tell you what happened?"

"She told me she'd been a teenager during the Second World War. Poor. She'd met an American soldier stationed near London. He was an artist, working with the British Army, sketching, documenting the war in England."

"Sounds like a romantic movie."

"It does. And, at least at first, they were happy. The times were awful, but they shared them. He even asked her to marry him. But then she found out he was already engaged to a woman back in the States, and she broke off the relationship."

"So no happy ending."

"No. And by that time she was pregnant."

"Did she tell him?"

Sarah nodded. "He even sent money for a few years. Money for his son. But postwar England was hard for an uneducated woman with a child but no husband. She told me that when her son was five she was desperate. She'd lost her waitressing job and couldn't pay for her flat. Her little boy was hungry, so she gave him to the social services ladies. They promised it would be a temporary placement. Her son would be cared for while she saved enough to start over."

"Did she ever see him again?"

"Once or twice. Then one day when she arrived at the children's home where he'd been living he was gone. They told her there'd been a measles epidemic. They were sorry. He'd died."

"How awful for both of them! And she never married?"

"No. She wrote to Bob—that's what she called him—and told him their son was dead."

Sarah's hands were clenched. "She wouldn't tell me what she did after that. I don't think she had a good life. At the nursing home they said she'd been a charwoman until she was too old and weak to work anymore."

"So sad."

"I was furious," Sarah said, getting up and striding from one side of the room to the other as though she'd like to hit someone. "This poor woman—my grandmother!—had lived a horrible life, and even lost her son, all because she'd fallen in love. If only I'd known sooner, I might have been able to make her last years a little easier. But I hadn't known." She turned to me. "She died a month after I met her."

"At least she died knowing she had a granddaughter."

"Yes."

"And she gave you the picture."

"Her nurse did, after she died. I'd been my grand-mother's only visitor. She gave me the photo, and several letters my grandmother had kept."

"Letters?" I leaned forward.

"They were crumpled and faded and hard to read. But they were from a man named Bob. She'd kept them all those years. They were postmarked 'Haven Harbor, Maine.'"

"Did she know her Bob had become rich and famous?"

"All she knew was he was an artist," Sarah said. "When she knew him, that's what he was. An aspiring artist. That's all I knew about him then, too. But after she'd died and I'd seen the letters, I decided to go to Haven Harbor. I knew he'd been here in the early nineteen fifties. He could have left long ago. But it was a clue. After all, I'd already traveled from Australia to England. Flying across the pond was simple. I wanted to find my grandfather, wherever he was, and tell him what had happened to my grandmother and to his son." Sarah paused. "Tell him he had a granddaughter."

"That's why you came here."

Sarah nodded. "I got here about five years ago, checked into one of the B and Bs, and asked my host-ess if she'd heard of a Bob Lawrence. She laughed—said everyone knew who Robert Lawrence was. But I'd missed him. He'd died fifteen years before."

"You must have been so disappointed."

"I went to the library and looked up his biography. Dozens of books and magazine articles had been written about him and his art. I read everything I could find, but none of them mentioned my grandmother, or anything about that period in his life except that he'd served in the armed forces in England during World War Two. After he came home he married and he and his wife—probably the American fiancée—had a son, Theodore. Ted. By the late nineteen-sixties his paintings had become famous."

"Did you tell Ted Lawrence who you were?"

"I couldn't just walk in and announce that I was the daughter of his father's illegitimate son born at the end of World War II. The only proof I had was the picture of my father. And a story. And the letters, of course. But I'd found out what I wanted to know: who my father was, and where he'd come from." She smiled. "And I'd fallen in love with this town, and its people. I'd cut my ties to Australia. I kept thinking that Haven Harbor was where my family was from. I didn't think it was important that Ted Lawrence knew I was his niece. What was important was that I knew who my family was. Who I was."

I nodded slowly. "I think I understand."

"Then I met your gram at church. I knew I wanted to stay here, but I didn't know how I could support myself and become part of the community. I told Charlotte about my grandmum and her business, and she encouraged me to use what I knew about antiques and the money I had left to start my own business. Antiques are popular in Maine. And when she expanded the Mainely Needlepointers I was one of the first to volunteer to help. Doing needlepoint made me feel closer to my grandmum in Australia. Somehow it brought the two threads of my family together. I was—content."

"How did Ted Lawrence find out who you were, then?"

"That's the next part of the story," said Sarah. "Maybe the strangest part. Shall I put together the other pizza?"

Chapter Three

"Children, farewell, your sleep is sweet,
Yet still the silent tear will flow
'Tis well you were not doomed to meet
Life's chequered scenes of care and woe."

—An elaborate family register surrounded
by roses. A list of family members, many
of whom had already died, enhanced by
a painted scene of a large home and a
weeping willow, created by Janet Carruthers.
Janet was born in Scotland in 1809. She and
her family (her father was a minister)
arrived in America in 1813.

Sarah picked up the empty platter that had held the
first pizza she'd made. We must have finished it. I'd
been so focused on her story I hadn't noticed. But the
lingering taste of oregano and cheese reminded me
that we'd met to have dinner as well as talk.

"More. Yes," I agreed.

She moved to the kitchen. I watched her quickly stretch the dough into a quirky circle on a pizza stone and cover it with a light layer of tomato sauce, several handfuls of grated cheeses, and sliced mushrooms.

Neither of us said anything until the pie was in the oven and she'd returned with another beer for each of us.

As the pizza baked, she continued her story.

"I'd gotten to know Ted Lawrence a little," she said. "After all, his gallery is just down the street. I'd gone in a few times to see the paintings and I went to openings before the Chamber of Commerce suggested all Haven Harbor stores should stay open late on Thursday Art Walk nights, and I had to be at my store. I'd asked about his father's paintings. My grandfather's paintings, of course, although he didn't know that. He told me about the hours each day his father had spent in his studio. That his paintings were based on real places, but their colors and shapes and energy were the way he saw them in his mind. He'd called more realistic paintings 'postcard art.'" Sarah smiled. "Ted said his father taught him to see the world through shades and forms and emotion. But he knew his paintings would never be as great as his father's."

"Does he—Ted—still paint?"

"Not as much as he used to. He's spent his life ensuring that his father's work won't be forgotten. Although his gallery here on Main Street shows a dozen other artists, the private gallery at his home is devoted to his father's work. He says he's too old and tired to focus on his own painting. His father's legacy is his work."

What if Sarah had known her grandfather? Would he have taught her to paint too, as he had his son?

Would she be an artist today instead of a dealer in antiques?

My thought was interrupted by the beeping of the oven timer. As Sarah went to get the second pizza, I stared at her Robert Lawrence painting. I knew he'd based it on the Haven Harbor Light. But the closer I looked at it, the more I realized the lighthouse had never looked the way he'd painted it. His lighthouse was a swirl of shades of white and gray, as though winds were surrounding the building, above the force of the breakers arching toward the ledges below it, daring ships to approach.

Sarah's pizza was delicious. No wonder we'd finished her first pie so quickly. "When did you tell Ted?" I asked. "Tell him his father was also your grandfather."

"After you came back to Haven Harbor in May," Sarah said, "I started thinking about families again. Charlotte—your gram—welcoming you home, and you searching for the truth about your mother reminded me of my grandmum, and my searching for my dad's family. For *my* family. That's when I decided to tell Ted."

"So you told him 'way back in May? Four months ago?"

"Not until early July. Late one afternoon I went to his gallery. I told myself I was going to look at the paintings, but really I was getting up enough courage to talk with him. He isn't at the gallery all the time; Jeremy takes care of most of the customers. But that afternoon they were both there. Ted and I were talking about the paintings as usual, and then, suddenly, he suggested I come back to his home to see his other, private gallery, where he kept his father's work, including pieces he owned that he didn't plan to sell. It was where he took his best customers."

"The ones who could afford his father's work."

"Some of them, of course. But also people he thought would understand the paintings. Would appreciate them. Jeremy told me later than many of the guests invited to The Point, the Lawrence home, were artists themselves, looking for direction. Ted thought his father's work might help them to find their passion."

"And so you went to The Point," I said, wanting Sarah to hurry. To tell me less about the art and more about her family.

"I did. That day was the first time I saw this painting." She gestured at the lighthouse. "And he showed me many more. And even, after a while, some of his own work." She took a sip of beer. "Ted didn't paint the way his father had hoped, or the way he'd aspired to paint. But I liked his work. His paintings were quieter than Robert's, more delicate. They had a different sensibility."

"And?"

"We drank wine, and ate shrimp he defrosted, and he asked the question you've wondered about: Why did I come to Maine? How did I end up in Haven Harbor? I told him my story, the way I've told you today. At first I didn't tell him that my dad's father was his father. But then he guessed."

"He guessed?"

"He told me to wait. Then he went to a small room between the main house and the gallery, and rummaged through a lot of paintings and sketches. He was gone maybe twenty minutes before he came back with a small painting. I knew immediately it was a portrait of my grandmother. She was young and her hair was curled up and under, the way women did it in the forties. She looked the way she had in the photograph of her and my father."

"What did he say?"

"He told me that after his father died he'd inventoried all the work that was left. A lot of pieces had been done years before; his father hadn't wanted them exhibited or sold, but kept them for sentimental reasons, or to remind him of techniques he'd used years before. Ted found the portrait among those. At first he didn't think anything about it. It was dated 1944 and he knew his father had been in England then. He'd found other sketches of England, too. But no other portraits." Sarah threw her head back a little, as though remembering. "Ted also found several letters from England that his father had saved. One of them included a picture of a young boy, maybe two years old."

"So Ted knew!"

"He suspected his father had an affair when he was overseas, and there had been a child. But that's all he knew. He had no proof. No return address. And by that time both his parents were dead; he had no one to ask. But he saved everything. He said he hoped someday the mystery would be solved."

"And it was. You solved it."

"He had no doubts." Sarah's smile was wide. "He welcomed me, the way I'd dreamed he would. Said he'd always wanted a brother, and wished he'd known my father. Said my eyes were like his father's."

"How incredible. You must have been walking on air."

"I was. Haven Harbor had seemed like home from

the beginning, you understand. But now I had a family. An uncle!"

"How could you have kept it a secret for so long? I'd have wanted to shout it to the heavens!"

"That first night, that's exactly how I felt! Ted got out old books of photographs and started introducing me to my family. It was all so amazing. I couldn't keep all the stories straight, and we laughed . . . but even that first night we both realized there might be a problem."

"A problem?"

"Ted has three children. None of them are artists, or are involved with his business, or live in Haven Harbor. He hardly ever sees them. But Ted's house alone must be worth a fortune. His father's paintings certainly are. And here I'd just arrived and we'd decided I was a member of the family. A member no one had known about. Ted immediately said I should share his father's estate. That I was Robert's grand-daughter, and that was only fair."

"Wow! You'd be rich!"

Sarah shook her head. "I told him I wasn't inter-ested in the money. I had a life. A business. A cat. Ruggles is hiding under the bed, by the way. I'd been looking for a family. For connections to the past. Not for an inheritance."

"And he said?"

"He insisted. He said I was blood, and my father and I hadn't had what he and his children had grown up assuming was their due. That he was going to change his will no matter what I said."

"But let me guess—he wasn't sure that his children would want to share with you."

"Exactly. Plus Robert Lawrence is famous. What I

knew about his life, even if it was a short episode, was an unknown chapter. A scandalous one. If people found out I was his granddaughter, they'd want to know all the details. Ted's children—my cousins—wouldn't be the only ones questioning someone appearing out of nowhere and declaring they were related to one of America's most famous artists."

"You could have DNA tests," I suggested.

"At first we didn't want to do that. Ted said he believed me, and the tests would take an amazing story and turn it into a clinical analysis. I said it was up to him. But after a while we both realized that for other people, for legal reasons, we needed more proof than old letters and an untitled painting. So we went ahead and had the DNA tests, Angie. Robert Lawrence was definitely my grandfather, and Ted Lawrence is my uncle."

"So when are you going to tell people?"

"Very soon. That's why I'm telling you now. Ted's invited his children to his seventy-fifth birthday party. He's going to introduce me. Tell them who I am." Sarah looked at me. "I don't know what's going to happen, Angie. His children have their own, very different, lives. How will they react to having a new cousin? You met Ted at the Wests' home last month."

I nodded.

"He liked you, and he knows you and I are good friends. I asked him if you could be at the birthday party, too."

"Me?"

"Angie, I'm really nervous. All my life I've wanted to be part of a family. Now, at least biologically, I have one. I love being Ted's niece. He hasn't been feeling well in the past month, and I've loved being able to help him a little. But after all these years, I've just found him. I don't want to lose him, the way I lost my grandmother in England. Now I'm afraid the joy of finding my uncle will be lost if his children reject me. I'm scared. I don't want to face them by myself. Please, Angie. Be my friend. Come to my uncle's seventy-fifth birthday party with me."

Chapter Four

"While education cultivates the mind,
  May sacred virtue lead to joys refined."

—Verse stitched (in addition to three
  alphabets) by Mary Rhodes of
  Southampton, Long Island, New York,
  in 1806. Mary was eleven years old, and
  her work was done predominantly in
  cross-stitch and queen-stitch.

Ted Lawrence's seventy-fifth birthday party turned out
to be a birthday weekend. His children, Sarah explained, lived too far away for the event to be just an
evening, or even just a day. I reluctantly volunteered
to help her prepare Ted's house for the event, and
his gallery employees, Patrick and Jeremy, were also
recruited to prepare for the big day.

An early fall nor'easter had taken down one of the
oldest maples in my backyard that week, the maple I'd
built a tree house in when I was nine. The tree house

I'd escaped to after Mama disappeared and I didn't even want to talk to Gram.

The tree house was long gone, but I mourned that tree, and the memories it had held. And as a practical issue, I had to cut up the branches and trunk and get the wood out of the yard and into the woodpile. Plus, to add to my tasks as a new homeowner, the maple had fallen on top of the old stone wall separating my home from my neighbors'. Granite doesn't crumble, but a few of the stones had now cracked, either from the blow of the tree's falling, or from water that had filled and frozen in openings decades before and, given the right pressure, now had split them. Dozens of rocks that a few days ago had been carefully balanced and settled in the wall were now covering part of my yard.

I'd made a start on cutting up the tree, beginning with the smaller branches, using the chain saw Reverend Tom, now my step-grandfather, loaned me. I'd decided to rebuild the wall myself. After all, my ancestors had built it to begin with. I was up for the challenge. Not to mention it would be a lot less expensive than hiring someone to do it for me.

My neighbors had left early for their winter home in Florida. I had time. I'd been looking forward to starting on the wall. But how could I say I'd rather build a stone wall than help my best friend? The stones would be waiting for me after the birthday weekend.

Jeremy was going to close the downtown gallery early Friday afternoon in honor of the occasion, while the rest of us prepared The Point and its grounds. Ted didn't seem concerned about the details. He'd clearly turned them over to Sarah. I hadn't realized he was depending on her that much.

While she bustled about with lists and schedules,
Ted insisted the sixty-degree day was chilly and asked
Patrick and I to keep the wood box next to the living
room fireplace filled. As hours passed Ted sat quietly,
not saying anything, but occasionally throwing another
log onto the fire.

Sarah cornered me in the kitchen. "I'm worried,
Angie. Ted should be excited and looking forward to
his children arriving. But he's hardly said anything."

"Are you afraid he's getting cold feet about telling
his children about you?"

"I don't think so. But something's on his mind."

"He *is* seventy-five," I pointed out. "Maybe he's tired,
and resting up for the weekend."

"That's what he says. But he's changed over the past
few months. There's something he's not telling me."

"You're just nervous about the weekend," I cautioned. "You're hoping your cousins will love you and
be thrilled you've appeared, but you know they may
not be. You have to be prepared for anything, Sarah."

She nodded. "'When I hoped, I feared—Since I
hoped I dared.' That's what Emily wrote. I keep
hearing that line of hers over and over in my head."

"And you are daring," I said. "You've been incredi-
bly brave through everything—leaving Australia, finding your grandmother in England, coming here. . . ."

Sarah glanced into the hallway. "Shh! Patrick or
Jeremy might hear. Nobody knows but you and Ted
and me."

"Soon, Sarah. They'll all know soon. He's going to
tell everyone tonight, right?"

"That's the plan. With the champagne and before
the birthday cake."

"Only a few more hours to hold on, then," I said,

trying to be reassuring. "Now, what else can I do to help? If we keep busy the time will go faster."

"Would you mind putting clean sheets on the guest room beds? I dusted the rooms yesterday, but didn't have time to make the beds."

"No problem," I said, groaning inwardly. I hated making beds. "Which bedrooms?"

"All of them," she said. "Except Ted's, of course. We won't even go in there."

"But when you walked me through the house earlier today didn't you show me six bedrooms? I thought he had three children."

"He wants all the beds made," she said. "One room's supposed to be for me, but I don't want to stay here with the family. Even if they are technically my family, I don't know them. I want them to have time to talk with each other when I'm not here. Plus, I want to be able to escape, to go home and feed Ruggles and sleep in my own bed. I told Ted, but he insists I might change my mind. So three bedrooms for his children and their husbands, one for me—and an extra, I guess."

"Here're the orders from the patisserie," said a tall slender man, walking in and balancing a stack of boxes in his arms. "Sarah, you ordered bread for tonight, and pastries for breakfast, right? And the birthday cake." He put a large square box in the middle of the whitewashed kitchen table and turned to me. "You must be Sarah's friend, Angie Curtis." He held out his hand. "Jeremy Quill. I work for Ted down at the gallery."

His handshake was firm, his hand surprisingly smooth, and his tan slacks and pink oxford shirt, open several buttons at the top, fit perfectly. His thick wavy blond hair was immaculate, and he wore one small gold earring. He looked like someone who worked in a gallery. A perfectly arranged piece of art.

"Good to meet you," I answered. Sarah'd told me Jeremy had worked for Ted for at least ten years, maybe more. (*He once said Jeremy was like a son. A son who was interested in art.*) "The big weekend is about to start."

Jeremy glanced at his large gold watch. "And I need to get going. The New York City crew is due at the Jetport in a couple of hours, and I want to get a good parking space. Anything else you need done right now, Sarah?"

"Nothing; everything is on schedule. Thanks for stopping at the patisserie."

"Not a problem," said Jeremy.

"You're picking Ted's sons up?" I asked.

"Seemed the right thing to do. Ted said they could rent a car, but it seemed more personal for me to get them."

"Do you know them?" I asked. I didn't, of course, and neither did Sarah or Patrick. I'd wondered about Jeremy.

"I've met Luke and his husband," he said. "They came up for a few days several years go. Never met Michael or Abbie." Nothing in Jeremy's expression told me anything more than the facts.

"I'm looking forward to meeting them all," I said.

"It should be an interesting weekend," he said, raising his eyebrows a bit. "The gathering of the clan." He headed for the door. "I'm on my way. Should be back with the crowd by seven, Sarah."

"Great. Abbie and Silas are driving. They should be here by then too," she agreed.

Jeremy waved and left.

"Tell me again about the three of them," I said.

"Then I promise I'll do the beds." Maybe talking would help Sarah relax.

"It's not complicated," Sarah said. "Abbie's Ted's oldest, and only daughter. She and her husband, Silas Reed, are driving from Caribou."

"That's up in the County," I confirmed. (In Maine, "the County" always refers to Aroostook, the northernmost part of Maine.)

"Right. About a seven-hour drive, I think. They're "back-to-the-land" ers. Raise sheep and chickens and farm potatoes. Abbie teaches kindergarten. They'll be staying in the rose bedroom. It was Abbie's when she was growing up."

Ted's children had grown up in this house in Haven Harbor, as I'd grown up in the house I'd always thought of as home, and now was mine. Gram had hung photographs of Mama and me in almost every room of our house.

No photos were hanging here. You couldn't tell by walking through The Point that Ted even had children.

Sarah was continuing. "Luke's an investment banker. His husband, Harold, is an actor. They live in New York City. Michael's the youngest. He lives in New York City too, but from what Ted's said, I don't think he and Luke are close."

"So Luke and Abbie are both married. What about Michael?"

"All Ted told me was that Michael had a serious relationship with his bar bill at a Greenwich Village tavern. He's a poet. Had two poems published in a small quarterly several years ago, but none since. He's been a graduate student at NYU for ten years or so."

"How old is Michael?" I asked, incredulously.

"I don't know exactly. Ted said they're all older than me."

Sarah was thirty-three. I was baffled. Did Ted's children have anything in common other than their biological parents? Michael, the poet, was the closest to having an artistic gene. And from what both Jeremy and Sarah had implied, the three weren't close to either each other or their father.

I headed upstairs to make beds. Luke and Harold were assigned the large blue room in the front of the house called "the nursery." Clearly that name dated from a much earlier time.

Michael was to have the room next to his father's, over the kitchen, and down the hall from Abbie's.

That left the two unassigned bedrooms, the yellow room for Sarah and another room, pale blue with red accents.

No grandchildren, I thought, as I walked through the upstairs, checking that all was in order and up to Sarah's standards. *Ted has no grandchildren. At least not so far.*

Sarah had put fresh flowers in every room, even the unassigned bedrooms, and bowls of candy and fruit on each bureau.

I couldn't miss the spectacular quilt hanging in the yellow room. I'd admired it in Sarah's antique shop about a month ago. Ted must have bought it.

It was a "crazy quilt," pieced from different colors and shapes of velvets and velveteens. That would have been spectacular enough. But on almost every patch a different woman or girl had embroidered—some in cross-stitch, some in needlepoint, some in simple outline stitch, and others in a combination of stitches— what Sarah had decided were memories. Her research had indicated the quilt was most likely made as a wedding gift, perhaps for a young woman whose marriage would take her far from home. I'd been fascinated by the quilt the first time I'd seen it, and immediately went to look at it again. Ted had framed it carefully, to protect it. I looked for my favorite patches—a gull. A robin. Daffodils. A compass. A schooner. The North Star. Strawberries. A house, with an ell and a barn. A pine cone. A lighthouse. The ell pointed to Maine origins—few houses outside of early-nineteenth-century Maine had ells. And the lighthouse and schooner would only have been meaningful to someone whose roots were on the coast.

Each carefully stitched patch had also been initialed in now-faded ink. The quilt had been a treasure when it was made, perhaps a hundred and fifty years ago, and it was a treasure today.

Each patch told a story, now long forgotten. I wished, not for the first time, that the patches could talk. That there was a key to the meaning of the pictures.

Perhaps the bride had held that key in her heart.

I touched the nonreflective glass now covering the quilt. Its condition proved it had been treasured. I hoped its owner's life had been long and valued. Clearly her friendships had been.

Reluctantly I finished making the beds.

The upstairs looked perfect. More like a hotel than a family home.

I went back downstairs. When would Abbie and Silas arrive? I couldn't see anything else in the house that needed to be done. Patrick was dusting and vacuuming the private gallery and Sarah was conferring with Ted about something. I didn't interrupt them.

She'd been right when she'd told me this house and the land it stood on were valuable. The main house, designed so most rooms had views of the sea, opened to a wide porch overlooking the ocean and a gently sloping lawn that led down to a boathouse and dock and small sandy beach. (When I'd marveled at the sand, a feature not common on nearby rocky Maine beaches, Sarah told me her grandfather had created the beach fifty or more years ago, and Ted now replenished it regularly, after high winter tides and storms pulled the sand out to the north Atlantic.)

Two barns, one on each side, were connected to the main house by a series of small rooms that curved slightly inward, toward the ocean. The whole series of attached rooms and buildings was a *C* shape, protecting the porch and garden areas near the house from any winds not coming directly from the water. The gallery, which looked like a barn but was designed to display two levels of large paintings in a climate-controlled environment, was on one end. Next to it was additional space for storing paintings, and Ted's studio, which I suspected had once been his father's. On the other end of the house was a real barn, designed, not for horses or cows, but for several cars. It now held a small tractor and snowplow and a workbench that didn't appear to have been used for years. Camping and sports equipment hung on the walls and large cabinets held gardening supplies and smaller items. Unusual for such a large Maine complex, every room in every building was heated. And even the barn was immaculate.

Ted referred to the main house as his "cottage," the classic Maine word for a large vacation home. Perhaps at some point in the past his famous father had only used it seasonally.

I walked down to the gallery. Patrick had opened its wide doors to fall breezes.

"Hi!" I called out.

Patrick started; he must not have heard me coming. He turned quickly, dropping the broom he was using to sweep the polished pine floor.

Reddening with embarrassment, he picked up the broom. It wasn't easy. He still had trouble holding things.

"Hi! Did Sarah release you from chores?"

I grinned. "She's a bit uptight about this whole weekend."

"She shouldn't be. It's Ted's party. We're just friends helping out. As soon as his children arrive I assume they'll take over."

Patrick didn't know about Ted's announcement tonight. He didn't know why Sarah might be nervous.

"Looks like you've got the gallery in order."

"It wasn't hard. I'll admit I took as long as I could cleaning up the nonexistent dust. Just being in the same room with these paintings is an experience."

I hadn't looked around until then. "Are they all Robert Lawrence's work?"

"Most are. A few are Ted's, and he's even got a few Andrew Wyeths over on the back wall. From the inscriptions, I think Andrew gave them to Robert."

"Incredible. I hope he has this place insured."

"For sure. And there's a major security system. Although no insurance could replace what's in here. We're lucky just to be able to see this work up close. Most of Robert Lawrence's paintings are in museums or major private collections."

"I don't know much about art. But"—I turned slowly, looking around me—"even I can tell these paintings are amazing. Very different from yours, though. And I love your work."

"The work I did before the accident." Patrick winced

a little. "But I'm honored by your comparison." He bowed in my direction. "I'm not exactly in the same class as these guys."

"That painting in your living room is fantastic," I declared. "I love the colors and textures and . . . I just love it. I haven't got the right words to say why."

"I'll take 'love it.' And thank you." He looked out the wide doors toward the ocean. "I hope soon I can paint again." His tone was bitter, as he glanced at his deformed and scarred hands.

"You will. I'm sure of it."

He sighed. "I hope you're right. In the meantime I'm glad to be helping out at Ted's gallery downtown. In the past few weeks I've learned an incredible amount about what it means to be a gallerist. What has to be done to find excellent work, to market it—and, ultimately, to sell it. I'd always seen galleries from an artist's point of view. Ted and Jeremy have a very different perspective—one I really appreciate. Plus spending all day with different types of paintings has itself been educational. I can almost inhale the paintings hung there, and talking with possible customers makes me more conscious of what people are looking for when they're ready to purchase."

"Lighthouses and surf as souvenirs?" I guessed.

"Sure, that's what some customers look for. Nothing wrong with that. But Ted has other work in the gallery, too. Different artists. Different styles. What amazes me are the people who come into the gallery looking for, say, an eight-foot-long painting—because they have an eight-foot couch."

"I'd never have guessed that."

"It's true; believe me. In any case, the paintings in this gallery aren't for over couches."

I walked over to admire one of a sunrise over the ocean. At least, that's what I thought it was. The colors were stunning, as they merged with each other into glorious shades of pink and white and orange. How much would a painting like that cost? "I don't see any price tags."

"Not one," he agreed. "As they say, if you have to ask, you can't afford it."

"How *is* your own painting coming?"

Patrick glanced down self-consciously at his hands. "I'm still healing, they say. I started a couple of canvasses, but they didn't turn out the way I'd hoped. I don't have the control over my fingers—or my brushes—that I used to take for granted. But working at the gallery gets me out of the house, and talking and thinking about art. It's tiring—I'm still not as strong as I like to think I am. But it's a good transition until I can paint again." He winked at me. "Only one problem."

"Oh?"

"It leaves Bette alone a lot of the time."

Bette was Patrick's kitten, my Trixi's sister. We'd adopted our housemates in August.

"How's she coping?"

"I suspect sleeping most of the time. Although sometimes I come home and find a drawer pulled open a bit, or cat toys blocking the front door."

"Sounds normal to me! Trixi's decided the bottom drawer of my file cabinet makes a great bed. I'm just afraid someday she'll get stuck in there. Kittens!"

"And I haven't had a chance to invite any friends over to have dinner with me recently, either," he continued. "I'm now allowed to drive, so maybe I could find a pretty lady to go restaurant exploring with me in October, when the gallery business slows down a bit."

"Sounds possible." I smiled back. "I could probably think of someone who'd like to do that. Especially if a gentleman artist were to invite her."

"Hold that thought for a few days," he said. "Right now I'm focusing on this weekend." He opened an almost-invisible door in the wall and put the broom away in a closet. "So tonight we'll celebrate Ted's birthday. Do you know the schedule for tomorrow? Ted said he wanted Jeremy and me to be around, available."

"I don't know what's scheduled for Saturday morning or early afternoon, if anything. Later in the afternoon Sarah said he planned to have a lobster bake down on the beach. I guess that's something his family did a lot when the children were growing up."

"I suspect Jeremy and I will be assigned to buying lobsters and clams then," said Patrick.

"You sound very knowledgeable about lobster bakes," I teased. He'd been to his first bake just weeks before. That one had been catered.

"I'm a fast learner," he agreed.

"I'll be dispatched to the farmer's market for fresh corn and potatoes," I guessed.

"Makes sense. Besides, you can't come to the coast of Maine from New York City and not have lobster. Even the County isn't the best place for fresh seafood."

He *was* learning fast. *The County*, eh? Pretty good for someone who'd just moved to Maine a few months before.

Sarah stood in the doorway, looking at both of us. "I can't stay still," she blurted. She glanced at Patrick.

"Ted just told me he has *several* important things to say tonight," she said, looking at me. "And that he's bought a few fireworks to set off on the beach tomorrow, after the lobster bake. I'm just hoping we don't have any unexpected explosions tonight."

Chapter Five

> *"On Earth let my example shine*
> *And when I leave this state*
> *May heaven receive this soul of mine*
> *To bliss divinely great."*

—Sampler decorated with flowers in vases and
a blooming tree, made by eleven-year-old
Sally Martin Brown in silk thread on linen
in Marblehead, Massachusetts, about 1800.

Patrick held up his hand. "I hear a car. Or is that a truck?"

"Abbie and Silas!" Sarah turned and raced through the connecting rooms toward the main house.

"I guess Ted's birthday weekend has officially started," said Patrick.

"Might as well go meet the guests," I agreed.

"They can wait a minute." Patrick looked into my eyes, and moved toward me. As his arms surrounded me, my mind filled with a kaleidoscope of images.

The first time he'd kissed me. The feel of his body next to mine. The hope that he wouldn't let go.

But then he did.

"I couldn't wait any longer. I've been wanting to do that ever since I got back from Boston," he said, his lips touching my hair.

I reached up and kissed him, gently. And then not as gently.

Then I stepped back. "Sarah will wonder why we haven't joined her."

"I wasn't thinking about Sarah." He looked down at me and kissed my forehead. "But you're right. Let's go." He put his hand lightly on my back as we walked through the connecting rooms toward the main house.

All I could think about was turning around and kissing him again.

But I didn't. Not now.

In the living room Ted was awkwardly hugging a plump middle-aged woman whose hair and makeup were immaculately arranged, but whose hands were chaffed and red.

"Abbie, thank you for coming," said Ted. "And Silas, too. It means a lot."

Silas, a huge bear of a man, complete with black beard, worn jeans, and a flannel shirt, nodded in response. "We made good time. Leaves haven't turned so far. No leaf-peepers on the turnpike."

"Can I get you something to eat? Or drink?" Sarah said. She stood in the hallway between the living room and kitchen. I assumed she'd already been introduced.

"No need," said Silas. "We stopped at the Micky D's right outside town. We're set for the moment. Although

I could always do with a beer, if you've got any. Or some Bradley's with milk would taste real good."

Maine's favorite drink: Bradley's Coffee Flavored Brandy. Fishermen added it to their hot coffee and teenagers snuck it into milkshakes. I hadn't thought of it in years.

"I'll get you something," said Sarah, turning toward the kitchen.

"Good-lookin' housekeeper you've got," Silas added to Ted.

"Sarah's not my housekeeper. She's my . . . friend," said Ted. "I invited a couple of friends to help out this weekend. Those other two young folks in the hallway there are Angie Curtis and Patrick West. Com'on in. Meet my daughter, Abbie, and her husband, Silas."

"Nice to meet you," said Abbie. Then she turned to her father. "I thought this was going to be a family gathering."

"These folks are my Haven Harbor family now," said Ted firmly. "I can't run both galleries and the house by myself anymore. These three friends, and Jeremy, keep my life in order."

He'd exaggerated my relationship to the group, but hey. It was his family, and his birthday.

"Jeremy? That strange fellow who used to work for you is still around?" said Abbie.

"He's not strange, and yes. Jeremy's been with me almost fifteen years now. Couldn't run the gallery without him. You'd know that, Abbie, if you visited more often."

"We got crops to get out, Ted," said Silas. "And this time of year Abbie's busy with her teaching as well as the canning and freezing and such. Wasn't easy to take the time to get down here now. But you seemed to think it was important."

"I brought you two jars of my bread-and-butter pickles," said Abbie. "They're in the kitchen. I remembered how much you loved Mother's pickles."

"Thank you, Abbie," said Ted. "Kind of you to think of that."

"Here's your beer," said Sarah, handing Silas a tall frosted glass.

"Can would've been good enough," said Silas.

His wife shot a look at him.

"But thank you, Sarah." He took a long drink. "Where is it you started out? Wasn't in Maine."

"I was born in Australia," said Sarah.

"Long way from here," said Abbie, smiling at her.

"It is," Sarah agreed. "Can I get anyone else something?"

"Scotch would be good," said Ted. "You know how I like it."

Sarah nodded. "And you, Abbie?"

"Maybe a diet soda? I'll come with you and see." She followed Sarah to the kitchen.

"So where're the newlyweds?" asked Silas. "Limo hasn't arrived from New York City yet?"

"Jeremy's picking Luke and Harold and Michael up at the Jetport," said Ted. "They should be here in a couple of hours. We'll have dinner after they arrive."

"Abbie and me usually go to bed by about nine-thirty or thereabouts," said Silas.

"Well, I hope you'll be able to stay up a little later than that tonight," said Ted, sitting back down in his chair by the fireplace. "For the occasion."

The floor-to-ceiling bookcases on either side of the fireplace were filled with large books on art and artists.

I wondered how often Ted's children had looked at
them when they were growing up.

"Why don't I get you a drink, Angie?" Patrick asked.
"I think I'd like one, too."

I nodded. "White wine, please."

He followed Sarah and Abbie to the kitchen.

"So, Angie. Where're you from?" Silas asked.

"Right here. Born in Haven Harbor," I said. "You?"

"Presque Isle. Seven generations of Reeds up there.
Lots of Reeds down here on the mid-coast, too."

"I suspect there are," I agreed. "So you're a farmer?"

"Organic. Only way to go," he said. "Some folks
don't believe it makes a difference. But Abbie and me
want things as natural as we can get 'em. Healthier,
you know. And when we sell the crops, we can ask
more for 'em. It's harder to grow organic vegetables,
and have free-range chickens. Always chasing those
chickens out of where they shouldn't be. But they eat
the bugs, and that's good for the crops, and good for
us. Nothing healthier than eating a chicken raised on
bugs!" He grinned.

Where was Patrick with my wine? I hadn't imagined
any of Ted's children would be like Abbie and Silas.

Abbie was making an effort, I could tell, by the way
she'd dressed and put on makeup. But her husband
was from another part of Maine. Many Mainers were
farmers. Silas just wasn't what I'd expected someone
in the elegant and prestigious Lawrence family to
be like.

The Point was spectacular, and I assumed Ted had
plenty of money. But it didn't look as though Abbie or
Silas were benefitting from any of it.

"Where did you and Abbie meet?" I asked, as Abbie

rejoined us and Patrick pressed a glass of wine into my hand and disappeared back into the kitchen.

"Orono."

"You both went to the University of Maine?"

Silas laughed loudly, and slurped his beer before putting his glass on a mahogany table.

Ted winced. That glass would stain.

"Nope. I was taking an extension course on new methods of potato farming. Good course, as I recall. Abbie came for the weekend to hear a rock concert at the university. That's where we met."

"At the concert?"

"Right. Love at first sight." He looked over at Ted, who was staring into the fireplace. "She was a real looker then. Prettiest girl I'd ever met. Not fat, like she is now."

Abbie's smile froze.

Silas didn't seem to notice. "We got married two weeks later. Didn't even tell her dad what we were doing."

"They surprised me, for sure. But Abbie promised she'd get her degree, and she did," said Ted, turning toward us. I couldn't tell if he were proud of his daughter, or still incredulous that she'd married Silas.

"She was real good about that promise," Silas agreed. "I'll admit I wasn't too happy about it at first. I could've used her at home more then, to help out. But she went to UMPI and got her degree and certificate, and that teaching has come in handy in tough crop years."

"UMPI?" asked Patrick, coming back into the room and handing Ted his scotch.

"University of Maine in Presque Isle," explained

Abbie. "Those first few years were a bit rugged, but we're still married."

"Sure are," agreed Silas.

"Dad, I'd like to go upstairs and rest a little before the boys arrive. Okay with you?"

"You do whatever you want, Abbie. After all, you're at home now." Ted's smile said that so far, all was well.

I hoped it stayed that way.

As Abbie and Silas picked up their bags and headed up the wide staircase, I looked past Ted to the painting over the fireplace. I'd only been in the living room briefly before, and I hadn't paid attention to it.

"Is that Abbie?" I asked, pointing at the portrait of a seated woman and a young girl leaning against her.

Ted looked up. "Abbie and Lily, my wife. Dad painted it. He said they both glowed."

"They do," I agreed. Lily was stunning. Her long blond hair was curled slightly at the ends, and it exactly matched her daughter's. Artists might exaggerate beauty in a portrait, particularly a portrait of someone they loved. But both mother and daughter in this painting were exceptional. Patrick or Ted, the artists in the house, might give technical explanations for the way both Lily and Abbie glowed, but they'd be wrong. The mother's and daughter's love for each other was what made the painting come alive. "They were both beautiful."

"Abbie grew up to look just like her mother," Ted said, raising his glass to the painting, and then to his lips. "When she was younger."

Then Silas had been right. Abbie had indeed been "the prettiest girl" he'd ever met. What had happened since then? Time, I suspected. And hard work. The Abbie I'd just met wasn't unattractive, but her hair color had darkened, her figure had thickened, and her skin was already lined.

She was probably ten years older than I was. Maybe a little more.

I resolved to go back to using the sunblock I'd slathered on daily in Arizona. I'd never been beautiful the way Lily and Abbie had been. But I wasn't ready to be middle-aged. I sipped my wine. Not that I'd have a choice in a few years.

"I still miss her," said Ted. He was still looking at the painting. "When Lily died, the love went out of this house."

Chapter Six

"We stand exposed to every sin
While idle and without employ
But business holds our passions in
And keeps out all unlawful joy."

—Sampler stitched by twelve-year-old Sarah
Todd in 1807. Sarah probably lived in
northern Massachusetts or southern
New Hampshire. She stitched a wide border
of flowers and birds around her sampler of
alphabets and numbers.

"Angie, would you help me with supper?" Sarah called
from the kitchen.

"I've been summoned," I explained to Ted. I left
him staring at the painting over his fireplace.

He nodded, but I wasn't sure he heard me.

"I thought we had supper under control," I said
to Sarah.

"We do," she agreed. "But I overheard you talking with Ted about Lily. Tonight he has to focus on today, and the future. Not on the past."

"When did she die?" I asked, as Sarah handed me a large bowl.

"In 1981. Fill this with chowder crackers. Ted said you could never have too many."

Sarah was focused on today. But I didn't know the Lawrences, and I was curious about them.

"Is Patrick back yet?" Sarah asked, looking out the back kitchen window.

"He left?" I asked. "He was just handing out drinks in the living room."

"I checked. We only have seven bottles of champagne, and there'll be ten of us. Plus, Silas wants Bradley's Coffee Brandy. I asked Patrick to make a run to the State Store."

"Seven bottles of champagne sounds adequate. Especially since some people are drinking already." I put down my wineglass.

"I don't know how much these people drink. And Ted and his family will be staying here tonight. They won't have to drive. I told Patrick to get two cases of champagne, and several bottles of Bradley's."

"That much?"

Sarah shrugged. "I don't want Ted to run out. And there are only six bottles of champagne in a case."

Of course. Everyone knew that. I always ordered my champagne by the case.

"Sarah, you've got to relax!"

"I know, I know. I'll feel better when supper is ready. So fill the bowl with crackers!"

I obeyed. It wasn't an exacting task. "Is the table set?"

She nodded. "Since this is family, I thought each

person could fill their bowls out here in the kitchen and carry them to their places. If they want more, we can leave the pot on low."

Sarah had borrowed Gram's classic (and delicious) recipe for haddock chowder, but also planned to add lobster, shrimp, scallops, and mussels, which she'd already prepared and were in a large bowl in the refrigerator. I peeked into the refrigerator. "No clams?" I teased.

"I couldn't find any for some reason," she said.

"The chowder smells wonderful."

"All I have to do is add the rest of the seafood and heat it," she said, as though reminding herself.

"It will be fine, Sarah. Really, it will be."

"Ted insisted on chowder. He said Lily always had a pot of chowder on the stove when company was expected. She said it was easy, she could heat it up whenever the guests arrived, and it tasted of Maine."

"Gram does the same," I agreed. "It's a New England thing. But her chowder just had haddock. Your chowder will be over the top." And not authentic, I said to myself. But maybe the way Lily had made it. "You didn't tell me. What happened to Lily?"

"She drowned."

"A boating accident?"

"She was swimming." Sarah pointed generally in the direction of the Lawrences' private beach. "I don't know any details. Ted doesn't want to talk about it."

That I understood. "Thanks for telling me. I almost asked him in there, when he was telling me about her portrait."

"Beautiful, isn't it?" said Sarah. "It's hard to believe she isn't still alive, and right here in the house with us."

I felt a slight chill. "Are you saying her ghost is here?"

I'd lost Mama when I was ten—maybe close to the age Abbie had been when her mother died. But although I often thought about Mama, I'd never thought of her still being in the house with me.

"I don't believe in ghosts," Sarah said. "But I think Ted feels Lily is still with him, one way or another."

Chapter Seven

"Jesus permit thy gracious name to stand
As the first efforts of Rebekah's hand.
And while my fingers on the canvas move
Incline my youthful heart to seek thy love,
With thy dear children, Lord, give me a part
And write thy name, blest Saviour, on my heart."

—Sampler worked by Rebekah Ursula Ousby
of Raleigh, North Carolina, when she was
twelve years old, in 1834.

"Here's the first carton," said Patrick, putting the champagne on the counter. "Do you want all the bottles in the kitchen?"

"Please," said Sarah, as she opened the carton and started trying to find places for the bottles in the wine refrigerator.

"They won't all fit in there," I pointed out.

"You're right. We'll put the others in the pantry.

When there's space we'll fill in the empty spots. Champagne we don't drink tonight can be for the lobster bake tomorrow."

A weekend of champagne. And I'd been tempted to dig up rocks and rebuild a stone wall instead. Clearly I'd had my priorities confused.

Patrick dropped the second carton of champagne and a bag of Bradley's bottles on the kitchen table. "Anything else need doing?"

"Someone could bring me another scotch!" Ted's voice came from inside the living room.

"Right away," said Patrick, heading for the corner of the large kitchen equipped with cabinets of glasses, a small sink, shelves of bottles, and a large wine refrigerator. I'd seen restaurant bars less equipped.

Sarah was now putting the extra champagne in the pantry, a small pine-paneled room next to the kitchen. She'd made room for the Bradley's on the bar.

"The wine refrigerator's full," she said, over her shoulder. "And some people will want wine."

Like me. I took another sip. Usually I'd have finished my glass by now. But the evening was full of uncertainty. I wanted to be totally together if Sarah should need me. And I was several miles out of town. I'd have to drive home.

The back door opened again.

"Ted, they're here!" Sarah called out.

She and I stood out of the way as Ted greeted his sons. No hugs for them.

"Luke, you've been putting on a little weight," said his dad, looking him over and grinning.

So Luke was the slim (despite his father's comment) dark-haired one wearing what Brooks Brothers probably sold in their "casual" department: a maroon cashmere sweater, over a tan Oxford shirt and tan slacks. He looked fine to me. "Good to see you, too, Dad. Harold's too good a cook, and I've been skipping workouts."

"So where's that husband of yours?" asked Ted.

"He sends his apologies. He couldn't make it this time. He got a part in a show down on Bleecker Street—near Michael's place, actually. The show must go on, you know."

"Good for him. You tell him he was missed. But you're here, and that makes me really happy." Ted clapped Luke on the shoulder.

"Michael's here, too," Luke pointed out.

"Glad you could make it, too," said Ted, putting his hand out for Michael to shake.

Instead of returning the gesture, Michael pointed at the bags he'd dropped on the floor. "I think I'll take these upstairs. What room have you assigned me?"

"The one you had when you were growing up," said Sarah, from the corner.

"Fine. I'll be down in a few minutes." He looked over at the bar. "Have any single malts?"

"Several," Patrick answered. He seemed to have taken over bar duty. "Oban okay?"

"Perfect. Pour me one. Straight."

Jeremy finally came in, carrying a garment bag.

"Would you put that in my room?" Luke asked, as though Jeremy was a porter.

"Sure," said Jeremy. He shrugged at Patrick and followed Michael up the stairs.

"A drink for you, Luke?" asked Patrick, who'd just poured Michael's Oban.

"Wine's fine. Malbec, if you have it."

"No problem."

"Flight all right?" asked Ted.

"Cab to LaGuardia took longer than the flight to Portland. Longer still to drive here. You didn't need to send Jeremy for us, Dad. We could have rented a car."

"Jeremy volunteered. Glad you were both able to get on the same flight."

"I booked our tickets. It was easier that way," Luke explained.

Patrick handed him his wine.

"Why don't we go and sit in the living room and wait for Michael to join us? Abbie and Silas are here, too. They went up to rest before you boys got here."

"Haven't seen Abbie in years," Luke said, following his dad into the living room.

"Living in the County's a little different from living on the Upper East Side," Ted pointed out.

Sarah and Patrick and I stood in the kitchen, looking at each other. No one said anything. A few minutes later Jeremy joined us.

"How does it feel to be treated like help?" he asked, looking at all of us. "You'd think those men thought I was their chauffeur."

"And I'm the bartender," said Patrick. "Although I suspect they could all fix their own drinks more easily that I can."

I'd noticed he'd had trouble opening Luke's Malbec bottle. I made a mental note to help when it was time for the champagne toast.

"He didn't even introduce me," said Sarah, "except to Abbie, who thought I was the housekeeper."

Or me, I thought. But I wasn't important to this weekend, or to Ted's life. Sarah was.

"Should be an interesting evening," said Jeremy. "Hey, bartender. How about a vodka martini for the chauffeur? Straight up."

"Right away," said Patrick. "And a refill, Angie?" I put my wineglass on the bar.

"That martini sounds good," said Sarah. "Make that two."

It was going to be an interesting evening.

Maybe more interesting than I'd anticipated.

Chapter Eight

"Map of the State of New York"

—This unusual embroidery, now owned by
the Cooper-Hewitt Museum of Design in
New York City, was stitched by Elizabeth
Ann Goldin in New York and dated May 21,
1822. It outlines not only New York State,
but all of its counties and bordering lakes,
rivers, and parts of New Jersey. Elizabeth
Ann also included historical facts about the
state and its population: 1,372,812 in 1820.

By seven-thirty everyone was downstairs, relatively
lubricated, and ready for supper.

Abbie and Ted had taken a short walk together, but
after that all the Lawrences had stayed together in the
living room.

Michael had been doing more drinking than talking. Luke focused the conversation on his father,
asking about the gallery, recent sales, and the art

market. If he hadn't been Ted's son, I would have thought he was thinking of buying a painting.

Sarah smiled a lot, but spent most of her time adding the finishing touches to the dinner. She had me remove the place setting planned for Harold and polish the champagne glasses to be brought out when the cake was served.

I didn't think the flutes needed polishing, but I did it anyway. Whatever helped Sarah relax.

Patrick had continued playing bartender and refilling glasses as needed.

Jeremy was sitting near Ted in the living room, but saying little unless Ted specifically drew him into the conversation. He didn't look any more comfortable than I felt. Or that I knew Sarah was. But he'd positioned himself with Ted and his family, not with those of us in the kitchen.

Patrick was the only one who seemed totally at ease. Occasionally he'd flash me a smile and I'd feel the same warmth I had when he'd kissed me.

I wished he'd kiss me again.

But this definitely wasn't the time.

While Sarah added sherry and cream to the chowder, along with the rest of the seafood, I put together individual salads. Sarah'd decided the salads would be served at the same time as the chowder. The bowl of chowder crackers and two loaves of the patisserie's French bread were in the middle of the table.

I watched the family from a distance. Had they any clue about what their father was going to announce tonight? I didn't think so.

What I overheard of their conversation seemed stilted, and emphasized how out of touch they'd all been with each other. I heard Abbie lament the lack of a new tractor, and Michael mention (several times) how expensive it was to live in Manhattan.

"How close are you to getting your doctorate?" Abbie asked him the third time Michael mentioned how high his expenses were. "When you're Dr. Lawrence you could get a job teaching in some place less expensive, like Iowa. Or you could come back to Maine. I hear Portland's changed a lot since we were growing up, and several colleges and universities are near there."

"The power of New York City's excitement and diversity feeds my creativity," said Michael as Patrick silently handed him what was at least his fourth Oban. "I'd feel stifled anywhere else."

"Some of us manage," was all Abbie had to say in response. Then she added, "But I guess we don't all have creative minds to feed. Just hungry stomachs."

I could tell Silas was about ready to bring up organic food as a way to feed both your brain and your body when Sarah stood in the doorway and announced, "Supper's ready. Chowder's self-serve, in the kitchen. Salads and bread are on the table."

Sarah had (I assumed at Ted's request) put place cards on the table. Ted, of course, was at the head of the table. The rest of us, family or "outsiders," as I was pretty sure the family saw the rest of us, were alternated at the table. Sarah was given the place of honor at Ted's right hand.

I was sitting between Silas and Jeremy, wishing one of them had been Patrick.

No one questioned serving themselves chowder.

"Excellent chowder," said Luke, nodding at Sarah in thanks.

"It's not the way Mom made it," said Abbie. "But it's not bad."

"It's the way I like it now," Ted said quietly. "Your mother's been gone a long time."

Which initiated the first toast of the evening. "To Mom!" said Michael. "Gone, but never forgotten."

We all raised our glasses. "To Lily, my love, who gave me three children, but not enough years," Ted added.

Sarah had done a masterful job with the chowder. I made a mental note to ask for her version of Gram's recipe. Patrick had filled wineglasses at each place setting, and for the most part the table was quiet as the chowder and bread and salad disappeared. Several people took their chowder bowls back to the kitchen for refills. Sarah refilled Ted's bowl for him.

He was quiet; perhaps tired, or perhaps he too was nervous about the announcement he'd promised to make tonight.

When everyone was finished Sarah and I took the dirty dishes to the kitchen to be washed later, and Patrick distributed the champagne flutes. I stayed in the kitchen and opened a couple of bottles.

"Wow. We really are celebrating tonight, Dad," Abbie commented. "I haven't had champagne in years."

"Then it's about time," Ted said, smiling. "And after all, I'm only going to have one seventy-fifth birthday. Who knows when we'll all be together again?"

"It's a celebration of family, then," put in Luke. "I so wish Harold had been able to be here. He's the only one missing. He'd really have loved Sarah's chowder."

I could tell Sarah was pleased. I didn't know what she was thinking about these cousins of hers, but so far Luke had been the most polite to her.

As Patrick poured the champagne, Sarah brought in an enormous birthday cake. Different colored brushes were painted vertically around the sides and on the top it said, simply, "Happy 75th."

"There's only one candle, Ted," Sarah explained. "Because you often say, 'Just take one day, one year, at a time.'"

"And so I do, dear Sarah," said Ted. He stood and blew out the candle.

"And a toast to Father. With thanks for years well lived, and hopes of many more to come," said Luke. We all stood and drank the toast together.

"Sarah, would you mind cutting the cake for me?" asked Ted.

She handed around pieces of the lemon cake with raspberry filling.

I wasn't sure I could eat anything more until I tasted it. Nicole at the patisserie had outdone herself.

I'd almost finished my piece when Ted stood again.

"I called you together this weekend not just to celebrate my birthday, but because I have a few things to tell you."

Chapter Nine

*"While God Does Spare
For Death Prepare."*

—Part of Mary Batchelder's elaborately
stitched sampler, which includes birds
and flowers. Mary also listed her birthdate
(June 13, 1757) and the year she completed
her work (1773).

"Patrick, would you mind refilling everyone's
champagne glasses?" As Patrick did, Ted continued.
"First, I want to thank all of you for being here tonight, whether you came from down the street or
from hundreds of miles away. You are my family,
whether by birth or by friendship, and no celebration
of my birthday would be complete without every one
of you. And Luke—Harold would also have been
welcome, as I think you know."

He took a sip of his own champagne. "Thank you
to Sarah and Patrick and Angie and Jeremy who made

this weekend possible. They cleaned this old house of ours and ordered or made the food. They brought in all the libations we're enjoying tonight. And, most important, they're the ones I depend on every day to help with the many parts of my life and business that are not celebrations. They deserve to be here."

Not me, I thought. But I do have a role to play. I'm here for Sarah. When was he going to tell them about Sarah?

"Now, I told you I had some announcements to make tonight. And I do. I want you to hear me out, because what I have to say is important to all of you."

He looked around the table.

"I've been around this planet long enough to know that speakers often have to choose whether to announce the good news or the bad news first. Tonight I have some of each. But before I start, I want you to know I've thought through what I'm going to say, and I've made my decisions. This is not a weekend to negotiate with any part of life. It's a weekend to celebrate family, and the past, and think a little about the future."

"Oh, shit," Silas whispered. "What does he want?"

"First, the good news. You've all met Sarah Byrne tonight. You've complimented her on her chowder. And some of you have wondered what a young Australian woman is doing in our home in Haven Harbor. Well"—he smiled down at Sarah, whose hands were clasped tightly together in her lap—"it turns out that my father, your grandfather, had an adventure when he was serving in London during World War II. He and a young English woman fell in love, and she had a child. I'm sure you'd like to know more details, and we have the weekend to explain this whole amazing story, but Sarah's father was my half brother. A brother I never had the privilege of knowing. But I'm very happy to now know his daughter. Sarah is my niece and yes, Abbie and Luke and Michael, she's your cousin."

"A story is all well and good, but what proof do we have that this woman isn't just conning you?" Michael interrupted. "She doesn't look like us. Hell, she doesn't even sound like us. What right has she to pop up in Haven Harbor and claim she's a member of our family?"

I glanced around the table.

Silas's hands were clenched. Abbie looked furious. Jeremy was flushed. Luke drained his fresh glass of champagne.

Patrick refilled it.

Ted wasn't finished. Ignoring Michael's outburst, he continued.

"As I said, we can get into the particulars of Sarah's story, and her journey to find us, later this weekend. But for now, just know I believe with all my heart that Sarah is my niece. And that, because I knew questions would be asked about such an amazing story, I convinced her that we should have DNA tests. And, yes, they proved that, despite her name and accent, Sarah is a Lawrence. I might add that during the few months I've known her she's more than proven herself worthy of our family. Sarah"—he raised his glass—"I drink to you, and officially, in the presence of my children, welcome you to our family."

No one else said anything. Then Jeremy also stood and raised his glass. "To Sarah."

The others followed, slowly.

So far this was not going as well as I'd hoped.

Ted motioned everyone to sit. "Sarah, as you've probably guessed, knew I was bringing you all together and was going to introduce her to you. But I have several other announcements no one knows about."

Jeremy sat up straight.

Luke and Abbie glanced at each other. Silas and Michael finished their latest glasses of champagne. Sarah looked puzzled as Patrick continued filling glasses. He was holding the bottles with two hands, I noted. He hadn't spilled a drop.

"My second announcement, although it shouldn't come as a shock to any of you, considering that we've just eaten a good part of my seventy-fifth birthday cake and that no one lives forever, is that I'm dying."

Gasps all around. Jeremy paled.

"No!" said Sarah, rising slightly.

Ted gently pushed her down. "I have stage four lung cancer. Yes, I've seen doctors. No, there's nothing to be done about it. I've accepted that I won't be around much longer. I haven't been the best father." No one commented on that. "And I wasn't a great artist, like my father. But I was lucky enough to be loved by a wonderful woman, and to have had responsibility for bringing the genius of Robert Lawrence's work to the world. I've had the joy of working with creative people, and of living in this wonderful home, in this spectacular state. And of being a parent to three children, all of whom I love, and whom I hope love me in some way."

None of Ted's children looked at each other. Jeremy crumpled his napkin. Sarah started crying.

"I wouldn't be a very wise man if I didn't know that my children expected to receive a fair degree of wealth after my death. None of you have settled in this part of Maine. You've all made your own lives. So after I'm gone, this home, and all that is in it, will be sold, and the profit divided evenly between the three of you. That's the first part of the plan."

"Grandfather's paintings?" Abbie asked.

"I've thought hard about those," Ted said. "Over many years all of us in the family have benefitted from the sale of Father's paintings. This house was his; his paintings paid for us to continue living here, for the schools you went to or"—he looked at Michael—"still attend. They paid for me to open my gallery in Haven Harbor. The paintings of Robert Lawrence have supported everyone in our family for over fifty years." He paused. "Everyone in our family except Sarah."

Sarah started shaking her head. Abbie's mouth was actually open.

"So at my death, all unsold Robert Lawrence paintings will go to Sarah, except for the portrait of your mother and Abbie. That will go to Abbie."

"What will happen to the gallery?" Jeremy asked. "To both galleries?"

"The gallery in this house will be emptied of the Lawrences—the Robert Lawrences. Any paintings of mine that my children or Sarah would like they can have. The others will be sold or destroyed, as they see fit. I suggest any of my paintings or, Sarah, any of my father's that you choose not to keep, be sold one at a time, or given to the Portland Museum of Art. They've been hounding me for years to give them my collection of Lawrences."

"And your gallery in Haven Harbor?" Jeremy looked ashen.

"I haven't decided what to do with the gallery. You've worked for me for many years, Jeremy. You know the artists we represent and their work. Whether you continue that gallery, or whether it's sold as part of my estate and you start over somewhere else, you have the knowledge and skill to be an excellent gallerist."

Jeremy sank back in his seat. His face had turned from ashen to red.

Sarah just sat, tears dripping down her face. She looked as though she was in shock.

Luke was the one who spoke. "That's what you 'plan,' Father? Have you already rewritten your will?"

"Not yet, son. I have an appointment with my lawyer on Tuesday. But I wanted you all to know what I was going to do, and why. If any of you have questions, we have the weekend to talk them through. But right now I'm a sick old man, and I'm going to bed. Tomorrow afternoon we'll have a lobster bake down on the beach, for old times' sake. I haven't planned anything until then." He looked around the table. "I suspect some of you may want to talk about what I've just said. That's fine. But don't wake me until the morning. Then you can ask me any questions you've come up with."

Wasn't anyone going to react to Ted's news that he was dying? Were they all just concerned about his will? I waited for someone—anyone—to say something.

But everyone sat silently as Ted walked around the table and into the hall. We could hear his footsteps slowly heading upstairs, and the door of his bedroom closing.

Then everyone spoke at once.

Chapter Ten

"Leah Gallagher and Rachel Armstrong the Daughters of George and Sarah Bratten was born at one birth near Wilmington (Del). They opened School in Lancaster (PA) on the First Day of May 1792 and had this sampler made by one of her scholars viz Sarah Holsworth in the year of our Lord 1799."

—This sample is part of the American needlework collection of the Winterthur Museum in Delaware. In addition to the words, it pictures the Lancaster County Poorhouse, with birds on its roof.

"Who the hell are you, to come out of nowhere and mess up our father's life?" Michael looked at Sarah, but didn't wait for her answer. He threw his napkin down on the table and stomped off.

"He said they had DNA tests!" Abbie called after him. She turned to Sarah. "We should at least listen to your story."

"She's not even an American." Silas stood up. "Is any Bradley's on that bar?"

This time Patrick didn't volunteer to get a drink for him. "Yes," he replied calmly.

Before Silas got to the dining room door, Sarah had broken down, her quiet tears turning to sobs.

I went to her immediately and put my hand on her shoulder. "Sarah, they don't mean it. They're in shock."

"I don't care about them, or his paintings, or any of it." She looked up, her face red and wet with tears. "Didn't any of you listen? Ted's dying! I spent all those years trying to find my family, and now he's dying."

Luke and Abbie exchanged glances.

"Sarah, why don't you come into the living room? Maybe Patrick could get you a cognac or something else you'd like. I'd like to hear your story," said Luke.

"I agree. We're all in shock. This is a lot to absorb. A new cousin, and Dad sick," agreed Abbie.

"Plus the changes in what we all thought were in the will." That was Jeremy. "He'd promised me a share of the paintings, and the gallery. All the years I've worked for that man and a pretty face shows up and everything changes." He got up and left the room. We heard the kitchen door slam.

Sarah's cheeks and nose were red. She looked on the verge of hysteria.

"Come on, cousin," said Abbie. "Come talk with us."

Sarah got up. "I should have guessed he was sick. He's been so tired recently, and he's asked me to help him with the house, and with this party . . . things he'd always done himself. I just thought he was getting old. I never guessed he was dying!" She looked at me. "I never should have left Australia. As soon as I find a relative, they die. I've had too many deaths."

Abbie went over and put her arm around Sarah. "Come with me. Come and sit down and tell us about it."

She and Luke led Sarah out of the dining room.

Patrick and I just looked at each other.

"Did you know he was sick?" I asked quietly.

"Not a clue. Did you know Sarah was his niece?"

"She told me ten days ago and swore me to secrecy. She was afraid of how Ted's children would react."

Patrick looked after them. "Well, now she knows for sure."

"What can we do?"

"We can start by cleaning up the dinner."

I nodded. "Ted has a dishwasher, and leftover chowder can go in the refrigerator."

I could work faster than Patrick. I had two good hands. Together we managed to clean the dining room and put the kitchen back into a semblance of order. Every time I walked past the living room door, I eavesdropped for a few seconds. Sarah was telling her story, and the others seemed to be listening.

I hope they believed her, for all their sakes.

"So, now everyone will know but me. How are Sarah and Ted related?" asked Patrick.

For a rich guy, he knew how to wipe down counters and fill garbage bins, I noted. He'd even separated the recyclables. I wasn't always good about that.

"Robert Lawrence had an affair when he was stationed in London during World War II. His girlfriend got pregnant, but he was engaged to someone here at home, so they broke up. She sent him pictures of her son, and he sometimes sent money. But those were the late forties and early fifties, before he was famous. I suspect he didn't send much. By the time the child was five or six his mother was destitute. She took him to a children's home, a place he could be cared for until she got her life together. When she went back to see him, she was told he'd died."

"That's awful." Patrick sat at the kitchen table while I finished washing the last of the pans. "So the child died."

"No, actually, he didn't. It's complicated, but there was what they called a 'child migrant' program in the UK then. They sent children to British colonies. Robert Lawrence's son was one of those children."

"But I thought he'd died!"

"That's what they told his mother. And she told Robert. The social service people told the boy that he was an orphan, and he was sent to Australia. Eventually he grew up, married an Australian woman, and had a daughter. But his wife died when the baby—Sarah—was very young, and then he committed suicide."

"What a horrible story."

"Unbelievable, actually. Except for that DNA proof." And a photograph and a painting.

"So how did Sarah end up in Haven Harbor?"

"Her grandmum, as she calls her, her mother's mother, raised her in Australia. After her grandmother died she contacted the social service organization to see if they could find her biological family in England. After two years, they found her father's mother."

"That's a miracle in itself."

I nodded. "Sarah went to England, but her grandmother there was very ill and died soon after they'd met. When she was there she found out Robert Lawrence was her grandfather, and saw letters from him postmarked in Haven Harbor. So she came here."

"And found Ted."

"Robert Lawrence had already died. Sarah was shy

about introducing herself to Ted, as a relative out of nowhere—tonight you could see why. Especially since by then she'd learned her grandfather had become a famous, and wealthy, artist. She lived here for several years without telling anyone who she was—including Ted."

"And?"

"She told him earlier this summer. He believed her right away, because he'd found a portrait of an English woman his father had painted, and several letters which mentioned their son. Sarah had a picture of her grandmother and her father, and a couple of letters from Robert. She told me Ted was prepared to accept her immediately. But he was afraid of what his children would say, so they had DNA tests to make sure."

"And the tests confirmed it."

I nodded. "He even gave her one of Robert Lawrence's paintings."

"I did know that. Jeremy and I took it to her apartment and hung it there. I thought it was strange; maybe it was a loan? Clearly Ted liked Sarah, and she was hanging around the gallery a lot. But I only met Ted in August. You were there when my uncle introduced us. For all I knew Sarah'd been his friend for years." He looked embarrassed. "I guess I wondered if that's all they were. Friends, I mean."

"I suspect you aren't the only one in Haven Harbor who's wondered about that," I agreed. "I thought of it, too. But, of course, he's so much older than she is. . . ."

"And he's leaving her all his Robert Lawrence paintings? Sarah will be a millionaire if she sells only one or two."

Patrick had plenty of money himself. He would know.

"Paintings like that are an immense responsibility. No matter what she decides, in the meantime she'll have to find some climate-controlled place to store or hang them." Patrick sat back a moment. "Maybe I could help her with that."

"She's going to need help, for sure," I agreed. Patrick was an artist, and I trusted him. He'd have contacts who could help Sarah.

He glanced toward the living room. "I hope they're being kind to her. She's in a difficult position."

I nodded. "She wanted so much to have a family. But families aren't always easy."

Chapter Eleven

*"A Sampler resembles an elegant mind,
 Whose passions by reason subdu'd and refin'd,
 Move only in lines of affection and duty,
 Reflecting a picture of order and beauty."*

—From sampler stitched by Lucy Turpen in
   1815 in Woodbury, New Jersey.

"This is where you guys are." Sarah looked pale and exhausted, but she was smiling as she entered the kitchen.

"How's it been going in there?"

"Abbie seems nice," Sarah whispered. "She's a needlepointer, too. Silas passed out on the couch. Michael didn't want to talk much, but for some reason he took notes when I was telling my story. Then he went upstairs. Luke's being almost too nice to me. I don't know whether to believe them when they say kind things." She paused. "I hope they're accepting me, but I don't think any of them are going to be my best friends. And Ted's dying. . . ." Her eyes filled up again. "It's all a dream turned into a nightmare."

I gave her a hug.

Footsteps clomped down the main staircase. Seconds later Michael appeared, carrying a towel. "Late-night swim, new cousin? Lawrence family tradition."

"The water's cold in September. And this time of night it's not safe," Sarah answered.

"Sure it is. I've been swimming at night down at our beach since I was a kid." He rummaged through a closet in the hallway and emerged holding a large flashlight. "Maybe I'll write a poem in your honor. "'Out of the night she came, forgotten family returned.'" He flicked the torch on. "Let there be light! But if you're chicken. . . ." He dangled the light in front of Sarah's face. I could smell the alcohol on his breath from where I was sitting.

"No, thank you. Not tonight."

"Maybe tomorrow then. I'll see if any of the others are game." He headed for the living room.

Sarah looked after him. "'The Things that never can come back, are several—Childhood—some forms of Hope—the Dead—'"

Quoting Emily was a good sign Sarah was beginning to cope.

"I think it's time I went home," I said, checking my watch. It was close to eleven. I'd been at The Point all day. No wonder I was exhausted. "Trixi needs to be fed."

Patrick nodded. "Makes sense to me. We're expected back here tomorrow morning, right, Sarah?"

"About nine should work."

"Coming?" I asked.

She hesitated. "Maybe I should stay."

"Why don't you let them be on their own to talk?

It's late; they'll be going to sleep soon anyway. Didn't Abbie and Silas say they usually went to bed early?"

Sarah grinned slightly. "Silas is already in the land of the unconscious. And I sure don't want to go midnight dipping with a drunk, even if he is a poet. And a cousin. Okay. You're right. I'm coming, too."

The three of us headed for our cars in the parking area in back of Ted's house. As I drove down his long drive I saw the light from a flashlight moving down the lawn toward the beach.

Michael was heading for his midnight swim. Maybe it would sober him up.

It had been an exhausting day. I suspected tomorrow would be one, too.

Chapter Twelve

"*Now, when she had dined, then she might go seke out her examplers, and to peruse which worke would be beste in a ruffe, which in a gorget, which in a sleeve, which in a quaife, which in a caule, which in a handkerchief; what lace would be best to edge it, what stitche, what seme, what cut, what garde; and to sit her downe and take it forthe little by little, and there with her needle to pass the afternoon with devising things for her own wearynge.*"

—Description of woman consulting a sampler to decide which stitches to use for her next project. Written by Barnabe Riche (1540-1617), an English author and soldier, in his *Of Phylotus and Emilia*, in 1581. This is one of the first literary references to samplers.

Trixi's tongue, earnestly trying to clean my face, woke me at six in the morning. "It's too early," I moaned.

She purred in response. Clearly it was not too early for her. And where had I been most of Friday, when I should have been at home, providing strokes and entertainment? And, most important, a consistently full dish of her favorite canned food: salmon pâté.

Her morning ablutions proved successful. I groaned, stretched, got up, and washed my face myself before stumbling downstairs. Trixi was already sitting patiently next to her food dish, in case I hadn't remembered. She got her pâté and some dry food before I turned on the coffeepot.

I read somewhere—probably at the vet's office—that you might own a dog, but a cat owned you.

Trixi would have shrugged and thought, *"As it should be."*

What had happened at the Lawrences' house after Sarah and Patrick and I left last night? I'd find out this morning. Sarah had said to be there by nine.

I scrambled a couple of eggs while the coffee was perking.

Thanks to Trixi, I had a couple of hours before I'd have to make myself presentable and appear at The Point.

Time enough to clear a few feet where the stone wall had stood.

I threw on my grungiest work clothes. "Sorry lady. Too many cars and wild creatures out here that would make short work of an (almost) three pound kitten like you."

I was determined Trixi should be an indoor cat, but she was also a Velcro cat. She wanted to be wherever I went.

I headed outdoors. Trixi meowed in protest, but settled by the kitchen window, where she could watch me.

The uprooted maple had knocked about half the stones off the old wall. Some had scattered, pushed by the tree's branches. Others lay in a heap next to where the trunk of the tree had lain a week before. I'd removed most of the tree, leaving a messy combination of large and small rocks, small branches and green leaves that had been severed too early to have turned red.

Unlike modern walls built by stone masons with rocks and stones graded and smoothed at a quarry, whoever built this wall most likely used rocks dug from the large kitchen garden that had once taken up most of the space between our house and barn.

The garden was smaller now. Gram had grown peas and beans and zucchini and summer squash, along with tomatoes and several types of leaf and head lettuce, plus her favorite herbs. I'd been trying to maintain what she'd planted in the spring, but weeds had already overgrown part of it. Gardening required constant attention, and this past summer I'd had other parts of life on my mind.

Maybe next summer I'd have the garden and yard more under control.

Four months had passed since I'd come back to Haven Harbor. I'd only promised to stay and run Mainely Needlepoint for six months.

I suspected now that those promised six months were only the beginning of my new life as an adult in the place where I'd gown up.

Memories of my childhood here still interrupted my dreams and blew through ordinary conversations with people who hadn't known me then. Or I'd turn a corner and run headlong into my past.

But it was all getting easier. The past was over.

Except for those memories.

I got a crowbar from the barn and started moving

the heavy pieces of granite and sandstone, slate and basalt. It wasn't easy.

Some rocks had been scarred from the collapse of the wall. Many were slippery with mosses and streaked red from iron or glittered with the mica that had been part of them for hundreds of years, maybe thousands, before they'd been unearthed and positioned in this wall by one of my ancestors. The smaller, smoother, stones had probably been lugged up from Pocket Cove Beach to fill spaces.

I didn't know a lot about building walls. But if the stones weren't level they'd fall off the first time a chipmunk scampered along them, or another nor'easter blew.

I wanted my wall to withstand time and weather. My predecessors had used balance and patience and taken the time to find the perfect rocks for their dry stone walls. Using mortar felt like cheating.

I took a break and looked carefully at the rest of the wall. The intact part.

The stones had been placed crosswise, not lengthwise, as I'd first assumed. And the wall was slightly narrower at the top than the bottom.

That made sense. Smaller stones filled in the spaces left by the larger, irregularly shaped ones. I'd have to sort the displaced stones.

A few larger stones remained in place, on what had been the base of the wall.

I decided to leave them there, to build on. But the broken stones, and the smaller ones, had to be removed before I could start again. I got back down on my knees and started clearing spaces for new stones, and leaving heavier ones for the crowbar.

Half an hour later I looked down at my hands.

Abbie's hands yesterday had been red and rough. I said a silent apology to Abbie for having noticed. Now my fingernails were broken and my hands filthy. I'd clean up before I went back to The Point, but my hands wouldn't look manicured for a while.

Which reminded me I couldn't work on the wall for too long. Using the crowbar, I lifted one more rock out of the dirt it had been half-hidden in and shifted it to the side.

The hole it left was deep, but I'd have to even it out before I put that stone, or another, back in its place. I stood up and stretched. It was time to stop work for the day anyway.

I picked up my red crowbar and then glanced down. Something that didn't look like a rock was in the soil below where I'd just been digging.

Curious, I dropped down on my hands and knees again and started uncovering it. Who knew what I might find that had been buried for close to two hundred years?

As I worked to move more dirt away, I felt a chill. The more I dug, the clearer it was.

The stained gray fragment hidden for years under my family's stone wall was a bone.

Chapter Thirteen

"(over the mantel in Charlotte Palmer's bedroom there) still hung a landscape in coloured silks of her performance, in proof of her having spent seven years at a great school in town to some effect."

—From *Sense and Sensibility* (1811) by
   Jane Austen (1775-1817).

I carefully pulled the bone out of the earth. It was small, maybe from an animal of some sort. One end was fragmented.

I took it inside and, to Trixi's fascination, washed it in the kitchen sink and left it to dry.

Over the years Gram and I had dug chips of old pottery and handmade square-headed iron nails out of the yard. We'd even found a few coins from the late nineteenth and early twentieth centuries, and a pewter spoon. Once Gram had found a bullet.

She'd called the police that time, to make sure the bullet wasn't dangerous.

They'd assured her it was not.

Maybe I should call the police about the bone? But if it was from a dog or cat or other small animal, they'd laugh.

Instead, I called Gram.

"Good morning, Angel! I thought you were spending the weekend at Ted Lawrence's with Sarah."

Of course, Gram didn't know what had happened last night. So I told her.

"Sarah is Ted Lawrence's niece! I know people say everyone in the world is only six connections apart. But—Sarah and the Lawrences! What a story. However did she keep it quiet all this time?"

I smiled. All the questions I'd asked when I'd first heard. "Last night Ted told his children. They didn't seem thrilled."

"Ted's always had issues with those kids of his," Gram shared. "After his wife died, he mourned too long. Maybe he's mourning still. Some said he blamed himself for Lily's death. His children grew up pretty much on their own. Oh, he made sure they had food and went to school. Had a housekeeper most of the time to watch out for those details—Lizzy Davis lived there for some years as I recall. It was a while back. Abbie was such a beautiful girl, and a beautiful teenager. Everyone in town said so. But she ran off and got married when she was a freshman or sophomore in college. The boys moved out as soon as they could, too."

"Sad. Then Ted never married again?"

"Not even dated, so far as I heard. Funny, since he had a reputation as a bit of a ladies' man when he was married. Some folks tried to set him up, you know, after Lily died. They figured he could use company out at that place of his. But he wasn't interested." She paused. "Maybe he'd already sown his wild oats."

"He's leaving Sarah all his Robert Lawrence paintings," I blurted.

"What? *All* of them?" said Gram. She wasn't often surprised. "Sarah will be a millionaire—a billionaire—if she sells them."

"I don't know what she's going to do," I said. "It all happened so fast last night." I glanced at the kitchen clock. "I have to get cleaned up and get over to Ted's again. I promised Sarah I'd help for the weekend. But I called to ask you about something."

"Yes?"

"You know our old maple fell in the storm last week."

"Tom loaned you his saw to clean it up. You didn't hurt yourself, did you?"

"Nothing like that, Gram. I've finished cutting up part of the tree, but unless Tom needs his saw back right away, I'd like to keep it another week or so. But when the tree fell it knocked down part of the stone wall between our house and the Smarts' house."

"Not surprised. It was a grand old tree. Sad to see it go."

"I've decided to rebuild the broken part of the wall."

Gram hesitated. "Building a stone wall's harder than it looks, Angel. You could hire someone to do that for you."

"I'd like to do it myself. Get in touch with my Maine roots, I guess. Anyway, I was just outside, clearing away some of the stones and rocks so I could start. And I found something weird."

Gram was silent for a moment. "What did you find?"

"It looks like a bone. A small bone. It was under the wall."

Gram's deep breath was audible through the phone line. "Why don't you just put it back there, Angel. Put it back where it belonged. Sometimes it's better not to disturb the past."

"I wondered if I should call the police."

"It's been there for generations. No need to bother anyone. Just put it back."

I heard Tom's voice in the distance.

"I have to go. Tom's reminding me it's Saturday. Time for choir practice. But don't worry about what you found. It's from a time long past."

Gram hung up.

That was strange. I looked at the bone, now drying in the dish drainer next to my sink.

I didn't want to put it back in the ground. Besides, I didn't have time now. I had to shower and get the earth of ages cleaned off my hands before I headed over to help Sarah at The Point

The bone was probably buried by an animal, maybe a pet dog, a century or more before.

Gram was right. It wasn't important. It'd be embarrassing to ask the police about it.

If it was an animal bone.

Chapter Fourteen

"Gossamer: A rich silk gauze, so-called from its resemblance to the finely woven silken thread spun by spiders, and which seems to derive its name from the fact of its being chiefly found in the Gorse or Goss. According to an ancient legend Gossamers were said to be the raveling's of the Blessed Virgin Mary's shroud on her Assumption which fell from her."

—From *The Dictionary of Needlework: An Encyclopaedia of Artistic, Plain, and Fancy Needlework*, by Sophia Frances Anne Caulfeild and Blanche C. Saward, London: L. Upcott Gill, 1882.

Patrick must have been waiting for me. He walked outside as soon as I'd parked near Ted's house and gallery.

"Am I the last to arrive?"

"You are," he said, reaching down to push a strand of hair behind my ear and kiss me lightly. I touched his arm in response, wishing I could touch more of him. But anyone in the house could have been watching. Patrick's and my relationship, whatever it might turn out to be, was too new to flaunt. Or even disclose.

"Where is everyone?"

"Michael survived his late-night swim. He's sitting on the front porch, looking at the ocean and nursing a nasty hangover and a Bloody Mary. Silas is drinking coffee and Bradley's and generally complaining about life. Luke and Jeremy just went to the barn gallery with Ted."

"Luke's seemed interested in art the past couple of days."

"Maybe he's newly cultivated an interest in his grandfather's work since he found out it will all soon be Sarah's," Patrick commented. "But everyone's being civil. Jeremy's practically fawning over Ted."

"He really wants to inherit the downtown gallery," I noted. "He's worked there long enough. I wonder what he'll do if Ted doesn't leave it to him? Last night Ted left that up in the air."

Patrick shrugged. "The world is full of opportunities. Many of them are outside Haven Harbor, though. I've gotten to know Jeremy a little since I've been helping out at the gallery. I think he has a friend in Scarborough he wants to stay close to."

"Galleries in Portland would be closer to Scarborough."

"Most of those are operated by their owners. Not a lot of jobs for someone with Jeremy's background."

We'd almost reached the house. "And Sarah?"

"Sarah's back in organization mode. She and Abbie are planning the rest of our day." He opened the kitchen door for me.

Sure enough, Abbie and Sarah were bent over

a legal pad, making lists. Sarah looked up. "Good morning! You're a little late."

"Sorry. I decided to do a little yard work this morning and got more involved than I'd planned." Like, in finding a bone under my stone wall. This didn't seem the time to share that mystery. "What's happening here?"

"We're planning this afternoon's lobster bake," Abbie said, as though she and Sarah had been working together for weeks.

"Giving out assignments?" Patrick guessed.

"Very soon," Sarah agreed.

"We all ate breakfast late, and there's plenty of Sarah's wonderful chowder left if anyone's hungry in the next few hours. Because sunset is about six-thirty tonight, we want the lobster bake to start early enough to eat at about five o'clock. That means getting the fire started around two," Abbie explained.

Sarah had figured all that out days ago, but I was glad she was now getting Abbie involved.

"Dad wants us to do the bake the way we always did—dig our own clams and pit. Plus we'll have to gather driftwood and rockweed. So we'll have to get started now," she added, glancing at the clock. "It's low tide, so we don't want to waste any time."

You couldn't dig for clams or collect rockweed if it wasn't low tide. Sarah hadn't done a lobster bake before, so far as I knew, but certainly Abbie had.

I kept my mouth firmly closed. I was a guest, not a member of the family, old or new.

"I thought maybe you and Patrick could go to the co-op to get lobsters," Sarah added. "And if you leave now you can get to the farmer's market for the potatoes and onions and, I hope, late-season corn, before the market closes at noon."

"I wish I'd known we were going to have a bake," Abbie added. "Silas and I could have brought our own potatoes and onions to contribute."

None of his children had brought their father birthday gifts, I realized. Although Abbie had given a couple of jars of her homemade pickles to Ted. I'd noticed one was open on the counter. Someone, probably Ted, had sampled them.

Maybe gifts weren't the custom in this family. Or maybe he'd asked them not to bring any. Still, it seemed odd. I couldn't imagine not giving Gram a gift on her birthday. In August I'd found a vintage needlepoint sign that read HOME SWEET HOME surrounded by roses, and added a note saying how glad I was to be home again after ten years. She and Tom had hung the sign in their kitchen.

"Angie? Are you listening?" Sarah was asking.

"Right. Lobsters at the co-op and vegetables at the farmer's market. Got it." I started toward the door and then turned around. "What about drinks? Eggs for the bake? Mussels?"

"We're good for eggs," said Sarah. "Mussels might be good." She glanced at Abbie. "In case the clam diggers don't come up with enough for all of us. We have champagne, but maybe we could use a case of beer. What's Silas's favorite, Abbie?"

Her husband had been the only one drinking beer the night before.

"He usually drinks Allagash White. But I don't think he'll want beer. Today he's switched to Bradley's. We could use a couple of extra bottles of that."

More Bradley's? A couple of extra bottles?

"No problem," said Patrick calmly. "Is everyone else going digging for clams?"

"Luke and Michael and Jeremy, for sure," Abbie said. "Last I heard, they were arguing about which flat to go to."

"I'm staying here with Ted," Sarah explained. "And packing up the plates and glasses and paper towels and such we'll need for dinner."

Abbie stood. "I'll round up the clam buckets and forks and the hip boots for the diggers. There should be enough for an army in the barn. Then I'll start collecting seaweed and driftwood. I'll tell the clam diggers to get back in time to help dig the pit."

"Ted said he has dry wood set aside if there's not enough driftwood," Sarah put in.

"Good. And unless he's reorganized the barn, the shovels and tarp and drum to soak the corn will be there."

Patrick held the door for me. I was halfway out when I turned around. "Dessert? Shall I pick up something for after dinner?"

"Pies, if you see any good ones at the market. Or at the patisserie," confirmed Sarah. "We have some birthday cake left, but there were nine of us . . . and some nibblers late last night."

Abbie laughed. "I wouldn't count on finding much of that cake left."

Just one big happy family. How long would that last?

Chapter Fifteen

"How fair is the rose, what a beautiful flower
In summer to treasure and feel
For the leaves are beginning to fade in an hour
Still how sweet a perfume it will yield."

—Martha Elizabeth Spicer of Muskingum
County, Ohio, stitched this verse on her
sampler in 1851, surrounding it with
roses and baskets of roses.

Patrick held the door of his navy BMW open for me.

"You're sure you don't want to take my car? Lobsters
and mussels will stink up your new one."

"It's used," he assured me. "A year old. And when
have lobsters ever had a bad smell?"

After you've worked over a steamer for nine hours a day, I
thought to myself. "Did you just buy it?"

"Two weeks ago, when I got the go-ahead from my
occupational therapist that I could drive."

Before that, Patrick's mother, Hollywood actress Skye West, had hired a driver for Patrick. Ted Lawrence's wealth wasn't a novelty to Patrick, nor was his art. No wonder Ted had hired Patrick to help at the gallery. They had a lot in common: both had inherited wealth from parents, and both were artists.

I glanced at Ted's hands.

I hoped he could be an artist again. If his hands wouldn't do what he expected them to do, how would he cope? His new job at the gallery would be disappearing. Both Ted Lawrence and his gallery now had expiration dates.

"Where's the co-op Sarah mentioned?" he asked.

"Downtown, next to the town wharf. But the farmer's market closes at noon. Let's head there first."

"Where's that?"

"Haven Harbor Elementary School parking lot," I said. "I'll get us there." I'd been a student at Haven Harbor Elementary, a few years back. Jungle gym climbing, dodge ball, playing tag during recess. . . . Did students today do those same things? Or did they text their friends at recess?

"Yes, ma'am. Elementary school next stop." Patrick smiled at me, and I smiled back. I couldn't help hoping his hands really were all right to drive. I hadn't driven with him since before the accident, back in June.

But he seemed in control of the car. I relaxed after he expertly backed the car out and made the first few turns.

"Ted's kids seem to have accepted his illness, and their new cousin."

Patrick looked dubious. "It looks that way. I can't help thinking they're putting on a bit of a show for their dad. Last night they were more upset about

Sarah's inheriting their grandfather's paintings than they were about Ted's cancer."

"I wonder what Sarah's thinking. She's gone from not having a family, to being caught in the middle of a family that seems to squabble over everything."

"Except lobster. I didn't hear any complaints about the lobster bake."

"We left before anyone was assigned to dig for clams, remember," I pointed out. "I can't see elegant Luke putting on high rubber boots and mucking about in mud flats."

"He did it as a kid, from what I gather. Maybe it will bring back happy memories," Patrick reminded me.

"Maybe. And maybe Michael will take along some encouraging libations."

"No wonder Sarah agreed we should pick up some mussels. I don't think we can count on those guys coming back with a bucket of clams."

"I'll bet none of them get town licenses, either. Although a few towns around will let individuals dig a peck without a license, especially if they're just around for one day. I'd be surprised if any of those guys come up with even half a peck."

"How much is a peck?" asked Patrick.

"Two gallons," I answered. "Not that many. I've done my share of clamming, and it's not easy. I'm glad we were assigned shopping."

Patrick grinned. "Agreed." We were silent for a few minutes, both thinking. Then Patrick said, "I still can't believe Ted was able to hide stage four cancer from those of us who've seen him almost every day."

"You're sure he's not having chemo, then. Or surgery. Or radiation." What else did people do who were fighting lung cancer?

"I talked to him briefly this morning. He's decided

to let the cancer take its course until he's in pain. Then his plan is to call hospice." Patrick shook his head. "He has it all planned. He's even written his obituary and planned his memorial service. He said he didn't want to be a trouble to anyone."

"How long does he have?"

"Under six months. Doctors don't like to be pinned down about things like that."

"What's sad is that I suspect those who will mourn him most are Jeremy, who's worked closely with him for years, and Sarah, who's just found him. His own children haven't kept closely in touch. Unless they're all great actors, they don't seem grief-stricken."

"Maybe that's why he wants the end to go naturally and quickly. Not to fight. He even said he was looking forward to being with Lily again."

"If Gram had cancer, I'd be fighting it with her," I declared.

"That's the way I feel about my mother," Patrick agreed. "But Ted's the one who has to make the decision. He seems comfortable about what's happening. All he wants is to get his will rewritten, and then get on with the business of dying." He paused. "He may have the right idea. If I were dying, I'd want to make the decisions. Not have someone else make them for me."

There wasn't anything else to say. We were both silent as we pulled into the school parking lot.

Sarah was right. The farmer's market was beginning to close down. People in Haven Harbor shopped early on Saturday mornings.

I headed for a farm stand I hoped would still have late-season corn. They'd started packing their truck, but one partially full basket of corn was still out.

"Wait!" I called to the husky teenager hoisting a heavy carton of summer squash. "We need corn!"

He sighed and put the carton down. "How much, lady? We're almost out."

I glanced at Patrick. "Two dozen ears?"

He nodded.

The young farmer looked doubtful. "Count 'em yourself. Might have that many left. It's the end of the season, you know."

I nodded and started counting. Twenty-one ears were left. Some small, but they were fresh and they were corn. I couldn't hope for more today. "I'll take all you have left. All twenty-one."

Patrick pulled out his wallet. He saw me looking. "Before you got there, Sarah gave me shopping money. It's Ted's. I'm not being sexist."

"I never thought that!" I lied as the vendor handed me a large paper bag of corn and gave Patrick the change.

"We need potatoes and onions, too," he added.

We walked past almost-empty booths of pastries, dried fish, Chinese egg rolls, homemade cookies, and boxes of multicolored squash and pumpkins. Finally we found a tent with both potatoes ("We need small to medium sized red ones. They cook faster.") and onions, and bought fifteen of each. "There are nine of us, but someone might want more than one," I pointed out. "Or one of the potatoes might explode."

Patrick picked up the bags, holding them against his chest. His fingers didn't close well. I bit my lip and didn't ask if he needed help. He needed to manage his own way.

We loaded up the trunk of the BMW and headed for the parking lot on Water Street.

"I wonder if we should get clams, too?" Patrick

asked as we headed to the wharf where the co-op was busy serving steamed lobsters and fried clams to people sitting at picnic benches on the pier. The place where I'd worked as a teenager.

I headed us away from the restaurant over to the small building housing the lobster pound. "We said mussels," I said. "Maybe bringing clams would be insulting the clam diggers."

"On the other hand, maybe they'd be grateful," he said, opening the squeaky old screen door for me. The lobsters were sized in large metal tanks. I glanced at the day's selection. Most vacationers preferred two smaller lobsters to one large—not only did they feel more privileged to have two lobsters, but (as those in the know were aware) the smaller lobsters were younger, and often tasted better. Most important today, they'd cook faster at a bake.

"Eighteen pound and a quarter soft shells," I ordered.

"Streamed or to go?"

"To go. Do you have mussels?"

"Yup. How many you want?"

I thought quickly. If the others hadn't dug many clams . . . "Thirty pounds."

"Having a bake?" the oilcloth-clad lobsterman who was weighing our lobster order asked.

"Yup. Sure are," I said. "What about clams?"

"No clams today. Sold out early. Brought 'em up from Rhode Island, too."

Importing clams to Maine? That only happened for one of two reasons. One was a heavy tourist season demand. The other was Red Tide.

"Any safe flats around?"

"Sure. A few. But it's simpler to truck 'em in this time of year."

Good. The clammers weren't in danger of bringing home shellfish that could be dangerous to eat. Red Tide was the nickname for Paralytic Shellfish Poisoning, a bacteria that was sometimes found in clams. When Red Tide was near a flat, that flat was closed to digging.

"So, no clams," said Patrick. "Red Tide? I haven't seen any red water around." He picked up the large bag of lobsters, who were thrashing about at the indignity of being out of the water.

I took the mussels. "Red Tide doesn't always turn water red," I explained. "And mussels are good, too," I said. "Most of those sold here are farmed. Clean, and no problems."

"People better be hungry tonight," Patrick observed as we added sixty pounds of seafood to the trunk of his car.

"Can't think of any reason they wouldn't be," I said as we headed to the patisserie to pick up blueberry pies (might as well be traditional) and to the nearest package store for Bradley's Coffee Brandy before driving back to The Point.

Chapter Sixteen

"Barnard Andrews, Embroiderer and Box Maker, on Sixty Street, three doors above Market Street. Works, mends, and cleans all sorts of embroidery in the newest and neatest fashion, such as any kind of clothes for gentlemen and ladies, pulpit cloths, &c, either in gold, silver or silk, with all sorts of tassels. If there are any ladies that have an inclination to learn embroidery or any of the above-mentioned work, he will either attend them at his house or their houses."

—Advertisement placed in a Philadelphia newspaper in 1768.

"Great!" said Sarah, looking at the piles of food in the back of Patrick's car. "Abbie's gone to pick up the clammers. When they get back they'll start digging the pit."

"Did they get any clams?" I asked, glancing over at Patrick.

"Not many, they said when they called," said Sarah.

"But I suspect they did find a lot of mud. I got the hose out to rinse off their boots and arms and anything else necessary."

"Luckily it's a warm day for September," I said, not cracking a smile.

"It is. Close to seventy, I think," she agreed.

"There're a couple of gardening wagons in the barn. Put the food in that and cart it down to the beach," directed Ted, who'd walked out to join us. "Then bring the wagons back for the coolers for the champagne and ice."

"And the pies," said Sarah, lifting the patisserie boxes out of the car. "Let's not get these mixed up with the seafood. Plates and paper towels and glasses are on the kitchen table. Everything has to go down to the beach."

"And don't forget the fireworks. They're in the barn, too," Ted added, surveying the piles of food.

"I'll make sure we get them," Patrick assured him.

"Before you go down to the beach yourself, Sarah, I'd like to talk to you for a moment," Ted said.

Sarah and I exchanged glances. Then Patrick and I headed for the barn, while Sarah went back in the house with Ted.

"Wonder what that's all about?" I said.

"Could be anything. Maybe he forgot something else, or just wanted to thank her for all she's done this weekend. She's certainly worked hard enough."

"Plus closing her store for a couple of days. Ruth Hopkins was going to sit in for her there, but she had an arthritis flare a couple of days ago, and has to stay home."

"Must be hard for Sarah to run the business alone."

"She does most of her buying in the winter when

she either doesn't open the shop, or keeps short hours."

"Guess she won't have to worry about that anymore," said Patrick. "The sale of one of those paintings she's going to inherit could support her for years. She won't have to worry about living on the second floor of that little shop anymore."

"I wonder what she'll do. I can't see her sitting around looking out at Haven Harbor."

"Travel, maybe? Support a foundation or two?"

Patrick had experience with the challenges of having too much money. I couldn't begin to guess what they would be.

Several wagons were in the barn. We each took one, planning multiple trips each. The path to the beach wasn't smooth. And we didn't want to pile too much on each wagon.

As we were loading up, Sarah ran out of the house. "Angie! You won't believe what Ted just did!"

"What?"

"He gave me the portrait of my grandmother. The one his father painted in London in 1944! I'm thrilled!"

Patrick looked at her. "But Sarah, last night he said he was leaving you all of the Robert Lawrence paintings. You would have inherited it anyway."

"I guess. But it's so much better that he chose to give it to me now. It's not just one of a bunch of paintings."

I could see Patrick wince at her word *bunch*.

"It's a family portrait. I've never dreamed of having anything like that." Her grin was contagious. "And he wants me to take it home with me today. Now! He's wrapping it for me. Will you come and help me carry it to my van, Angie? I'm so excited I might drop it.

And I want to pad it with blankets and . . . I am so excited!"

"I can see that," I said.

"Don't worry. I'll take the first wagon of food down the hill, and come back. If you finish securing the painting, you can join me then," said Patrick.

"Thank you, Patrick! Come on, Angie!"

Abbie drove in with two of the clammers as we headed into the house. Jeremy must have taken his own car.

I followed Sarah into the house and through the rooms connecting the main house to the studio and storeroom. Ted was there, wrapping the painting in layers of padded brown paper.

"Just about got it covered for you, Sarah. Be careful now. It's never been framed, so there's nothing to protect it."

"I'll be so careful. I'll cherish it forever!" Sarah hugged Ted so hard, I was afraid he'd fall down. "I'm so thrilled. You're so kind, to let me have her. You have no idea how much she means to me, because of who she is—and who painted her—and because you gave her to me!"

Ted was clearly delighted with her reaction. "This is probably my last birthday, Sarah dear, but you've made it the most special one I've had in years. You pushed me to get my family together, and ordered everything and made it work. I even think, despite the occasional grumbling, that my kids have enjoyed the weekend, too. A few months ago I'd never have believed all three of my children would be digging a pit for a lobster bake, just like in the old days."

"I'm so glad it's worked out," said Sarah. "Because you're the best uncle ever!" He held her back as she flew at him again, clearly wanting to hug him.

"Calm yourself, girl. I'm an old man. Don't want to die of a heart attack before the cancer gets me." His smile was clear. He and Sarah may only have known each other for a few months, but they'd clearly grown close.

"Now, you and Angie take your grandmother out of this house and put her in your van. She belongs with you, not with anyone else. Not even with me, although I wish I'd known her and your father. They must have been special people to have resulted in you." I saw tears in his eyes. "Now scat! Get that out of here!"

The painting wasn't large—maybe two by three feet—but the packing made it larger. Sarah picked up one side and I took the other, and the two of us walked carefully through the rooms into the house, being very careful not to knock the painting against any doors or walls.

I held the painting as Sarah unlocked her van.

Patrick and the clammers had already disappeared, most likely down to the beach.

Sarah debated for a few minutes where the painting would be safest, and then put it, painting side in, on the front seat, covered it with the blankets she kept in her van to pack around her antiques purchases, and fastened the seat belt over the blankets. It looked strange, but safe.

The sound of running feet stopped both of us. We turned toward the house. Silas Reed was running toward us. He was waving a gun.

Chapter Seventeen

"Behold this early sampler may
Show Readers on a future day
That I was taught before too late
All sorts of idleness to hate."

—Sampler stitched by Susanna Muhlenburg of
Trappe, Pennsylvania, in 1790. In addition
to the verse she stitched a lengthy family
record and three alphabets within a
strawberry border.

"Stop! Stop, or I'll shoot!" Silas's words were slurred,
but his weapon was serious.

I stepped in front of Sarah and her painting, wishing I'd brought my Glock with me.

But who brings a Glock to a lobster bake?

Silas did.

"Whoa! What's wrong, Silas?" I asked.

Silas stood a few feet away, still pointing his gun at us.

"Ted Lawrence said he was changing his will, sure

enough, and that supposed new relative of his was going to inherit it all. But he ain't dead yet. She's stealing one of his paintings. Sent us all down to dig a damned hole in the beach; thought none of us would know what was happening here? Well, I came up to the house to get some Bradley's and found you out. You may be able to con that old man, but you can't fool me. You give that painting back, and any others you've got in that van. Do it now, or you'll be sorry you messed with my wife's family."

"I'm not stealing anything. I wouldn't do that. Ted gave me the painting. It's one his father did of my grandmother." Sarah's voice was firm.

"I don't care what the picture's of. It ain't yours. He said he was going to change his will. But unless he did it today, under our noses, he ain't done it yet. You have no right to that painting."

"Silas, it's all right. Ted gave the painting to Sarah. I was there; I saw him." I stepped toward Silas. He stunk of coffee brandy, but at four or five feet from us, that wouldn't interfere with his aim. I turned slightly. "Sarah, give me your keys."

She handed them to me, whispering, "I don't want that drunk driving my van!"

"Silas, Sarah and I aren't going anywhere. Neither is the painting. See?" I held up the keys. "These are the keys to the van. Now why don't we all go together and find Ted and ask him about the painting."

"That man never liked me. But I've taken care of his damned daughter all these years. Thinks she's so great, growing up in this place"—he gestured wildly with the gun—"but that father of hers never gave us nothing. Said we'd married without him, we could live without him. Figured someday he'd die and we'd get what was rightfully ours. But now he goes and gives it to some foreigner who don't even speak English right."

I could feel Sarah stiffen behind me.

"Silas, put the gun away. Let's go and find Ted. If he agrees Sarah's stolen the painting then I'll call the police myself. I promise."

He hesitated.

"Remember, I have the keys to the van. No one— Sarah or anyone else—can drive the van and the painting away while I have the keys."

"You'd really call the cops?"

"I would. You have my word on that. And if they find you waving that gun around, they'll arrest you instead of Sarah. You wouldn't want that, would you?"

He slowly shook his head.

Then he put his gun in the holster I now saw under his shirt. Had he worn the damned thing all morning?

"Let's all go together now. Slowly. Ted's probably still in the house."

The three of us moved cautiously toward the kitchen door. Inside the kitchen Silas stopped to pick up another bottle of Bradley's. Just what he needed. But I didn't object. "Ted?" I called. "Ted, are you here?"

No one answered for a few minutes. Then Ted started down the stairs from his bedroom. He'd dressed for the lobster bake in old paint-covered pants and a sweatshirt.

"I'm here. What's the problem?"

"Silas saw Sarah and I putting that painting in her van. He thinks she stole it." I turned to look at Silas. "He pulled a gun on us."

"Damn it, Silas, don't get involved with what isn't your business. I gave that painting to Sarah. It's a portrait of her grandmother my dad did back in the forties, not a multimillion-dollar seascape."

"You sure she didn't steal it?"

"Absolutely sure. Now, if you still have that gun on you, I want you to give it to me, right now."

Silas didn't move.

"Silas, I don't allow guns in this house, and you know it."

Silas slowly took the gun out of his holster and handed it to Ted.

"Now, I'm going to put this in my safe. I'll give it back to you before you leave tomorrow. In the meantime, I don't want you harassing Sarah or questioning what I choose to do with what's still mine. I'll be dead soon enough, and you and Abbie and the boys can fight for every can opener in this place. But for now I'm in charge, and if you don't do as I say, you can get your wife and the two of you drive back to the County tonight. Hear me?"

"I hear you, Ted." Silas looked as though Ted had just stuck a pin in him.

"Tell Sarah you're sorry."

"Sorry, Sarah." Silas's words were as clear as they could be after all he'd drunk, but I saw his eyes. He might be saying he was sorry, but he was furious. I didn't trust him an inch.

"Silas, you've got the bottle you came for. Why don't you go on down to the beach?" I handed the car keys to Sarah. "Sarah, lock your van. And why don't I go with you, Ted, to make sure that gun goes in your safe."

He looked at me questioningly, but nodded.

Sarah waited until Silas had started down the path to the beach. "Hide your car keys somewhere no one can find them," I advised her quietly. "Now, Ted, I'm sorry to bother you, but we'd better get that gun into a safe place. I want to make sure Silas doesn't come back for it."

The day was still young. I hoped for Ted's and Sarah's sake that we could all enjoy the lobster bake and that the trouble was over.

But I was wrong. Trouble was just starting.

Chapter Eighteen

"Teach me the measure of my days
Thou maker of my fame
I would survey life's narrow space
And learn how frail I am."

—From sampler completed by Fanny Rine.
Fanny was born in Lancaster, Pennsylvania,
on September 26, 1796, and stitched her
sampler at Mrs. Armstrong's School, also
in Lancaster, in 1808.

Sarah took Ted's arm as the three of us headed down
the worn rocky path toward the beach. Both of them
looked shaken, but all was well. Silas's gun was locked
away, as was Sarah's painting. Even I didn't know
where she'd hidden her van keys.

Maybe we'd seen the end of a family conflict. With
everyone around, Silas would be more under control.
I hoped.

Preparations for the lobster bake were in full force

by the time we got to the beach. The food was piled in bags and buckets to one side, a pit about four feet wide and two feet deep had been dug, and Michael, Luke, and Abbie were carefully covering the bottom of the pit with two layers of medium-sized sea stones. Jeremy, wearing a multipocketed fishing jacket that looked brand-new, was climbing over rocks on one side of the beach, tearing off handfuls of rockweed and tossing them into a large plastic garbage can.

Silas stood alone on the other side of the beach, looking out to sea and lifting his bottle of Bradley's to his lips.

"You don't need any more rocks than that?" Patrick was asking. "I thought the hole would be deeper."

"Pit doesn't need to be deeper. Just deep enough to hold the rocks and seaweed and food," Luke explained.

"What about all the wood?" Patrick pointed to a pile of driftwood and branches that I assumed had come from Ted's woodpile. "When you put the wood on the stones, you'll fill up the pit."

Michael grinned. "Watch and learn from the masters." He stood up and stretched. "If you feel the way I do, Luke, I'll be fighting you for a hot bath and painkillers tonight."

"If you went to the gym more often, your muscles wouldn't object as much," said his brother.

But he was stretching, too.

"You've done a great job with the pit and stones, boys. Time for the kindling, I think." Ted sat on a rock near the sea grasses. Someone had spread blankets on the sand for the rest of us.

"Yes, sir," said Abbie, grinning. "I brought a stack of old newspapers you hadn't recycled yet down from the barn. We can start with those." She tossed small stacks to Sarah and me, instructing us to knot them, and then put them on top of the stones in the pit.

I showed Sarah how. Then Luke and Michael covered our layers of newspaper knots with small branches, and then with medium-sized logs. The siblings might not have seen each other frequently, but they knew how to work together.

"Dad, I think you should light it," said Luke. "For old times' sake."

Ted pulled matches from the pocket of the old canvas jacket he'd put on over his sweatshirt and knelt to carefully light the newspapers in several places. Sarah helped him stand and we all watched as the papers caught fire and began igniting the kindling.

"When do we put the food on the fire?" Patrick asked.

Everyone smiled. But no one laughed.

"The fire has to burn for a while, Patrick. Maybe an hour. Maybe longer. When the wood is just about gone, and the stones are hot, you'll see. In the meantime, you folks need to collect more rockweed. I'll handle the corn detail and keep an eye on the pit," Ted pronounced.

I felt like saluting. Ted must have been a tough dad. Today no one was complaining about being given orders, likely because they knew it would be the last time they'd gather in just this way.

Patrick and I stayed back a little, picking up a couple of large garbage bags and knives then heading to the rocks at the edge of the water.

"What's 'corn detail'?" he asked as I bent down and showed him how to pull or cut off pieces of rockweed attached to rocks, or pick up pieces of kelp that had floated in from deeper waters. It was a harder job than it sounded. It was almost impossible to have too much seaweed for a lobster bake.

"Traditionally, people steam the whole ear of corn, with the husk, on top of the seaweed. But it's late in the season, and September corn is tougher. Ted's going to shuck the outer layers, leaving the thinner layers of the husk on the ear."

"Won't the husks burn?" asked Patrick. He was finding it difficult to loosen the rockweed from the rocks. His hands couldn't hold the knife tightly enough.

"He'll soak the almost-shucked corn in a garbage can filled with seawater. The saltwater will add some flavor to the corn, and keep it from burning." I stood up. "Do me a favor and hold the plastic bag open? My hands are slippery, and I have trouble opening it to put the rockweed in."

Patrick looked at me. "You can just say it. I can't scrape the rockweed with these damn hands of mine. Don't pretend, Angie. We both know what the problem is. Don't pity me."

"I know you're having trouble. But I'm not pitying you," I answered "I *am* struggling with the plastic bag. We can help each other."

Patrick stood up. "I don't want any special treatment, Angie. Not ever. Not from anyone. And especially not from you."

"Understood." I reached down, severed another piece of rockweed, and tossed it into the bag Patrick was holding. "Look—the others are going back to the beach. Maybe we have enough."

"We'll go see," Patrick agreed. "But if they need more, we're coming back." Then he smiled. "I'll admit, I had no idea how hard putting together a do-it-yourself lobster bake would be."

"Next time back to the caterer?" I smiled.

"Not sure about that. But this all better taste spectacular."

"It'll be memorable, no matter what," I said. "Your first authentic lobster bake, after all!"

"I'm grateful to you, and Sarah, and especially to Ted, for including me," he said as we headed back to the section of the beach where the others were gathering. "I know I'm an outsider. But I'm serious about making Haven Harbor my home. I want to learn about living here."

I didn't tell him that to most Mainers in Haven Harbor he'd always be "from away." Or that, despite her newly discovered roots, so would Sarah. But being from away didn't mean people wouldn't accept him as he was. He'd be different, but still part of the community.

"I'm glad you're here, too," I said. I wished my hands weren't full of knives and plastic bags full of salty-smelling rockweed. I wished I could hug Patrick, or hold his hand. The best I could do was touch his shoulder with mine as we walked across the sandy beach to where the lobsters' pyre was burning.

Chapter Nineteen

"Sweet music descend and bless the shade
And bless the evening grove
Business and noise and day are fled
And every care but love."

—The beginning of a poem stitched on the inner bed valance (so it could be read by those in the bed) by Mary Swett Bulman about 1745-1750. Mary, who'd been born in Boston, married Dr. Alexander Bulman in 1730, when she was fifteen. After his death in 1745 during the siege of Louisbourg she began needlepointing these elaborately flowered bed hangings, perhaps to keep her mind busy. Her set, including four curtains, a coverlet, headcloth, tester, outer and inner valances, is the most complete set of bed hangings from this period to survive. Today they are in the Museum of Old York in York, Maine.

"Getting close to raking time," Ted declared. "Corn's soaking, and looks like you have enough seaweed. It's a little early to open the champagne, but anyone want beer or wine?"

Silas, of course, had been drinking all along. He was focusing on his bottle of Bradley's. Michael poured several plastic cups of chardonnay and passed them around. I suspected he would have preferred scotch.

"To the lobsters!" toasted Ted. We all raised our glasses (or bottles).

The tide was coming in more quickly now, each incoming wave covering a few more inches of beach. We were all sitting safely above the high tide mark, but by the time the lobsters were red, most of the beach would be under water.

I inhaled the salt air and looked around.

The rock where Ted was sitting was at the top of the beach, almost to where gentle sea breezes were moving the now-yellowing salt grasses and sea lavender in gentle waves. Above him, on the hill overlooking the beach and the sea, stood the Lawrence cottage.

It had been the center of his family. I didn't know exactly when his father had bought or built The Point, perhaps when Ted was in his teens. But The Point had been designed to stand out. To prove Robert Lawrence's success to the world.

Maybe that was "the Point." A joyous declaration of accomplishment.

How many storms had it weathered since then? Nor'easters and blizzards. Pains and sadness of deaths. Joys of marriages and births. Adolescent rebellions and tears. And now more changes were coming. Ted would be leaving this place that he loved. Would one of his children buy it in from the others? He didn't expect them to. That had been clear last night.

Everyone else was sitting on blankets, looking at the sea, sipping their drinks. Maybe remembering other times on this beach.

Silas faced the sea, while Luke had turned toward the others on the beach. Michael sat alone. Would Luke have acted any differently if his husband had been here this weekend? I suspected not. But I didn't know.

Jeremy and Abbie sat on either side of Ted. Abbie was refilling his glass. Despite Silas's reaction earlier this afternoon, the weekend Sarah and Ted had planned seemed to be going as well as they'd expected, if not hoped.

Patrick also sat alone, looking out to sea. Was he thinking of paintings he hoped to do? Of his new life in Maine?

Or were we all just tired from foraging for supplies for the lobster bake? Tired, relaxing, and waiting.

Ted broke the silence. "The fire's burned down enough now. Who's got the rake?"

Michael stood and got a heavy iron rake from one of the wagons now lined up below the path to the house and started raking the pieces of wood in the pit.

Patrick leaned toward me and said softly, "What's he doing now?"

"Breaking up any pieces of wood still unburned, and making sure the coals fall between the rocks to keep them warm. Next . . ."

"Rock time!" Ted announced.

Each of us picked up several stones either near us, or in the pile someone had made earlier, and dropped them carefully on top of the other rocks and the hot ashes.

"Now the seaweed," Ted continued, almost in an incantation.

Abbie began, filling the pit with the rockweed she'd gathered. "Who has more? We need a couple of feet," she said. Luke tipped the seaweed-filled garbage cans into the pit as Michael raked it relatively smooth.

Patrick watched in fascination. "That's a lot of seaweed," he commented.

I just smiled.

"Now—clams and mussels!"

Jeremy poured the few clams they'd dug that morning, plus the mussels Patrick and I had bought, on top of the seaweed.

"Potatoes . . ." continued Ted. "And Sarah, take the corn out of the water and put it in now. Onions, too."

The layer of food was getting thicker.

"And now more seaweed!" Ted proclaimed as though he were announcing a tournament win.

I lugged the bags Patrick and I had filled over to the pit and Luke helped me empty them onto the food.

"What about the lobsters?" Patrick asked.

A few people laughed, but the laughs were good-natured.

"Best for last!" Ted bellowed. I had the feeling his proclamation and directions were part of the Lawrence tradition. "And now—the lobsters!"

We all stood around the pit and passed the bag of lobsters around, each placing two of the creatures, less feisty than they had been earlier, on top of the seaweed. Ted then stood up and added a half dozen eggs to different parts of the lobster layer, while Luke stood by with a large tarp. "Help me, Jeremy?" he asked.

Jeremy looked surprised to be asked, but he and Luke covered the pit, and everything in it, with the tarp. We all fastened the edges down with small rocks and sand so the tarp wouldn't blow away or let out the gathering steam.

"And now?" asked Patrick.

"Now we have more drinks," Michael explained. "And wait about half an hour."

"I remember"—Patrick turned to me—"when the eggs are cooked, so are the lobsters."

"You've got it," Luke agreed. "The hard work is done. Eating is ahead."

Of course, there'd be cleaning up, too.

But as the wine bottles made their way around the group, I had the feeling not everything would be cleaned up tonight.

"Finish up that wine," Ted said. "Champagne comes next. We'll gorge ourselves and drink champagne and then watch fireworks. It's going to be a night to remember."

Ted was right. He didn't know just how memorable

Chapter Twenty

*"Oh virtue, sorrowing man's relief
In pity by kind Heaven Sent
Thou takest away the thorn of grief
And Plants instead the rose content."*

—From sampler by Sarah Abbot, born March 6, 1806 in Concord, New Hampshire, and stitched in Bethel, Maine, where her family had moved, in 1823. Sarah married Timothy Capen, a farmer, had four children, and died in 1874.

Luke removed the trap, checked to see that the eggs were hard-boiled, and nodded to the rest of us. "Ready!"

Abbie handed him a plate. He served Ted first; then he and Abbie filled the other plates.

The champagne had been in several large coolers, on ice. It was fantastic, even in plastic glasses. ("Dad never allows real glasses on the beach. If one broke, we'd be cutting our feet for years," Abbie explained as she poured us each full cups.)

About ten minutes before we guessed the lobsters would be ready, Ted had put two pounds of butter in a paella dish on top of the tarp. By the time the lobsters and shellfish were ready to be eaten, the butter had melted. We passed the dish around, dipping our lobster claws and mussels and clams in it.

Maybe working for the food made it taste better, but everything was delicious. Even the end-of-season corn wasn't bad. I'll admit I put my onion and potato to the side. I planned to have a second lobster before eating my vegetables.

After all, despite the news about Ted's health, it was a party.

Everyone seemed to feel the same way.

"I wish Harold had been able to be here," Luke said as he broke the large claw off his lobster. "I don't think he's ever been to a real lobster bake."

"On Long Island they call them clam bakes," Michael said, slurping his champagne a bit as he tried to balance his cup and his plate.

"Doesn't make sense. Lobsters are the stars of the meal." Luke nodded. "But I agree. I've been to clam bakes on Fire Island. None as good as this, though. Maine lobsters are still the best."

Silas and Abbie didn't say much. But the pile of shells next to them was growing.

"Happy?" I asked Patrick.

"Happy," he agreed. "Can't imagine a better place, or meal, or"—he looked at me—"better company."

The night was magical.

Some of us were starting on our second lobsters when Ted stood, spilling his plate of food onto the beach. Another toast? But he wasn't holding his glass. He tried to say something, but he sputtered. He couldn't talk.

We all stopped. What was wrong? He pointed at his lips, and throat. Then his face and one of his arms started twitching. Jeremy and Abbie jumped up. Abbie put her arm around her father, and Jeremy held his arm.

"Are you choking? Do you need something to drink?"

Ted kept trying to talk, but only gurgles came out of his mouth.

"Who has a phone? Call nine-one-one," I said, remembering I'd left my phone in my car. Who'd want to be interrupted at a lobster bake?

Luckily no one else had worried about that. Almost everyone pulled out a phone. Luke got through first. "Emergency at Ted Lawrence's home, at The Point. My father can't talk." He looked over at Ted. "I think he can breathe. Maybe he's having a stroke. We're down at the beach, but we'll try to get him up to the house."

Lobsters and champagne were forgotten. With Luke on one side and Abbie on the other, half carrying their father and leading the way, we all headed up the rough path toward the house. By the time we got there Ted *was* having trouble breathing and could barely stand.

"Is he allergic to anything?" the ambulance attendant asked as soon as the EMTs arrived.

"Not that I know of," said Luke. "But he has lung cancer."

"We need to get him to the hospital," was all I heard anyone say as they strapped Ted onto a stretcher and slid him into the ambulance.

We could still hear the sirens when Sarah said, "We need to follow them. Who's had the least to drink?"

Patrick and I were nominated as drivers. I hoped no cop would stop us for a Breathalyzer test. Abbie and Silas ended up in my car.

"Do you think the old man's gonna make it?" Silas asked Abbie.

"I don't know. We don't even know what happened. He was sitting eating his dinner, and everything seemed fine. And then . . ."

"If he dies now, before he changes his will, we'll still be okay," Silas added.

"He was going to leave the pictures and money to me, not 'us,'" Abbie snapped. "Don't even think about that at a time like this."

They were both sitting in the backseat. In the mirror I saw her elbow him and point at me.

Patrick and I wouldn't be affected by Ted's will, either his current one or the one he planned to write. But everyone else at the dinner tonight would be.

For Sarah's sake, I hoped he'd be all right. At least well enough to change his beneficiaries in the way he'd planned.

He had his own reasons for leaving her his father's paintings, and he hadn't cut his children out. If they sold The Point, they'd each end up with a large amount of money. This house, in this location, with its history, would sell for millions.

But so might most of Robert Lawrence's paintings.

Abbie and Silas were silent the rest of the way to Haven Harbor Hospital. I was glad. I didn't want to hear any more about the will.

Ted was still alive. He was the important person right now, not his children, or Sarah, or Jeremy, who'd kept to himself for most of the day, but clearly hadn't been happy.

Death should be a time for cherishing, I thought. Remembering. Not anticipating gain after death.

But, of course, I'd never been in their position. I'd only been ten when Mama disappeared. Gram might have been concerned about money then, but she wouldn't have worried about missing out on a fortune. She would have worried about not having enough money to buy food and support me.

I pulled into the hospital parking lot in back of Patrick's car, and my passengers jumped out and headed for the emergency room entrance. I hung back a bit. After all, I wasn't a relative or even a close friend.

Patrick must have felt the same way. He came over and put his arms around me as we silently shared the horror of a beautiful day turned frightening.

"What do you think happened?" I said.

"I don't know. He could have had a stroke. He kept pointing at his mouth and throat."

"The EMT guy asked about allergies. A bad allergy could cause some of those symptoms, right?"

"Anaphylactic shock, like from a bee sting? Maybe. A friend of mine used to carry epinephrine, to inject if he were stung. He told me once when we were out camping, in case he got stung and couldn't get the pen out in time. He said he'd have trouble breathing, and swallowing, and probably collapse."

"That sounds like what happened to Ted," I thought out loud.

"There were no bees on that beach, Angie."

"Maybe he was allergic to something else."

"Champagne? Lobster? Mussels? I'll bet he's had all those things hundreds of times before tonight."

We started walking toward the emergency room entrance.

"But never when he had lung cancer. Maybe he's on some medication, and had an interaction. Or . . ."

"Or maybe we should leave the diagnosis up to the doctors." Patrick pushed the metal plate that opened the door automatically. "We got him here as soon as we could."

I nodded. But had it been soon enough?

Chapter Twenty-one

> *"'Tis education forms*
> *The common mind*
> *Just as the twig is bent*
> *The tree's inclined."*

—Stitched by Nancy Dearborn Thomas, who
was born in Brunswick, Maine, about 1816.
She dated her sampler in Bath (where her
family had moved) May 19, 1826. Nancy
also stitched a family register. She died
shortly after completing this work.

Everyone was clustered in the emergency waiting
room. Sarah looked up as Patrick and I came in.
"Where've you been?"

"In the parking lot. We thought the doctors would
only want to talk to immediate family members."

"Family." Sarah's eyes filled with tears. This was
not the way she'd envisioned this weekend, although

right now Ted's children seemed to be accepting her presence.

"What do they say?"

"Not a lot. It's too early. They're focusing on allergies. They asked exactly what he'd eaten in the past six hours."

"What everyone else ate, I assume," I said.

"Which is what we told them. I think they're focusing on allergies because none of the rest of us are sick."

I nodded.

"Do they have a prognosis?" asked Patrick.

Sarah shrugged. "No one's said anything. But I don't think it sounds good. Luckily Jeremy knew who Ted's oncologist in Portland was, so they're checking with him to find out what meds Ted was taking. One of them might have caused this." She paused. "Or interacted with the wine or champagne he was drinking. He might have been taking pain meds. I noticed he wasn't drinking as much as some of the rest of us."

"Then the doctors don't think it was a stroke?" All I could think of were Ted's slurred words.

"No one's mentioned a stroke." Sarah looked as though she might collapse. "I don't know what they're thinking. I'm just so scared."

I took her arm and helped her over to an uncomfortable orange plastic chair that seemed to be the only seating in the waiting room.

"I think all of us could use some caffeine. Why don't I find the hospital cafeteria and get coffee?" Before anyone could comment, Patrick left.

"We're probably all a little high," said Sarah. "I felt

relaxed and happy on the beach. Right now I feel as though we're in a nightmare."

Before I could say anything else, Dr. Karen Mercer came into the waiting room. I recognized her from the last time I'd been here, only a month before. That time I'd been with Dave Percy. He was now healing well. I hoped whatever had happened to Ted, we'd be able to say the same about him a month from now.

"All of you were with Mr. Lawrence today?" Dr. Mercer said, looking around the room.

Maybe it was a slow night. No one was waiting for any other patients.

"We were," said Luke, playing the role of eldest son. "We were all with him when he became ill, and one or more of us were with him all day. And for the past twenty-four hours," he added.

"Good. And none of you feel nauseated? Faint? Have trouble breathing? Feel as though you can't control some part of your body?"

Silas put a hand on his stomach.

"I don't mean have you had too much to eat or drink," Dr. Mercer added.

I almost smiled. We'd probably all had too much to eat, and some had had considerably too much to drink.

"You were having a lobster bake this afternoon," she said, looking at her pad of notes. "Right?"

Several people nodded.

"You had wine and champagne to drink. Lobsters, clams, mussels, onions, and potatoes to eat. Am I right?"

"Corn, too," added Abbie.

"Of course. And Mr. Lawrence has eaten all of those things in the past with no ill effects?"

"That's right," said Luke.

"Is everyone who was at the lobster bake here now?"

"Patrick West just went to get coffee for us," I put in. "Everyone else is here."

"Good. Because I want you all to stay here at least a couple of hours. We don't know for sure what caused Mr. Lawrence to collapse, but I want to make sure none of you get sick."

"What's wrong with Dad?" Abbie said. "Don't you know yet?"

"We're pretty sure," said Dr. Mercer. "We think he may have been poisoned by something he ate or drank, or by a combination of drugs and alcohol. We're investigating all possibilities and treating him the best ways we can."

"If it was something he ate or drank, why aren't we all sick?" I asked.

"That's the key question," said Dr. Mercer. "Unfortunately, right now I don't have a good answer for you. But I may soon. So relax, everyone, and get as comfortable as you can."

"Can we see Dad?" asked Michael.

"He's unconscious right now," said Dr. Mercer. "I'd prefer that you all stay out here."

Where the hospital can keep an eye on us, I thought to myself.

Poison? It didn't make sense.

I suddenly thought of Trixi. She'd need food. I'd been so involved with digging out my stone wall this morning, I'd fed her, but hadn't given her any extra before I'd left.

The stone wall. I'd found a bone under the stone wall.

This morning seemed so long ago.

I picked up my phone and called Gram. Several of my companions were also calling people. It might be a long night.

Ted's fireworks wouldn't be needed. We'd had our own version.

Chapter Twenty-two

"How blest the Maid whom circling Years improve
Her God the object of her warmest love
Whose useful hours successive as they glide
The book, the needle, and the pen divide."

—Verse stitched in Eliot, Maine, by Mary
Elizabeth Wentworth, born December 10,
1824, who completed it on her eleventh
birthday. By 1850 she was living and
teaching in Roxbury, Massachusetts. In the
late 1850s she married a Baptist minister
twenty-four years older than she was. Their
children were born in Maryland and Kansas.
By 1870 they'd moved to Red Bank, New
Jersey, where Mary again taught, before they
moved to Ossining, New York, where her
husband worked at the prison (Sing Sing)
and Mary opened her own school, the
Cedar Glen Seminary for Young Ladies. It
offered instruction in "all the substantial
and ornamental branches."

"Gram? I need a favor."

"What is it, Angel? And where have you been all day? I tried to call you a couple of times earlier and you didn't pick up. Tom and I wondered if you could usher tomorrow at church. One of our regular ushers is sick, and everyone else seems to be busy."

"I can't, Gram. Remember—I was going out to The Point. But now I'm in the emergency room. No! Nothing's wrong with me! But Ted Lawrence collapsed at the lobster bake late this afternoon."

"How is he?"

"Not good. He's unconscious. And Gram, the worst part is the doctor says he may have been poisoned."

"Poisoned!"

"Since we all ate the same food today, we have to stay here to make sure we're okay."

"How do you feel, Angel?"

"I'm fine. And so are the others—Sarah's here, and Patrick, and Ted's children." I lowered my voice. "And Jeremy, who works for Ted at the gallery. Just one big happy family."

"Have you called Dave?"

"Dave? Why should I call Dave?"

"Because if it's a poison, he might know what it was," said Gram. "Couldn't hurt to ask."

"You're right. I hadn't even thought of that. I'll call him. No one else in town has a poison garden. And Gram? The reason I called? Would you go over to my house and feed Trixi? I don't know how long I'll be here tonight."

"Not to worry, dear. I'll take a little walk and give her some dinner. Don't you worry. As long as she has food and a cozy place to sleep she'll be fine. But do call Dave."

"I will. Right away."

"And when you can, let me know how Ted is. And the rest of you, if anyone else is sick."

"I think we'll be fine, Gram. But I'll let you know."

Patrick handed us each cups of bitter coffee as I finished the call. If that wouldn't sober everyone up, nothing would.

"Any news?"

"We'll be stuck here a while. They suspect Ted was poisoned, maybe something he ate, so we're all guinea pigs. They're waiting to see whether any of the rest of us get sick."

Patrick frowned. "That's not a good sign. But what could have been poisoned? We were eating fresh seafood and vegetables and excellent champagne."

I shrugged. "Gram had a good idea. She suggested I call Dave."

"Dave? Oh—that friend of yours with the poison garden. I've never met him."

"Well, you may tonight." I put down my coffee and called Dave. "It's Angie. I'm at the emergency room. Dr. Mercer says Ted Lawrence may have been poisoned, and she's holding everyone who was at a lobster bake with him this afternoon captive. Sarah's here, too," I added, since both Dave and Sarah were Mainely Needlepointers and worked with Gram and me. "I thought you might have some suggestions."

"I'll be right there."

Short but sweet.

"Why does Dave have a poison garden?" Patrick asked. "That sounds a little . . . morbid."

"Unusual, anyway," I agreed. "Dave teaches high school biology, and he wants all his students to be aware of poisonous plants, and how to avoid them. So his garden is like a big science project."

"Isn't it dangerous?"

I shook my head. "The garden's fenced in and locked, and most people in town know about it. His students think it's pretty cool." And he's helped me solve a couple of murders, I thought.

We all sat, although not patiently. Luke tried to call Harold, but Harold was at the theater. It was Saturday night, and the show must go on. In the meantime Luke paced, making the rest of us nervous. Michael fell asleep. Silas and Abbie sat together, but didn't talk, or even look at each other. Jeremy followed Patrick's example. After we'd all finished our coffees he brought another tray of cups.

If I drank any more of that awful stuff I'd be showing symptoms of nausea.

Abbie redid her makeup, and Silas thumbed through an old issue of *Sports Illustrated* that was in the waiting room. Patrick and I just sat.

What was there to say?

Dave arrived a half later. I introduced him to Patrick; they'd heard about each other, and I could feel the testosterone rising as they looked each other over. Normally I'd find that amusing. Tonight I was too tired and stressed.

Dave got right to work. After all, poison was his thing. "Has anyone else shown symptoms?"

"No. We're all fine," Patrick answered.

"Did the lobster bake include clams or mussels?"

"Both," I said.

"Who bought them?"

Patrick and I looked at each other. "We did," we said simultaneously.

"Where?"

"Down at the co-op," I said. "But—no. That's wrong. We bought the lobsters and mussels there. They were out of clams. Jeremy, Luke, and Michael went clamming this morning and brought some back."

Dave got up and spoke to the man at the registration desk. A few minutes later Dr. Mercer came out to see him. She glanced at his leg. "No crutches? You're doing well, Dave."

"Thanks to your good care, and the surgery I had here," he said.

By now everyone in the room was listening. Sarah was the only other person there who knew Dave.

"When I was here last month, do you remember our talking about my garden?"

Dr. Mercer brightened. "Of course. You have a poison garden."

"Angie Curtis"—he gestured at me—"called me tonight and told me you suspected Ted Lawrence might have been poisoned. She thought I might be able to help. I may know why he's sick."

Dr. Mercer took a breath, and looked around the room. "I'm sorry. I was on my way to tell all of you. Mr. Lawrence died a few minutes ago. He never regained consciousness."

Sarah began crying. Michael looked as though he was in shock. "He's dead? Really dead?"

"I'm afraid so," said Dr. Mercer. "We don't have many people in Emergency tonight, so if any of you would like to come and see him, you're welcome to."

Luke and Michael went past her into the ER. Jeremy sat, staring at the wall. Abbie looked at Silas and said what everyone was thinking. "What do we do now?"

"There'll be an autopsy to determine cause of death," said Dr. Mercer. "We'll call the medical examiner tonight, but I doubt the exam will take place until Monday. You should be able to make funeral arrangements after that." She looked around the room. "I'm so sorry for your loss. Dave, would you come with me? I'd like to hear what you think."

He and Dr. Mercer disappeared into the Emergency Room.

"We're the drivers. We'll wait for Luke and Michael and then take everyone back to The Point," said Patrick quietly. "There's nothing we can do for anyone here."

I nodded.

A few minutes later Dave came back.

"So?" I asked. "Did you figure out what it was?"

"I think so," he answered. "Although we'll have to wait for the autopsy to make sure. It could be something else. But I think he died of paralytic shellfish poisoning."

"Red Tide," I said.

"It might just have been one clam. But his system was already weakened by cancer. Make sure no one eats any clams that might be left at the lobster bake."

I wasn't worried. I suspected the gulls had enjoyed the rest of our dinner. Had any of them died, too?

Toxic algae blooms didn't only kill people.

Chapter Twenty-three

"As this fair sampler shall continue still
The guide and model of my future skill.
May Christ the great exemplar of mankind,
Direct my ways and regulate my mind."

—Section of genealogical sampler stitched by
D.T. (Deborah) Phillips (1810-1885) in 1824
in Portland, Maine. Deborah became the
second wife of botanical physician Moses
Lunt in 1842.

Patrick and I drove everyone back to the Lawrences.

Those of us not staying at the house promised to
come back in the morning with trash bags to clean up
the remains of the ill-fated lobster bake. It didn't seem
right to leave that mess with the three who'd just lost
their father, even if their relationships with him
weren't close.

I worried most about Sarah. "Would you like to stay
with me tonight? Or have me stay at your place?"

"No. I just want to be alone. I need to think," she said, climbing into her van. "And I want to take my grandmother home and find a place for her."

The portrait. I'd forgotten about that. So much had happened in one day.

"I'll come back about nine in the morning?" asked Patrick.

"I'll be here," I promised.

Sarah nodded, and Jeremy shrugged. "Guess we'd all better come. There's safety in numbers."

Patrick and I watched as Jeremy headed for his car. "That's a strange reaction," I said.

"Who knows? Everyone's stressed tonight."

"I wouldn't be surprised if the Department of Marine Resources sent someone here tomorrow to find out where those clams came from," I added. "Ted's children planned to leave tomorrow. They'll have to make other plans."

"I suspect there'll also be a few discussions about the will Ted didn't have time to make out," said Patrick. "I'm assuming his earlier one, whatever it said, was more favorable to his children, since he didn't know Sarah then."

"We'll find out soon enough," I said. I hoped Patrick would suggest that he'd follow me home, or that I should follow him. But I understood. This was not a day to take another step in our relationship. This was a day to accept and go on, and do what we could for those who'd lost someone close to them.

True to her word, Gram had been at my house. She'd left the porch and living room lights on for me, and Trixi's food and water dishes were full. My little black kitten seemed glad to see me, rubbing herself around my ankles.

Then I realized I probably smelled of seafood. She

might be bonding with me. Or she might be hoping
I'd brought back some lobsters or mussels or . . .
clams. I didn't want to think about the whole situation
anymore. I wanted to take a deep bubble bath and
collapse into bed.

But I'd promised to call Gram.

"Are you home?"

"I am. Thanks for taking care of Trixi for me."

"That was simple. I was thinking of taking a walk
tonight anyway. How's Ted?"

I hesitated. But Gram always wanted news straight.
"He died, Gram. Dave suspects he ate a clam poisoned
by Red Tide. Your idea to call him was a good one.
There'll still have to be an autopsy, of course."

"Oh, no. I didn't know Ted well, but he and his
father have been assets to Haven Harbor for the past
half century. How awful! I assume someone went
clamming on their own."

"Three people, actually."

"They must feel awful. They probably skipped that
little nuisance step of getting a license or checking to
see what flats might be closed. Although closed flats
should have been posted."

"You're probably right. But Ted was the only one to
get sick."

"And to die right after he'd told his family about
Sarah. I don't know his children well—they went to
private school, and there was a bit of a scandal about
his daughter, when she got pregnant and took off to
marry someone she'd just met. But I suspect they're
not welcoming Sarah into the family fold with open
arms."

Gram was right. But I didn't feel like rehashing
the past two days. "Abbie was pregnant? She didn't
mention having any children."

"Well, maybe it was all gossip. It was years ago, Angel, but I'm pretty sure there was a child involved. I wonder if any of Ted's children will move back to Haven Harbor and live on The Point. Abbie lives up in the County, right?"

"Caribou. She teaches kindergarten there. The oldest son, Luke, works on Wall Street. He's married to an actor."

"Doesn't sound as though their lives would transfer to Haven Harbor." Gram paused. "Abbie was such a beautiful child. I remember thinking Ted's wife, Lily, had been reborn. She and Abbie looked like an ad for the perfect mother and daughter."

"I heard Lily drowned."

"Down at their beach. I've always told you, Angel, never to swim alone. That's what she was doing. Maybe she got a cramp, or an undertow pulled her out. They found her body tangled in a lobster line just outside the harbor."

I shuddered.

"Don't think Ted ever quite got over her death. Never had another woman in his life, far as I heard."

And if Gram hadn't heard Haven Harbor gossip, it hadn't happened.

"What's Michael doing these days?" she asked.

"Writing poetry. Going to NYU."

"Goodness gracious, girl, he's been doing that for twenty years. Man should get his life together and grow up one of these days."

"Maybe he will now."

"You're right. Maybe he will."

"And Gram, there's more. Right after Ted told us Sarah was his niece, he told us he had lung cancer. Stage four. He didn't have long to live. Maybe the wine he was drinking interacted with his pain meds. But even if not, his cancer might be one reason he died so quickly. His body couldn't fight back."

"So sad."

"And his dying tonight meant he didn't make out the new will he'd planned. The will leaving Sarah all of Robert Lawrence's paintings. Probably his earlier will left everything to his children."

Gram sighed. "So Sarah went from being an heiress back to being an antiques dealer in twenty-four hours."

"Right."

"How's she doing, Angie?"

"Pretty well, all things considered. I'm going to meet her at The Point tomorrow morning with Patrick and Jeremy to clean up what was left of the lobster bake."

"Gulls will have gotten most of it."

"I'll take garbage bags. Lots of garbage bags."

"I must say, Angie. Since you've come back to Haven Harbor, nothing here's been boring."

"Was it ever?" I said, remembering Mama. "Thanks again, Gram. Love you."

"Love you, too. As always, for always."

I hung up.

As always, for always. That's what families should be.

I hoped the Lawrences were supporting each other tonight.

Chapter Twenty-four

> *"May my fond genius as I rise*
> *Seek the fair fount where knowledge lies.*
> *On wings sublime trace Heavens abode*
> *And learn my duty to my God."*

—From sampler made in 1803 by Dorcas Shaw
  (1788-1879), probably at the school of
  Elizabeth Dawes in Portland, Maine. In 1810
  Dorcas married Samuel Marshall in Augusta.
  A few years later they moved to Corinth,
  Maine, where they lived for the rest of their
  lives and had five children.

The beach was as messy as I'd imagined, but we
weren't the first to get there. Two men from the Department of Maine Resources Biotoxin Monitoring
Program (it said on their cards, which they'd left
nailed to a white pine next to the path to the beach)
had arrived at The Point at dawn. They'd managed to

wake Luke, who'd told them they could take whatever they wanted from the beach.

They'd bagged all the clam shells (between the partiers and the gulls, they hadn't found any actual clams, but they had found one dead bird) and cross-examined Luke, and then Jeremy, who'd been the first of the cleaning volunteers to arrive, about exactly where they'd dug the clams so they could check the flats.

The clammers had tried several locations, so it wouldn't be as simple as the Marine Resources folks had hoped. They planned to post every flat a clam might have come from yesterday, and test them all. Apparently on general principles they also posted the Lawrences' beach, despite knowing no clams were there.

The rest of yesterday's mess was still on the beach. Patrick had trouble picking up garbage, so Jeremy and I did most of that, while Patrick and Sarah filled in the pit and pulled wagonloads of supplies and garbage up the hill to the Lawrences' barn.

Luke came outside and thanked us briefly before disappearing. We assumed the other Lawrences were either in bed or in mourning.

"Or hung over," Sarah commented.

By a little after noon we were all exhausted and filthy, and the beach was as close to clean as it would be until winter tides had swept over it.

"The other Lawrences," Jeremy said, "are probably toasting each other with the leftover champagne and congratulating each other on their inheritances."

"I wonder what Ted's earlier will said," I said, out of curiosity.

"I don't know," said Jeremy. "He never told me. He

once said I'd be a good person to take over his gallery someday, but I assumed he was referring to his retirement in the distant future, not his death."

"Most parents divide their estates between their children equally," Sarah pointed out.

"But Luke has plenty of money; Abbie works hard but has almost nothing—Ted pretty much cut her off after she married Silas—and he was still writing checks pretty regularly to Michael," Jeremy said.

"How did you know all that?" asked Patrick.

Jeremy shrugged. "I worked in the gallery for years. I heard a lot. And for the past couple of years I've been keeping the books for the business. I don't know everything, but I kept my eyes open."

"Interesting. Who was Ted's lawyer? He or she would probably have a copy of the will."

"Lenore Pendleton took care of his legal business," said Jeremy.

"Lenore Pendleton was murdered in early July," I pointed out. "I don't know who's taken over her practice."

Jeremy shook his head. "Ted sounded as though he was working with someone."

"Glenda Pierce might know what happened to Lenore's records," I mused. "She was Lenore's secretary."

"But wouldn't he have kept a copy of his will here, at home? Maybe in his safe?" asked Patrick. "My mother has several lawyers, for different parts of her business, but she always keeps copies—or originals—of important documents either in her safe in Los Angeles or at her bank. You don't expect your lawyer to be murdered, of course, but people do die or retire."

"I'm worried about the gallery," Jeremy admitted. "Should I open the gallery as usual Tuesday morning?

Or will Ted's children, who clearly know nothing about art, and care less about anything but money, assume I'm breaking in to steal their inheritance?"

Sarah hadn't said anything. Then, "We're standing here, outside their house. We've just cleaned up their beach. We should be able to ask them if they have a copy of Ted's will, and what will happen to the gallery. I know I won't be in the will. But Jeremy needs to know whether he should be looking for a new job."

Jeremy's skin noticeably paled. "You're right. You too, Patrick. You may not have a job anymore either."

We all knew Patrick's job wasn't necessary to cover his food and rent expenses. But yes: he'd been working at the gallery and I assumed he was being paid.

"Sarah and I don't have any reason to know about the distribution of the estate. But you both do. I agree. Patrick and Jeremy should knock on the door and ask them if they know what's going to happen. What *is* happening now. They deserve to know."

"And once they find out, I need to go home, take a shower, and open my shop," said Sarah. "I've already lost several days' income."

Sarah seemed the one of us most affected by Ted's death. She'd been holding up well, but her eyes kept tearing. She needed to get away from The Point and mourn in her own way.

Jeremy hesitated. "They could be in there right now, packing up all the Robert Lawrence paintings. Damaging them. Not one of them even knows how to crate a painting."

"Jeremy, those paintings aren't ours. They're responsible for the Lawrences now," Patrick reminded him.

"I've spent fifteen years of my life sitting in this dumb little town, taking care of those paintings. Protecting them for Ted, and for posterity. Those ingrates

are just going to ship them off to Sotheby's as a group.
I know it. They won't get top prices because they'll all
be sold at once. They don't know what they're doing!
I hate it! I hate them!" Jeremy sat down on a granite
bench next to the driveway. "I can't believe this is happening. It makes no sense. Ted would hate everything
they're doing."

"We don't know for sure what they're deciding,"
Patrick pointed out, putting his hand on Jeremy's
shoulder. "Why don't we go and find out?"

That was when we heard a gunshot, and glass
shattering.

Chapter Twenty-five

"The high honour bestowed upon Needlework in ancient days when it was considered one of the chief spoils of the conqueror, and a fitting gift to be presented to kings, is fully shown by its frequent mention by the sacred writers and by Homer, Pliny, Herodotus, and others."

—*The Dictionary of Needlework: An Encyclopaedia of Artistic, Plain, and Fancy Needlework* by Sophia Frances Anne Caulfeild and Blanche C. Saward, London: L. Upcott Gill, 1882.

All four of us ran into the Lawrences' kitchen, hoping no one was hurt. I touched the shoulder holster I'd put under my sweatshirt that morning. No, I don't usually wear my Glock when I'm planning on cleaning up a beach.

But Silas's threatening Sarah and I with his gun yesterday had made me uneasy. Very uneasy. When I feel that way, I carry. And since I didn't want anyone with me to know how uneasy I was, I concealed my weapon.

Maine law now let me do that.

Unfortunately, they let everyone else do it, too. Occasionally I walked through the supermarket, wondering how many shoppers and clerks were secretly armed.

Although I'd learned to shoot, and started carrying, when I'd worked for a private investigator in Arizona, I wasn't a fervent Second Amendment supporter. I wasn't against legal hunting. But truthfully, I'd feel a lot safer if, as Sarah had once said, our country was like Australia, and no one had guns.

On the other hand, as long as someone like Silas could drink and shoot, I wanted to be able to defend myself and my friends.

What was happening inside that house?

"Hello? Is everyone all right?" Sarah called out. The debris on the kitchen counters and table told us the Lawrence family, or at least some of it, had a late night. Bottles, glasses, and the empty cake plate were among the trash no one had cleaned up. Unless, of course, breakfast had involved scotch and Bradley's Coffee Brandy.

"Hello?" Sarah called again.

No one answered. And no one was in the kitchen or living room.

"I'll check the gallery," said Jeremy. Not surprisingly, his first thought was for the paintings.

"No one would shoot in the gallery," I hoped out loud. "What about upstairs? Sarah, come with me. You know the house better than I do."

She nodded. Patrick hesitated and then added, "I'll check the rooms between here and the barn."

Should all of us stay together? I didn't know what

we would find. Or who. But spreading out seemed to make sense. "Yell if you need help," I said as Jeremy and Patrick took off in opposite directions and Sarah and I started up the staircase to the second floor.

Abbie, wearing a faded flannel nightgown, her usually immaculate hair uncombed, came out of the rose bedroom as we reached the second-floor landing.

"What's happening? What are you doing here?"

"It's almost noon," I pointed out. "We cleaned up the beach. We were going to leave when we heard a gunshot."

"And glass breaking," Sarah added. "We wanted to make sure everyone was all right."

"I was sleeping," Abbie said. "I didn't hear anything." She looked around the landing. "Everything looks all right."

"Where are the others?"

"Maybe sleeping?" The only open bedroom door was Ted's. I glanced in. Unlike the rest of the house, his room was a mess. Bedding was on the floor, clothes strewn in all directions, books that might have been stacked had fallen over, and the closet door was open. Either Ted was a lot messier in his private life than he was in public, or his room had been trashed. Or searched.

"Luke was awake earlier, when the Marine Resources men were here," I prompted.

"Who was here?" Abbie looked confused. And hung over. Either she didn't know anything, or she wasn't going to tell us what she knew.

"Where's Silas?" I asked. After all, yesterday he'd had a gun. And he was her husband.

"I don't know. I told you. I don't know where anyone is."

"You weren't in the same bedroom?" Sarah asked.

"Not that it's any of your business. But no. We weren't. We had an argument last night. The last time I saw him he was asleep downstairs, in the living room."

I assumed "sleeping" for Silas was the equivalent of "passed out."

"He isn't there now," I said.

"I don't see it's any of your business where my husband or I sleep or don't sleep. And this is a private residence." She looked directly at Sarah. "You might have convinced Dad you were a relative, but you haven't convinced anyone else. Get out. Both of you. Or I'll call the police and report you for trespassing."

Sarah blanched, and dug in her pocket. "Ted gave me a key to the house a month ago. He said to use it if I thought he needed help, or there ever was a problem here." Abbie didn't know Patrick and Jeremy were also somewhere in the house. "Jeremy has a key, too."

"Dad may have given you that key. But he's dead. Gone. His permission ended at that hospital last night. So just get out. Now."

Sarah turned toward the stairs.

"And before you go, give me that key."

Sarah turned slowly, and threw the key on the floor. "You weren't here to take care of your father. You never even called to find out how he was. He needed someone to watch out for him. I did that. You have no right to treat me like this."

"And you were going to be well rewarded for being nice to the old guy. But it didn't work out for you, did it?" Abbie reached down and picked up the key. "He died, and everything he had belongs to his children, as it should be."

Sarah stopped back toward her. "I didn't cook and clean for him and keep him company for any reward. I was as surprised as you were when he announced he was changing his will. I didn't expect anything. He was kind to me, and trusted me. He knew you and your brothers might not believe who I was, which is why we had those DNA tests. All I wanted was a family."

Sarah's eyes filled, but she was angry as well as hurt. As she turned and headed down the stairs I realized none of the other bedroom doors had opened. Could anyone have slept through Abbie and Sarah's argument?

I glanced one more time at Abbie, who was fingering the key to the house as though it was a talisman. The way sometimes I rubbed the gold angel on the necklace Mama had given me when I was nine.

It was the only thing of any value Mama had ever given me. Abbie's father had given her everything when she'd been growing up, except maybe as much love as she'd needed. Now she'd inherit millions.

I didn't feel sorry for her.

But I wanted to know where her husband was.

"Angie!" Sarah's voice from downstairs sounded urgent. "Come on!"

"Just get out of this house," said Abbie. "Now." She went back into her bedroom and slammed the door after her.

Chapter Twenty-six

"Thus when my draught some future time invades
The silk & figure from the canvas fades,
A rival hand recalls from every part
Some latent grace and equals art with art.
Transported we survey with dubious strife
Each form & figure start again to life."

—Harriet Wells (1796-1814) of Woodbury,
Connecticut, and New Hartford, New York,
stitched these words on her delicate sampler
in 1806, when she was eleven years old.

"Angie! Now!"

I took a last look at the closed doors on the second floor, and raced down the stairs. Sarah sounded anxious.

She was standing in the hallway between the living room and kitchen, looking down toward the gallery wing. "I heard something down there."

A door closed in back of her, and Patrick joined us.

"No one, and no broken glass, between here and the barn," he confirmed. "How about upstairs?"

Sarah and I looked at each other. "Abbie's up there," I said. "She just woke up. I don't think she knows anything."

"But I heard voices, and something falling down toward the gallery," Sarah said.

Jeremy had gone that way. Who else was there?

"No other shots?" I asked as we ran toward the rooms that held the studio and painting storage as well as the gallery.

"I didn't hear any," said Sarah.

The sound of our footsteps stopped whatever was happening. All was silent.

Where was Silas? His gun was in Ted's safe. Abbie said he'd been sleeping in the living room last night, but no one was there now. Luke and Michael must be somewhere, too.

Every time we opened one of the wing's connecting doors, I expected to see someone. Without thinking, I'd drawn my gun. Sarah didn't seem to notice, but Patrick looked startled. He knew I'd been a private investigator. Guess I'd never gone into details about what that entailed.

This wasn't the time for a heart-to-heart talk.

"The paintings," Patrick said urgently. "They mustn't be damaged. We can't let anyone hurt the Robert Lawrences."

I'd been thinking more about people, but Patrick was right. The paintings were treasures. I'd been more impressed by them and by Ted himself than by any of Ted's children. Or by Silas, who was the one I expected to see behind each door we opened.

But it wasn't Silas. Luke was the one with a gun, standing over Jeremy, who was huddled in the corner of Ted's office, kneeling in shards of colored glass from a broken stained-glass window above him.

"He tried to shoot me," said Jeremy. "He did!"

That didn't make sense. Jeremy had been outside when we'd heard the gunshot.

"I didn't. But I just might," said Luke. "I found him trying to open Dad's safe."

Sure enough, a safe was behind Jeremy.

"Luke, put the gun away," I said, pointing mine at him.

Sarah and Patrick had retreated to the door, but hadn't disappeared. I wasn't sure which of them looked more surprised at what was happening.

"Gun down," I repeated. "I want to hear from both of you what happened."

"You're not the police," said Luke.

"Nope. But I'm a good shot."

"If I put my gun down, will you put yours down?" he negotiated.

"After I hear your stories," I promised. "And make sure no one else is hurt."

"There's no one else here," said Luke. "Abbie's still in bed, I guess. Haven't seen her today. Michael went for a walk."

"And Silas?"

"I took his gun last night. This gun. He was acting crazy. He was screaming at Abbie, saying he'd tell everyone what she'd done. He wasn't making sense. He probably won't even remember. I didn't get him to bed until early this morning. He's probably still there, in the guest bedroom."

"I saw Ted put Silas's gun in his safe yesterday afternoon."

"That must have been another gun," Luke said drily. "Did you or Dad ask him if he had more than one?"

I shook my head.

If Luke was telling the truth, then we needed to hear what was going on here.

"And the gunshot? The one before Jeremy got here."

Luke gently put his gun on Ted's desk. I reached over and took it, removed the bullets, and handed it to Sarah, who clearly didn't want it. "Just hold it," I said.

"Last night we all talked a lot. About Dad, and art, and what it was like growing up here. What was going to happen to this place, and to the paintings. We didn't make any decisions. Dad hadn't made out a new will—he'd said so Friday night. We assumed his earlier will divided everything between the three of us. His children. But we didn't know for sure. We didn't even know who his lawyer was. This morning Michael and I talked to those Marine Resources guys, and after Michael left for a walk I thought of Dad's safe."

"He's always had one?"

"I remember it from when I was a kid. I used to steal chocolates from a stash he kept in the bottom drawer of his desk." Luke pointed at a drawer. "He put them in the safe, to keep them away from me. I knew they were there. But when I asked for one he'd just say, 'They're safe.' And laugh."

I couldn't help smiling. It sounded like a father's response. Jeremy sat up a little and leaned against the wall, but didn't get out of the corner.

"So you remembered the safe."

Luke nodded. "I'd only been up here a few times in the past dozen years, and I certainly hadn't checked out the safe. But I suspected it was still here. I thought maybe he'd have put a copy of his will inside."

"You decided to find out."

He nodded.

"With Silas's gun?"

"Last night, after I took it from him, I hid it in a cabinet in the kitchen. I didn't want the gun. I just didn't want Silas to have it. He was drunk, and talking nonsense about how he and Abbie had waited long enough for their share of the Lawrence money, and how they deserved it, because they weren't rich New Yorkers, like Michael and I."

"Rich New Yorkers."

"That's what they said. When Michael's been whining all weekend that with Dad gone he won't be able to pay his rent. Apparently Dad's been paying Michael's expenses for years. Without monthly checks, he has no income." Luke sighed. "I told him it was time to grow up. That even if he was going to inherit a lot of money, it would take months for the estate to be settled."

At least six months, in Maine.

"Michael started asking me for money. A loan to get him by until his publisher came through with his advance."

"He sold a book of poetry?" asked Jeremy, who was still crouching on the floor.

"I guess." Luke shrugged. "I was pretty pissed at him by then. He's been drunk most of the weekend and he stunk of Scotch. I told him he had to grow up and get a job. If he couldn't get a job teaching, then maybe he'd be a good bartender. He certainly knew enough about drinks." Luke looked embarrassed. "Guess I came on pretty strong. He was furious. Said I was a selfish bastard, just like our father. That's when I got Silas to bed. I left Michael downstairs, opening another bottle of scotch."

"You haven't said why you fired the gun this morning."

Luke's shoulders slumped. "Guess I've watched too many movies. I found the safe, and tried to open it. Tried all the combinations I could think of, but nothing worked. Even tried to pick the lock with a paper clip."

"That wouldn't work!" said Jeremy, who'd been listening carefully. "Ted had a double combination. You needed both sets of numbers to open it."

"Well, anyway, I was so frustrated, I shot at the lock. Guess that doesn't work like in the movies. The safe didn't open. The bullet bounced off and hit the stained-glass window above it."

"That window was custom made for your dad," said Jeremy. One of his hands was dripping blood. "It was of Saint Catherine. She's the patron saint of artists."

"I didn't know that. But I knew I'd been stupid. I went out through the gallery to get some fresh air. Then I came back in here . . . and found that idiot"— he pointed at Jeremy—"fumbling with the combination lock."

Jeremy stayed on the floor, as though protecting himself, or the safe. "I wasn't fumbling. Ted gave me the combination because he trusted me. He kept checks in there from this gallery, and sometimes petty cash. But he was most worried about his customer lists and tax records." Jeremy looked at all of us, as though asking for understanding. "Gallery records. They're critical. Irreplaceable."

"So what are you doing here, trying to open this safe now?"

Jeremy brushed the pieces of glass off his legs, staining his jeans with streaks of blood as he stood up. "Same as you, I guess. I thought maybe his will was in there. I wanted to know what he'd planned to do with the gallery."

"So why didn't you ask? Why sneak in here?"

"I didn't plan to. I just came in, and saw the glass, and thought of the will, and tried."

Luke walked closer to the safe. "But it isn't open."

"You did a good job with that gun, Luke. You messed up the lock. The combination doesn't work anymore. Maybe a locksmith could help. But the combination won't help now."

"Shit," said Luke. "What a way to begin the day."

"We heard the gunshot and were afraid someone was hurt," I explained. "We hadn't planned to come into the house or bother you."

"I'm bleeding," Jeremy pointed out, glaring at Luke. "I need to wash my hand and get some bandages. I know where they are in the kitchen."

We all headed back to the kitchen, where Sarah bandaged Jeremy's hand.

"There's a glass replacement place out on Route One. They make house calls for emergency repairs to windows. You should probably call them," I suggested. "They can at least make sure rain doesn't come in. If you want the stained glass repaired, there's a guy down in East Boothbay who could do that for you."

Luke nodded. "Thanks. I'll do something."

"We came here this morning to clean up the beach," said Patrick. "It's done. All the tools and wagons are in the barn, along with bags of garbage."

"Thank you for that," said Luke. "And sorry for what happened this morning." He looked over at Jeremy. "When we find that will, you'll hear about it. In the meantime, would you keep the gallery downtown open? I assume you have a key and can do that on your own."

"I'd be happy to," said Jeremy.

"Good. Now I suggest we all take the rest of the day off," Luke said.

"It's a sad time," said Sarah.

"It is," said Luke. "Tomorrow's Monday. I've already made arrangements to stay here a couple of extra days. We'll find Dad's lawyer and get this will situation straightened out so everyone can relax a little."

Sarah was family, and the others didn't want her here. We needed to leave the rest of Ted's family alone with their empty bottles and their memories.

Chapter Twenty-seven

"Let ev'ry virtue reign within thy breast,
That heaven approves, or makes its owner blest.
To candour, truth and charity divine,
The modest, decent, lovely virtues join,
Let wit well temper'd meet with sense refind'd,
And ev'ry thought express the polished mind."

—Hannah Graves (1806-1864) made this
sampler in 1818 in Whately, Massachusetts.
(It is now in the collection of Historic
Deerfield.) Hannah was the oldest of
eight children. When she was eighteen
she married Banister Morton in
Hatfield, Massachusetts.

Maybe I shouldn't have let Sarah drive off alone.
Jeremy was upset, too. I didn't know how they felt—
but I was on the verge of tears.

And it hadn't been my uncle who'd died, or my
cousins who'd thrown me out.

My mind kept swirling around issues that didn't make sense.

I understood Ted's body was weakened from cancer. But what were the chances that he would die from a "bad clam," as folks around here would say, and no one else have a twinge of trouble?

Yes, Dr. Mercer had said that could happen. But was it logical? I kept going over Saturday in my head. The clammers *had* said they'd gone to several different places. Maybe they'd only dug one clam in a bad flat and Ted had been unlucky enough to eat that one.

It could have happened that way.

I found myself driving to Dave's house. He hadn't been involved in this whole mess. Maybe he'd have the answers. And I wouldn't have to explain the situation to him: he'd come to the hospital last night when I'd needed him. We'd needed him.

Dave was working in his poison garden. "Preparing for winter?" I called out.

"It's that time," he said, limping as he came toward me. "Covering some of the more delicate plants, the ones not native to Maine." He was wearing a Save the Cormorants baseball cap. An increasing number of stores were carrying them. That campaign was one of the differences the Mainely Needlepointers were making: reminding people that nesting grounds for endangered and threatened seabirds should be preserved. Shops couldn't get enough of the needlepoint signs and pillows we were stitching with the slogan and a spread-winged cormorant.

"Thank you for coming to the hospital last night."

"Not a problem. Of course, I don't know for sure Red Tide was the reason Ted Lawrence died. But the clues, as you might put it, headed in that direction. I just reminded the doctors of that." He paused. "Plus, it was an excuse to see Karen Mercer. She was calm in the face of all the craziness after I was shot last month. Special lady."

"Married?" I asked. I'd never heard Dave mention a woman in that tone of voice.

"Not wearing a ring." He grinned. "But no match-making right now, thank you. I have enough problems getting this leg of mine to heal."

He closed the gate to the garden in back of him and sat down heavily in one of his Adirondack chairs. "Glad you interrupted me. I can't do as much gardening at one time as I could before. . . ." He glanced at his leg.

"By next spring you should be fine."

"Next spring seems a long time from now," he said.

"I've been thinking about how Ted died," I started.

"Of course you have. No one in Haven Harbor dies without your questioning how and why, Angie."

"Not true!" Dave was joking, but there was some truth to what he was saying. I'd been back in town since May. Since then I'd gotten involved with one murder after another. "I don't think Ted was murdered."

"Good."

"But Friday night he told his family and close friends that he was going to change his will."

"Let me guess. Not everyone was thrilled."

I shook my head. "They weren't. I can't imagine anyone poisoning their own father . . . but it seems strange that we were all eating clams, and only Ted—the man so many people were upset at—got the toxic one."

"It could happen, Angie. Not everyone is murdered. Sometimes things happen by chance."

"The Marine Resources people were out early this

morning, collecting what was left of the clams from the lobster bake. They were going to post all the flats the clams came from, and start testing."

"Absolutely the right thing for them to do."

"I was wondering if there were any other poisons that would have the same initial effect as Red Tide."

Dave sat back. "Probably. The ME will do an autopsy and find out. But could be. You were there. How did Ted act?"

"He couldn't talk; he kept pointing at his mouth, and his neck. Then he started shaking. Twitching, almost. His cheeks, and his shoulders, and then one of his hands. And he had trouble breathing. I don't remember exactly what order that happened in; it was all so fast. We got him from the beach up the hill to the drive, where the ambulance picked him up. By then he couldn't stand on his own." I thought for a moment. "When the EMTs got him to the hospital he was unconscious. Three hours after that he was dead."

Dave frowned. "Still sounds like Red Tide to me. Red Tide doesn't always cause reactions that quickly, but Ted Lawrence was old."

"He was celebrating his seventy-fifth birthday this weekend."

"And you said he had cancer."

"Lung cancer. Stage four."

"That would explain how fast the toxins hit him, and his problems breathing. But yes, other poisons can act the same way." He paused.

"Like what?"

"Right off the top of my head . . . botulism. Some mushrooms. Arsenic."

"But where would those other poisons have come from?" I pushed Dave a little. I could almost hear his brain clicking through all he knew about poisons.

"Ted's daughter and her husband were farmers, right?"

"In Caribou."

"They might have had access to poisons in pesticides."

"They're organic farmers. They said that several times."

"I'll bet the daughter cans and freezes food, though."

Abbie had said she was putting food away for the winter. "Sure. But what . . ."

"If she didn't heat the vegetables enough, or something else went wrong in the preparation, there could be botulism. Did she bring any homemade goodies for her father? Maybe corn or green bean pickles?"

"Bread-and-butter pickles," I remembered. "I'm pretty sure someone had opened them. But I don't know if it was Ted."

"Pickles would be a possibility," said Dave. "Or someone could have put poison in something else Ted ate."

"I can't imagine how anyone could put poison in the sort of food we were eating. Lobster? Potatoes and corn steamed in seaweed? Clams? Mussels? Corn?"

"What was he drinking?" asked Dave.

"Wine, I'm pretty sure. But he didn't drink much. And most of us drank wine that came from the same bottle. Then we had champagne."

"Can't imagine what it was. Let me know if you hear the results of the autopsy. Now I'm curious, too. And don't be paranoid, Angie. The man could just have been unlucky and eaten the one bad clam. That's why I tell my students always to check with Marine Resources the day they go clamming. Or, better yet, buy their clams from a reputable dealer.

Any dealers that aren't reputable go out of business fast. Really fast."

I nodded.

"Relax, Angie. Not everyone who dies is murdered. Ted Lawrence wasn't a young man, and he already had a fatal illness. Screening his blood and the autopsy should be able to tell if he died for some other reason than Red Tide."

"Okay. Thanks for hearing me out," I said, standing. "Now I'm going home to work on my yard."

"You're gardening?" Dave grinned. "Last time I saw your garden, all you had were a lot of zucchinis and weeds."

"That's about right. But I lost a tree in last week's storm—that big maple in the backyard. Got it pretty well cut up, at least as a start, but it knocked down part of the old stone wall between my place and the Smarts'."

"Not surprised. Heavy tree, old stone wall. Probably chipmunks had secret passages in the wall that made it more vulnerable."

"Maybe," I agreed. "I decided to rebuild it myself. I haven't found any chipmunks. The only thing I've found that's a little strange is a bone."

Dave's head went up. "What kind of bone?"

"I don't know. About seven, eight inches long."

"Interesting. What'd you do with it?"

"Washed it. It's in my dish drainer right now, unless Trixi moved it."

"Was there just the one bone? Did you dig around it and under it to see if there were more?"

"No—one bone was enough. And I had to get over to the Lawrences to help with the lobster bake."

"Mind if I follow you home? You know me—biology's my thing. I'm curious about your bone."

"I figured it was from a dog, or cat, or something that died maybe two hundred years ago and somehow got buried underneath the wall."

"Could be. But amuse me. Let me look at it."

"Com'on over, then," I said. "I'll even throw in a toasted cheese sandwich. I'm about ready for lunch."

"You've got a deal."

I hadn't thought about that bone since yesterday. It hadn't seemed important. Gram had said to forget it. But if Dave wanted to take a look, what could be the harm? That bone had been in the ground a long time. We weren't exactly looking at a crime scene.

Chapter Twenty-eight

*"The Time will Come when We Must Give
Account to God How We on Earth Did Live."*

—Hannah Gore of Boston, Massachusetts, was
nine years old when she completed her
sampler in 1784. It includes a scene of a lady
(adorned with embroidered human hair)
holding a parasol and an elegant gentleman
with a walking stick going to a church. A cow
and two birds, one in a tree, are also in the
picture. Hannah married a baker in 1794
and they had four children. After she was
widowed she married again and had two
sons. She died in 1851.

"I'll make our sandwiches," I said to Dave as we entered
my house. Trixi met us at the door, reminding us that
her food dish could use replenishing.

Dave picked her up. "She's grown so much!" he
said. He was the one who'd rescued her and her

brother and sister. Her sister, Bette, was now living with Patrick, while their brother, Snowy, was, after a few weeks of visiting Gram, now back with Dave.

"Is she an inside cat?" he asked.

I nodded. "I live too close to the street. And fishers come into town sometimes. So far she hasn't complained."

"I'm keeping Snowy inside, too. Don't want him nibbling on anything in my poison garden." He put Trixi down. "I wonder if she remembers her brother and sister?"

"Maybe sometime we should schedule a reunion," I grinned. "I'm glad you got a chance to meet Patrick last night, however briefly."

"Seems like a nice guy."

"He is."

"While you're scrounging up some lunch, why don't I have a look at that bone you found?"

"Follow me."

It was where I'd left it, in my dish drainer.

Dave picked it up carefully (more carefully than I had) and looked at it critically. It wasn't white; it was stained with brown and a little green. Then he put it down. "Show me where you found it," he said.

I finished adding dry food to Trixi's dish and led Dave to the backyard, ducking through some of the downed branches I hadn't cut up yet. "Right here," I showed him. "I used a crowbar to pry up several rocks on the bottom of the wall, and saw part of it. I was curious, so I dug around it."

"Mind if I dig a little more?"

"No. If you find any good rocks for the wall, feel free to dig them out," I said. "I'll call you when our sandwiches are done."

Inside, I decided to heat some canned tomato soup, adding diced tomatoes and a little cream, and began toasting bread and slicing cheese, a process Trixi found fascinating. Once or twice I glanced out the window. Despite his sore leg, Dave was kneeling on the ground, using a small trowel I'd left next to the wall.

It didn't take long to fill two mugs with hot soup and two plates with grilled cheese sandwiches. "Dave!" I called out the back door. "Lunch is ready."

He held up his hand. "Be there in a minute."

I hadn't realized my discovery was that interesting. Then he called, "Come out here! You have to see this."

The soup and sandwiches would get cold. But he sounded insistent.

"I dug a little deeper and wider than you did," he said, standing and pointing down for me to see.

I saw. He'd uncovered a small skull and more bones. "They're human bones, aren't they?"

"An infant's," he confirmed. "An expert in forensic anthropology should take a look. I don't know enough to guess how old the child was, or how long the bones have been here. But yes. The bones are definitely human."

Chapter Twenty-nine

"Youth is the time for progress in all arts."

—Sampler stitched on linsey-woolsey in
Middletown, Connecticut, in 1810 by
twelve-year-old Charlotte Porter. The verse
is beneath a landscape scene including a
large house shaded by a tree, a woman
with a parasol, a shepherd and his sheep,
a church, a windmill, and a mountain. The
scene is surrounded by yellow flowers.

I shivered. "You're sure it's a baby?"

"Or small toddler. I'm no expert."

"The wall's been here for years."

"Would Charlotte know just how long?"

"I don't know. But I can ask. She might even have
some old pictures that would show it."

"When was the house built?"

"More than two hundred years ago."

We stood quietly. Reverently.

"Let's have lunch and think about what you want to do about it," said Dave.

"Shouldn't we cover the bones? Or something?"

"Do you have any tarps in the barn?"

"Sure." I ran to get one. I wanted those bones covered as soon as possible. Whose bones were they? How long had they been under my stone wall? I assumed my family had built the wall. Did the bones belong to someone I was related to? I shivered.

Dave and I covered the bones and put stones around the edges of the tarp to hold it down, just as I'd helped do at the lobster bake the day before.

By the time we went inside and washed up, the food was, of course, cold. I reheated the soup and stuck the sandwiches in the oven to warm them a little.

"Don't worry about warming everything," said Dave.

I heated it all anyway. I didn't want anything cold right now.

"I want to talk with Gram before I do anything about the bones," I said, finally. "She lived here before me. She might know more."

"I suspect those bones considerably predate Charlotte," said Dave.

"Do you know a forensic anthropologist?" I asked.

"Not offhand. But the University of Maine might. Or Maine's medical examiner."

The medical examiner in Augusta. Where Ted Lawrence's body was now.

"I'd guess to go through channels you'd notify our local police, and have them call the medical examiner's office to find out what they wanted to do."

"Or. . ." I said.

"Or?" asked Dave.

"We could just bury the bones again and not tell anyone."

He looked at me. "Is that what you want to do? Bury whatever happened again?"

"That child probably lived and died generations ago. There's nothing we can do about it now."

"Aren't you curious?"

Curious to find out about a child who'd been lying, buried, close to where I'd played as a little girl, and I lived now?

"I don't know. People used to have home burials, didn't they?"

"Sure. Still do. Maine has hundreds—maybe thousands—of family burying grounds. Most aren't in villages, though. I'd guess most people who died in Haven Harbor in the eighteenth and nineteenth centuries were buried in the graveyards near one of the churches. About eighteen-forty, some of those early graveyards got too crowded, and towns started creating cemeteries near the towns, but outside the city limits as it were."

"You're also an expert on burying grounds?"

"Always found them fascinating."

I shuddered. "Not something I'd put on my list of top ten interests."

"You don't have a poison garden, either," he pointed out.

"I'm going to talk to Gram. So for the moment—don't mention what we found to anyone, okay?"

"They're your bones," said Dave, throwing up his hands.

"Right now I don't want to think about death," I said.

"Then don't. Those bones have been there for a

while. They're not going anywhere you don't want them to go."

We finished our lunch, and Dave left.

I didn't call Gram. The rectory was only two blocks away. If she wasn't home, then at least I'd get some fresh air.

True, I'd been outside a lot in the past twenty-four hours. But today I needed the emotional relaxation of breathing sea air. And a little quiet time.

Right now two blocks would have to do.

Ted Lawrence's death was horrible enough. Not only because he'd collapsed in the middle of what should have been a celebratory party, but because of what his absence meant to Sarah.

She hadn't had long to think about how inheriting millions of dollars of paintings would change her life, and she'd been given two Robert Lawrence paintings I suspected she'd never think of selling, for sentimental reasons. But she'd wanted so much to have ties to a family. And although Ted had accepted her, his children hadn't. At least not so far.

And now Ted was gone.

I knocked lightly on Gram's door and walked in.

I heard voices. That's when I remembered it was Sunday. I hadn't gone to church. Gram and Reverend Tom probably were hosting some church meeting.

Luckily Gram was only having tea with Ruth Hopkins and Katie Titicomb, two of the Mainely Needlepointers, and Anna Winslow, whose husband, Captain Ob, was also a needlepointer. Sort of a family gathering without Dave and Sarah and me.

"I'll get another cup," Gram said as soon as she saw me, and gestured that I should join the other women. I loved that Katie had brought her needlepoint, and was working on one of the Save the Cormorants pillows. Gram gave me a quick hug. "So glad you stopped in, Angel."

"How are you all?" I asked. I'd seen Ruth and Anna relatively recently, but Katie had spent most of the summer in Blue Hill with her daughter Cindy's family. Cindy and I had been high school classmates, but now we only saw each other when she visited her parents in Haven Harbor. "How are Cindy and her kids?'

"All well, and the kids sprouting like witch grass," Katie said. "But they're back in school and day care now, and my husband was about to file for desertion if I stayed Down East any longer. Ruth and Charlotte told me about the cormorant situation, and I'm all in. Until you give me any more needlepoint assignments, I'm stitching cormorants."

"Love that," I said, accepting the cup of tea Gram handed me.

"How did the weekend go?" Gram asked. "I hope you don't mind, but I told everyone about Sarah. And Ted."

"Everyone in town will know soon. They say he ate a toxic clam at the lobster bake yesterday."

"Red Tide?" asked Anna.

"Let me guess. Amateur clam digging," said Ruth.

I nodded. "His sons and Jeremy, his assistant at the gallery, went out yesterday morning."

"Where were they digging?" asked Anna. "I thought all the affected areas around here were posted."

"I'm not sure. I know they divided and went to several flats. No one found many clams."

"Mackerel Point is posted," Anna said. "What time was this again?"

"Yesterday. Late morning," I said. "I don't know precisely."

"I was at Mackerel Point about noon yesterday,"

said Anna. "Hoped to get a few photos of migrating birds. This time of year we get some wonderful visitors, especially near the shore. That area was definitely posted. But I did see someone digging at the other end of the flat from where I was. Even with my glasses I couldn't see who it was, or even if it were a man or a woman."

"Sounds like the right time to have been one of the Lawrence clammers," I agreed.

"Didn't you tell them to stop?" asked Ruth.

"I headed down that way, meaning to point out the posted signs. But I'll admit I got distracted when I thought I saw a red-necked grebe." She shook her head. "I was wrong. It was only a horned grebe. It's still a little early for the red-necks. By the time I got to the end of the flat whoever had been digging was gone. I hoped they'd seen the posted warning on their way out and discarded any clams they'd gotten. They hadn't been there long."

"So sad about Ted," said Ruth. "I hadn't seen him recently. Arthritis keeps me to home a lot. But I would have called Ted and Lily 'close acquaintances' years ago. He never really got over her death."

"I heard she'd drowned," I said.

Ruth and Gram looked at each other. "That's right," said Gram. "She did. Ob's father was the one who found her, all tangled up in his lobster gear."

"Horrible."

"It was. And, of course, all the gossip didn't help Ted accept her death."

"Gossip?" My ears perked up. If anything had happened in Haven Harbor in the last hundred years, these ladies had heard it—directly or from their mothers, when they were children. Lily Lawrence had died in 1981.

Just a pebble in the stream to these ladies.

"There had been rumors," said Ruth. "Nasty rumors. Ted traveled a lot in those days, with his father. Robert was still alive then, and painting, and they all lived at The Point. Anyway, Ted and Robert went to galleries and museum openings, and sometimes they headed south in the winter, to paint."

"All Robert really cared about was his work. Ted painted too, of course, but he wasn't in the same class as his father. Robert's wife had divorced him years before, and then died a short time after that, so Ted spent a lot of time with his dad. In those days Ted was a handsome fellow, and a bit of a ladies' man," Gram added.

"Of course, then he married Lily. She was a beauty, no doubt. And so was little Abbie—took after her mother, that one. But with a big house to take care of, and people calling about Robert's paintings, and three little ones to take care of, Lily had a hard time of it," explained Katie. "She used to come to see my husband and beg him for pills. You know the kind—to help her relax."

"But your husband's a surgeon," said Gram. "Surgeons don't write prescriptions for frustrated women!"

"Well, he did sometimes. At least he did for Lily. Valium, I think it was she wanted."

Ruth pursed her lips in disapproval.

"Oh, he doesn't do that anymore. The rules about medications are so much stricter now, I don't think he'd dare. But back a few years, for a friend . . . anyway, so sometimes he gave her pills."

I thought of the portrait in the Lawrences' living room. I'd imagined Lily's life with Ted as idyllic. Money, a big house, some fame by way of Robert. A husband who adored her. I hadn't thought of her as someone who needed medication to cope.

"So that was the gossip?" I tried to get back to where the conversation had started. "That Lily Lawrence took pills?"

Ruth and Katie and Gram exchanged glances. Gram answered. "We probably shouldn't be talking this way, with Sarah now a Lawrence, and Ted passed away so recently, poor man. But no, the pills were just part of it. She also drank a bit more than most women. At least women around here."

I'd grown up in a house without a drop of liquor in it, despite Mama's working in restaurants and bars and my remembering her stumbling up the stairs late at night. But times changed. Now Gram and Reverend Tom had their own wine cellar. I had a feeling Gram's "a bit more" meant, "a lot more."

"So she took pills and drank. Not a good combination."

"Not at all. Those children weren't exactly neglected, but sometimes they were . . . forgotten," said Katie. "Once in a while one of them would show up at my house, because they knew me, you know. Lily'd forgotten to pick them up after Cub Scouts, or they'd been shopping together and she'd left without one of them."

"That's horrible!" I said. No wonder Abbie had married early and the boys hadn't stayed in touch.

"Haven Harbor's a small town. The Lawrences lived out on that Point of theirs, but the rest of us kept an eye on those kids. We all knew Lily was a little absentminded," said Ruth.

"You call it absentminded?" Katie shook her head. "That girl had problems."

"Well, despite everything, she seemed sweet to me,"

said Gram. "And everyone was upset when Ted and Robert came home that time—they'd been to Boston or somewhere on the Cape, I don't recall—and she was gone. Just—gone. The kids were there, but they didn't know where she was. They said she hadn't woken them up for school, and wasn't home."

"Ted was frantic. Do you remember?" asked Ruth. "Had the police out everywhere, sure she'd been kidnapped for ransom or something else horrible."

"Well, it was horrible," said Gram. "When Zeke Winslow found her body it was a shock to everyone."

Katie leaned over toward me. "But the biggest shock came later. See, they did an autopsy. Lily was pregnant."

"A fourth child? Why would that have been horrible?" I asked, not understanding.

"Because she was three months along. And three months before that, Ted and Robert were in Asia on some sort of tour. They were gone for almost four months." Katie sat back. "That child wasn't her husband's. No way."

"Did anyone know who the child's father was?" I asked.

Gram shook her head. "Someone must have known. But I never heard. I suspect Ted never knew either, although he might have had some ideas. Lily kept that secret the night she took those pills and drank scotch and went for a swim."

Michael had told us late-night swims were a family tradition. Had he been remembering his mother's death when he'd said that?

Chapter Thirty

"Last week our children had their examination and many from Lancaster who had girls in our boarding school came here to see and hear what improvement their children had made. They were examined in spelling, reading, German and English, arithmetic, grammar, geography, music, knitting, tambour, and embroidery or stain stitch as I believe you call it more properly."

—From a letter written by Sister Penny, a teacher at a Moravian school (Linden Hall Seminary) in Lititz, Pennsylvania, on April 18, 1801.

What a sad story. I immediately made a vow not to tell Sarah. She'd loved Ted. She didn't need to hear all his dirty laundry. Especially now. Lily's story wasn't about Ted. Although it did help explain how lonely he'd seemed to be, and maybe why he'd been so open to an unknown relative.

The ladies continued to talk, but about other people, other times. Town history.

But today my question was for Gram. I needed her advice.

I finished my tea, hoping the ladies wouldn't stay long. I wanted to check with Sarah too, and find out how she was coping.

Finally, cookies and tea finished, Katie offered Ruth a ride home and Anna left, too.

I breathed a sigh of relief.

As they were getting ready to go, I picked up the dishes we'd used and took them to the kitchen.

Gram joined me in a few minutes. "So, why are you here, Angel? You certainly got an earful about Lily Lawrence, but I'm pretty sure she's not the reason you stopped in this afternoon."

"No." Gram knew me better than anyone else in the world. I couldn't hide anything from her. Or, I thought, remembering a few high school escapades, I couldn't hide anything important from her.

I sat on one of the kitchen chairs. Juno, her Maine Coon cat who'd been hiding when the other guests were there, jumped up to check me out. She probably smelled Trixi. I stroked her a few times and she jumped down and settled herself on the bed Gram had put for her in the corner.

"It's about that bone I found under the stone wall."

Gram sighed. "I thought it might be."

"Dave Percy was over, and he took a look at it. Then he dug a little further."

Gram didn't say anything.

"He found more bones. He's pretty sure they're human. That they're a young child."

"What do you want from me?" Gram asked.

"Dave suggested I call the police. That the medical examiner's office would know a forensic anthropologist who could tell more about the bones—how old they were, for example. But I wanted to talk with you first."

"What do you want to know?"

"Anything that would help me understand what we found. How long has that wall been there? Who built it?" I hesitated. Gram wasn't acting as open as she usually was. "Do you know anything about the bones?"

"Angie, to begin with, no. I don't know anything about those bones. I didn't know they were there until you called me. The house was built in 1809, and I'm pretty sure the wall was built about that time, too. Probably the stones were dug out of the cellar space. New England ground is full of rocks. That's why we have so many stone walls. People built houses or barns or dug gardens, and needed a place to put the stones. Some places you'll see piles of them in the corner of property. Other folks built walls, for appearance and privacy. Stone walls in Maine are different from stone walls in New Hampshire, or Vermont. Rocks are different here, and people had different ways of putting them together."

"I knew that," I said. "But I never heard of anyone being buried under a wall."

"I haven't either. But I can imagine someone doing that."

"Because they murdered a child?"

"No, no, Angie. Nothing so dramatic. You just found out your mama was killed, I know. Maybe that's why murder is your first thought. Or maybe you read too many mysteries . . . and you've gotten involved in solving a few murders, too. Or maybe it's just that in today's world death, unless it comes in old age, is considered unusual. We want to know why someone died, and how. We even feel guilty that we couldn't have stopped, or at least delayed, it. When someone dies in a car accident we want to know whose fault it was. When someone gets cancer we wonder whether they were eating the wrong food, or smoking, or whether they had a bad genetic history. We ask God why the person we loved died before we were ready for them to go."

"Hasn't it always been that way?"

"People have always asked 'Why?' But in the past they accepted that they would never know. God-fearing people believed God took their loved ones. That they were now in a better place than in this imperfect world. Other people accepted, in their own ways, that wars and disease and accidents were part of life. Death was part of life."

"What has that to do with those bones?"

"I don't know whose bones those are, Angie. Maybe if you went back through all the family records you could figure it out. But I don't think that child was killed. Back when our house was being built, many families lost children. Women gave birth to five, six, seven, or even more children, not only because there wasn't reliable birth control, but because they knew perhaps a third, sometimes more, of their children wouldn't live to grow up. It didn't happen just in New England. It was the way families were everywhere."

"So why are those bones there?"

"What I suspect is that when our house was being built a young mother, probably someone in our family, lost a child very precious to her. She wanted the child to stay close, so, when men—perhaps her husband— were building that stone wall, they buried her baby under it. The stone wall was that child's grave maker. She could see it from her kitchen or bedroom window, and feel close to him or her."

"That's sad."

"Perhaps. But I'd like to believe she went on. That she had other children, who grew up in our house, and who played in that backyard, the way you did when you were young. That those bones have been there since the house was, and have had company . . . family . . . with them all these years."

"So you don't think it's a mystery."

"I think all families have mysteries, and secrets, and stories. I don't think they're all meant to be uncovered."

"So I should bury the bones again. Build the wall again."

"The house is yours now. It will be your decision. But yes. If it were my choice, I'd leave that child in peace."

Peace. I hoped Ted was in peace tonight too, even if his body was in Augusta with the medical examiner.

I couldn't help my small ancestor, but I could put him or her back in a place of rest.

Chapter Thirty-one

> *"Amidst the Cheerful bloom of youth*
> *With ardent zeal pursue*
> *The ways of Piety and truth*
> *With death and heaven in view."*

—From a sampler stitched in 1838 in wool on
linen using cross- and satin stitches by Sarah
Ann Dreisback of Bethlehem, Pennsylvania.
It also pictured a church, two houses, two
trees, sheep, and a bird. Sampler owned by
the Moravian Museum of Bethlehem.

At home, I looked at the tarp in my backyard, and the
bone in my kitchen.

Wrong or right, I liked Gram's version of what had
happened. I said a quiet prayer for the child whose
bones I'd disturbed, and for his or her mother and
father. Chances were they were all parts of my family.
And family should be treated with respect.

I'd rebury the bones, and rebuild the wall. Soon.

But I wanted to check on Sarah. It hadn't been an easy weekend for anyone—certainly not for Ted—but I was most worried about Sarah. Her high hopes had been shattered. How was she coping?

"Angie? I'm fine. Really fine," she assured me when I called her.

"You don't sound fine."

"I opened the store for a couple of hours, but there weren't many customers, so I'm at home."

"How about dinner?"

"I don't know if I can eat anything."

"No clams, I promise."

Silence. Clearly she wasn't ready to laugh about clams.

"I don't have much food in the house. I was thinking of getting something at the Harbor Haunts. Join me?" I didn't like the idea of Sarah alone, thinking of what might have been.

More silence. "I guess so," she agreed reluctantly. "But soon. I don't know how well I'll sleep, but I want to hide under the covers early tonight."

That didn't sound good. "I'll meet you at the café in fifteen minutes."

"Okay."

I glanced in the mirror over the sideboard where I kept my gun. Since I'd been home in Haven Harbor I hadn't even done any target shooting, and hadn't fired it in any other circumstances. But it had come in handy a couple of times. Like this morning.

What a strange weekend. I combed my hair, added lipstick, and decided the rest of me would be acceptable. The Harbor Haunts Café wasn't an elegant place. When Mama'd taken me there years ago, I'd always ordered milkshakes. She'd preferred chocolate sodas with coffee ice cream.

Now the Haunts had a bar.

Tonight I could have used a soothing milkshake.

Sarah was sitting near one of the windows. I headed toward her, but stopped on my way when I saw Haven Harbor Police Sergeant Pete Lambert sitting at the bar. Drinking coffee, I noted. He must be on duty and taking a break.

"Hi, Pete! Haven't seen you in a while."

"Most folks think not being in constant touch with law enforcement is good." He grinned. "Heard you and your friend Sarah were out at The Point yesterday when Ted Lawrence died."

"How did you know?"

He shrugged. "Unattended deaths get reported to the police. We called the Marine Resources guys to investigate the clams, and the medical examiner to confirm cause of death. Your name was on the report as being one of those present when Ted collapsed."

"I was."

"Sad situation. Marine Resources folks work hard to prevent that sort of thing from happening, and most Mainers are careful. Hasn't been a Red Tide death around here in years."

"Life is strange," I said.

"Death, too," Pete added. He saw me looking over at Sarah. "Two of you having dinner together?"

"It was an upsetting weekend. Good to get away from The Point."

"Understood. Enjoy!"

Sarah was waiting for me. She was sipping iced tea. "What did Sergeant Lambert have to say?"

I shrugged. "Not much. He knew we'd been with Ted last night. Said Marine Resources was concerned."

"Red Tide deaths don't help Maine public relations."

"True." A waitress appeared next to our table. She must be new; I'd have remembered her purple spiked hair.

I pointed at Sarah's tea. "Make it two. And a Caesar salad with shrimp. Have you ordered, Sarah?"

"Onion soup and a half haddock sandwich."

"Then you're both set." The waitress nodded and disappeared behind the counter.

"I can't believe this weekend," said Sarah. "Could anything else have gone wrong?"

"Your chowder was great," I said. "And the cake was gorgeous. Ted was pleased."

She nodded. "Until he was killed. By a clam!"

I thought of what Gram had said that afternoon. "Maybe it was fate." A woman I'd met in Arizona had wanted her husband investigated. She had lung cancer and was going to change her will if he had a mistress. He didn't, but I'd seen what stage four lung cancer looked like. "Ted died quickly. He'd done what he wanted to do: seen all his children, introduced you to them, made plans for the future."

"He hadn't changed his will."

"Does it really matter, Sarah? Inheriting those paintings would have changed your life."

The waitress put my tea on the table and I raised it to Sarah. "To survival."

"Survival," she echoed, unconvincingly. "I supposed having the paintings would have meant I could buy a house, and not spend all my time selling low-to-middle-end antiques to people who thought a Beatles poster was an antiquarian artifact."

"There is that," I agreed. "But it would have been a lot of responsibility, too. And you do have two of your grandfather's paintings."

"I'm so thankful he wanted me to take the portrait of my grandmother yesterday," said Sarah. "It was almost as though he knew that would be his last chance to give her to me."

"Have you hung her yet?"

Sarah nodded. "She's in my bedroom, where I can see her first thing every morning and last thing at night. She'll remind me of what one mistake can do to change your life. And how lucky I've been so far."

The waitress put our dinners in front of us. I was hungry. My lunch with Dave seemed a long time ago. "Lucky?" Sarah'd lost her parents and her grandmum, her grandmother, and now her uncle. She'd left the country where she'd been born to make a new life on the other side of the world.

"Lucky. Now I know where I came from, and where I want to live." She smiled into her beer, and then at me. "I have friends instead of family. But now I know what I missed, and it's really all right. Those cousins of mine might share my blood, but they're not like me."

"Luke wasn't too bad," I said.

"I guess not. Although I wasn't thrilled when he threatened to shoot Jeremy this morning."

"Jeremy was trying to open his dad's safe."

"He wouldn't have stolen anything. He wanted to see the earlier will. Luke did, too." Sarah shook her head. "I also learned I'd better be careful about alcohol." She raised her glass in my direction. "My father was an alcoholic, and Michael is certainly headed in that direction, if he isn't one already. Maybe it's a genetic thing."

"Silas was the one who drank the most, though," I said.

"No wonder Abbie wants to leave him," Sarah agreed.

"What? Where did you get that idea?"

"She told me, Friday night. You were talking with Patrick—cleaning up the kitchen, I think. Silas had already passed out, and Abbie'd been drinking, too. She said she'd married Silas because she was pregnant. Ted called her a slut and threw her out of their house. She was still mad at her father for not being sympathetic, or helping her."

"I thought Silas said they'd only known each other a couple of weeks before they'd gotten married."

"The baby wasn't his. But he didn't know that, and it turned out not to matter. The baby was stillborn. Very sad."

I thought of what I'd heard about Abbie's mother that afternoon. Sarah didn't need to hear that now. "Abbie never had other children."

"Intentionally or not. I don't know. But she hated living on a farm, and being up in the county. She'd finished college, like she said, because she hoped that would please Ted and he'd give her enough money so she could get a divorce. Leave Silas and Caribou. Start over. But that never happened."

"She told you a lot."

"She wasn't trying to be my friend, Angie. She was angry at her father, and at Silas, and she'd had too much to drink. I think she'd held on to the hope that when Ted died she'd inherit enough to change her life. And have proof Ted still cared about her."

"Friday night she found out that wouldn't happen."

"I told her she and her brothers could sell The Point. It might be worth a million or two, or more, and she'd get a third. But all she was focused on were her grandfather's paintings. They were what her father had cared about. Cared about more than he'd cared for his children, she told me. If he'd loved them, he would have left them the paintings."

I thought of Mama, and my absent father, and of the bones in my backyard. Families were complicated.

"I suspect living with Silas would be challenging," I sympathized.

"Abbie said the best part of her life was working at the kindergarten."

"I'm glad she has that, then."

Sarah nodded. We were quiet, eating and thinking. In the background I heard a phone ring. People should turn off their cells before they went into restaurants. They were annoying.

A minute later Pete appeared at our table. "Shouldn't be giving out information before we know the details. But thought you ladies would want to know. There's been another death up at The Point."

"Who?" I asked, thinking of the four people who were there.

"A Silas Reed."

"Silas is—was—Ted's son-in-law," I said. "His daughter, Abbie's, husband."

"What happened?" asked Sarah.

"All I know so far is I got a call from the hospital. EMTs brought him in. From the sound of it, he drowned."

"But?" I said, hearing Pete's unspoken words.

"But two unattended deaths in two days in one place is strange. Really strange. I'm on my way up there to investigate."

"Can we help?" said Sarah. "We know the family."

She didn't mention she was a member of that family.

"Not right now. I'm going to question them. And there'll be an autopsy, of course. Could be just a weird coincidence." Pete started to leave and then muttered, "I surc hope so."

Chapter Thirty-two

"Pompadour Patterns: The distinctive characteristic of the small floral designs so named is the combination of pink with blue in the colouring. All the tints were of very delicate hues and shades of the same. The style is named after the famous Madame de Pompadour, who appears to have been the first patroness of such a combination of colours in her costumes."

—From the *Dictionary of Needlework: An Encyclopaedia of Artistic, Plain, and Fancy Needlework* by Sophia Frances Anne Caulfeild and Blanche C. Saward, London: L. Upcott Gill, 1882.

Sarah and I parted company before seven Sunday evening.

Neither of us ate much after hearing Silas had drowned.

Sarah's original idea for the evening, "hide under the covers," was making more and more sense.

At home again, I turned off my telephone, made sure Trixi had clean litter and fresh food for the night, and went to bed.

Ted dying of shellfish poisoning. A child's bones in my backyard. Lily Lawrence's drowning, or maybe suicide. And now Silas's drowning.

Two of those events were long past. The other two were too recent.

I slept restlessly, my mind filled with visions of death, and dying, and trying to drive down a highway and having my vision blocked by a huge heart-shaped balloon hitting the windshield.

After that, I couldn't stay in bed any longer. I didn't want to dream.

It seemed as though Sarah and I'd been cleaning and getting ready for Ted's birthday party weekend at The Point months ago. But that had been Friday. This was Monday morning.

All over the country normal people were getting up, getting their children ready for school, and heading off to jobs.

Dave would be teaching at the high school. Sarah had a store to open. I'd planned to take the day driving between the gift shops Mainely Needlepointers supplied with Christmas ornaments, taking orders, listening to ideas, and making sure they knew about the Save the Cormorants campaign.

Too much had happened. I didn't want to leave town today.

I pulled out a file I'd started last week. Marie Meserve, from over to Newcastle, had asked me to find out about a half dozen matching napkins she'd inherited from her great-aunt. The napkins were edged with delicate embroidered blue and white flowers and marked with the letter *D* in the middle of

a wheel. She was curious about the napkins, and
where they might have come from, since *D* wasn't the
first or last letter of anyone's name in her family. I
should pull out my embroidery books and start
searching for information. But I couldn't focus on
work.

I checked the new Mainely Needlepoint Web site.
One customer had a question ("What size pillow
covers do you make?") that was easy to answer. No
orders. Our online sales department (me) was still a
work-in-progress.

I was restless. Those unsettling dreams still haunted
me. Maybe I should bury the bones now. But first I
needed to breathe fresh air and see that, despite all
the death I felt surrounded by, life was still good.

I'd gotten into the habit of taking an early morning
walk. Usually I ended up on Water Street, looking at
the harbor and the ocean beyond. If I were early
enough, I watched the lobstermen setting out.

Before I set out I checked my phone. I'd turned it
off the night before.

I had three texts. I almost didn't look at them. But,
like everyone else, I was addicted to my phone.

Sarah had texted right after I'd gotten home to
thank me for suggesting dinner out.

No problem there.

Dave asked what I'd decided to do with the bones.
I texted him back that I'd decided to rebury them. I
suspected he'd be disappointed, but I'd made my
decision.

The third message was from Patrick, only a few
minutes ago. He was at Ted's downtown gallery. It was
important. Could I join him there as soon as possible?

I'd been going for a walk anyway. I texted him back.
On my way.

What was he doing at the gallery early on a Monday morning? Usually the gallery was closed Mondays.

I pulled a heavy hoodie over my head. The fall morning was crisp. Soon I'd have to visit the outlets in Freeport or check the winter clothes at Renys to get some warm wools or flannels. The clothes I'd worn in Arizona wouldn't work for Maine temperatures or winds in late fall or winter. I'd been living in sweatshirts and sweaters I'd found when cleaning out Mama's clothes in June, but they wouldn't get me through the cold weather.

Outside I shivered in the stiff breezes. Was it really that cold? Or was my mind still in another place?

The lights were on in the gallery. I knocked on the locked door and Patrick came out, closing the door in back of him.

"Thanks for getting here so fast. I'm in a bit of a quandary, and you know Maine ways. I don't."

Why hadn't he invited me into the gallery? "So you came here?"

He gently touched my lips with a single finger. "I was just too wound up to sleep, so I thought I'd come down here and work."

"The gallery isn't usually open Mondays, is it?" I asked.

"No. But Ted gave me a key. And I didn't think Jeremy would be here today. Jeremy's job is taking care of the customers, unless they're important, or friends of Ted's."

I didn't correct his tense. Some customers probably still considered themselves friends of Ted's.

"Ted was teaching me the business side of the gallery. Contacts, contracts, marketing, setting up shows—that sort of thing. Since I was an artist, I'd seen it all from the other side. I found it fascinating to look at the retail world of art as a profit or loss business."

Patrick had brought me down here to tell me about how galleries were run?

"You've told me you liked working here."

"I've only been here less than a month, but it's amazing how much I've learned."

"So what can I help you with? I know a little about small businesses. But the art world isn't like a detective agency or a custom needlepoint business."

"I'm not looking for business advice, Angie. I've found Ted's will." He looked down the empty street, as if making sure no one else heard him. "If Jeremy shows up, I don't want him to know."

"The current will? The one he was going to revise?"

"I'm pretty sure it's current. It's dated less than a year ago. That lawyer you mentioned—Lenore Pendleton—the one who died earlier this summer? Her name is on it."

"Where was it?"

"A stupid place, actually. Under the old blotter holder Ted kept on his desk. No one uses blotters anymore, but his is Victorian. It has an elaborate brass frame and a heavy cardboard back. You slip the clean blotter into the frame."

"When you're writing with a fountain pen and need to blot it."

"That's the practical use. I've seen modern versions—now they're called desk pads—in offices of lawyers and judges and executives at theatrical agencies. Instead of brass, most of today's have leather edges. Or stainless steel. Some people put large calendars in them. Executives have them mainly because they make desks look impressive. My uncle has a set—

matching bookends, desk pad, pen set, blotter pad, pencil holder. . . ."

I resisted asking Patrick why he'd been in a judges' office. "So, Ted had one of these fancy blotter pads." I rubbed my arms. It was chilly outside. I assumed we weren't inside the gallery in case Jeremy showed up.

"A couple of weeks ago Ted asked me to read through his artist files. He wanted me to know which of the artists he represented were selling, and what they were selling, and for how much. He went off to have lunch with someone and left me in his office. The stack of files was on his desk, and . . . you know my hands still have trouble picking up things."

I nodded.

"I picked up the pile of folders, and I picked up the blotter pad, too. Of course, I put it right back. But before I did I noticed there were papers tucked behind the blotter."

"And you looked at them."

"Actually, I didn't. I saw an invoice on the top, from a lawyer. I might have looked further, I'll admit, but Jeremy came in to make a copy of an artist's statement for a customer, and then Ted came back from lunch. By the time I remembered the papers, I couldn't look at them."

"But you remembered them . . . ?"

"Last night. When I couldn't sleep. Everyone seemed so upset about the old will, and the possible new one. Neither of them had any importance to me, of course. But they did to all the Lawrences, and to Sarah, and even to Jeremy. So I was curious. I thought about where I would put private legal papers."

"In a safe deposit box," I suggested.

"Ideally, yes," he agreed. "But if Ted was going to rewrite his will next week—as he said he was going to do—then I guessed he would have gotten out his previous will, read it over, and planned what he wanted to change."

"That makes sense," I agreed.

"Usually an original will is left with the lawyer, or put in a safe deposit box. Legally, the Lawrences will have to find out where it is, and have it filed."

"But what you found in back of the blotter . . ."

"Is a copy of the will Ted made out last year. It answers the questions Jeremy and Luke were asking yesterday."

Chapter Thirty-three

"*Mary A. Tyson and Sisters' Seminary For Young Ladies, on F Street, north side, between 12th and 13th, where is taught a thorough knowledge of all the solid branches of education, and the French and Latin languages; Music on the Piano and Guitar; Worsted and Ornamental Needlework in all its various branches; also, the making of Wax Flowers, with a knowledge of the preparation of the wax.*"

—From an advertisement in the Washington (D.C.) *Daily National Intelligencer,* September 5, 1845.

"So—what do I do now?" Patrick looked at me. "I have something I shouldn't have. Wills are private documents. But I know the family wants to see it."

I sighed. It wasn't easy. "They've all had such an awful weekend." Did Patrick even know? "Have you talked to any of the Lawrences since we left yesterday afternoon?"

"Haven't talked to anyone," he said. "Except you, now. And Bette. She's very good at listening to my problems."

"Trixi's like that, too. Besides, it doesn't feel so strange to be living alone and talking out loud when you can say you were talking to a cat."

"Exactly."

"Then you haven't heard. Silas drowned last night."

"What happened? How?"

I shook my head. "I don't know any details. Sarah and I were at the Harbor Haunts last night for dinner. We saw Sergeant Pete Lambert there."

Patrick nodded. "Sure. I remember Pete."

"While we were having dinner he got a call about Silas from the hospital. He left, to question everyone at the Point. He said two accidental deaths in one place within twenty-four hours didn't sound right."

"Two of us. Two of the group that was together this past weekend. How could that be?"

"I don't know. You and I could come up with reasons people at Ted's birthday party might have wanted him to die before he rewrote that will. But he wasn't shot or strangled . . . he was killed by a clam. And I can't think of any reason to kill Silas."

"This past weekend I might have wanted to, a couple of times. That guy was a pain."

"He wasn't my favorite cast member in that family drama either. But until we know what happened, I don't think we should joke about it."

"Sorry. You're right. So what do we do now?"

"I think we should give whoever is still up at The Point the will you found. We don't have to say anything about Silas. It's just a strange coincidence that Sarah and I heard about him. They'll probably tell us."

I was interrupted by my cell. It was Sarah. "Angie, I couldn't sleep last night."

"I don't think anyone could."

"I kept thinking about Abbie. Her father died, and then her husband. She tried to be friendly this past weekend. She really did. More than either of her brothers. I've decided to go and see how she's doing."

Even when she threw you out yesterday?

"Patrick and I've just decided to go up to The Point, too," I told her. "Patrick found a copy of Ted's will."

Sarah ignored what I'd said about the will. But after all, it wouldn't have anything to do with her. "Do you think it would be strange if we all showed up?"

"Maybe. But they could throw us out again if they think so."

"When I couldn't sleep, I got up and made lasagna. And a maple cheesecake. I'm going to take both of them to The Point. Ted ate out a lot. There isn't much there to eat."

I couldn't help smiling. Taking foods to a grief-stricken family. Sarah was becoming a real Mainer. And her maple cheesecake was to die for. Although today wasn't the day to use that phrase.

"Why don't we all go together? Patrick and I are at the gallery. We'll meet you at the shop."

"See you then," agreed Sarah.

"All of us?" Patrick asked. "Together?" He looked doubtful.

"Safety in numbers," I said. "Sarah wants to talk with Abbie; they bonded a bit this past weekend. And she made lasagna and cheesecake for the family. You'll take the will; tell them you came to the gallery today to clean up some paperwork, and found the will under the blotter. Just as you told me. Ted probably didn't leave it here for long. Like you said, he was going to revise it and wanted to see what the wording on the earlier version was."

Patrick nodded. "This whole situation is awkward. But I heard what you said to Sarah. If they don't want us there, they'll throw us out." He hesitated. "Do you have your gun?"

"I do not. And I don't think I'll need it. We're just going to pay a friendly condolence call."

"Right," said Patrick. "And deliver the news about the will."

"Have you read it?"

"Enough. I don't think anyone's going to set off fireworks in celebration."

Chapter Thirty-four

> *"Short is our longest day of life,*
> *And soon its prospects end,*
> *Yet on that day's uncertain date*
> *Eternity depends.*
> *But equal to our beings aim*
> *The space to virtue giv'n,*
> *And ev'ry minute well improv'd*
> *Secures an age in Heav'n."*

—Sampler worked in 1834 by Eliza Jane
  Herbert, Portsmouth, Virginia, in the
  "Washington Navy Yard" style: a large
  central brick building with sheep grazing
  on its lawn, a flowered border, and vases
  of flowers. Samplers using this pattern were
  stitched at schools for girls who lived near
  the Washington or Portsmouth Navy Yards,
  perhaps taught by women whose husbands
  worked at the Yards.

Jeremy's car was in the driveway at The Point. So were the Reeds' pickup and Ted's sedan. The gang was all here.

We got out of Sarah's van and looked at each other. We were here. None of us wanted to be.

Sarah knocked on the door. Michael opened it. Even a couple of feet away, I could smell the scotch on his breath. He was holding a half-full glass.

"What d'you all want? We're in mourning. Again."

"We know. I brought you dinner. Homemade lasagna," said Sarah, pushing her way past Michael and clearing a space for a large pan and a smaller one on the kitchen table. "And a maple cheesecake." While he watched, she gathered the empty cans and bottles on the table and tossed them into the large plastic container in the corner labeled "Redemption."

In Maine you pay a deposit (incorporated in the price) when you buy alcohol or soft drinks. After the bottles are emptied you take them to a local redemption center and get your deposit of five or ten or fifteen cents back. The system keeps bottles and cans from being tossed from cars or left on beaches. People from away sometimes wondered whether all the "redemption centers" were a strange sort of Maine religious sect. But the Lawrences had grown up in Maine. They'd understand. Even if this weekend they hadn't always sorted their bottles and cans from the rest of their trash or recyclables.

Michael watched her, with a sort of awe. "Thank you. The food looks terrific. You heard about Silas?"

"We heard," said Sarah. "Where's Abbie?"

He pointed toward the living room. We followed Sarah there.

Abbie was sitting in the corner of the couch, staring

blankly out the window. Sarah sat next to her. "I'm so sorry, Abbie. We heard the news."

"The police were here. It was like Mom dying, all over again." Abbie let Sarah put her arm around her. They sat together, not saying anything.

"I saw Jeremy's car out there," I said to Michael. "Where are he and Luke?"

"Who knows? Those two. Always whispering and talking secrets," said Michael. "I think they're in Dad's office."

Patrick headed down the hallway in that direction.

"What happened last night?" I asked, trying to move Michael away from Abbie and Sarah. They looked as though they could use some privacy.

"Swimming. I went swimming, like I always do when I'm here. I asked if anyone wanted to go with me."

Friday night he'd done that. So nothing unusual.

"Silas said, sure, he'd go swimming. So we went down to the beach. I swam a little, but I was too tired to do much. I got out of the water, sat on the beach, and waited for Silas to get out." Michael took another gulp of liquor. "He never did. So I came back here. Abbie got hysterical, and said to call the Coast Guard or the police or something. Luke called nine-one-one. The cops came, with all their torches and stuff. They found him pretty quick. He was floating. They brought him in and tried to revive him, but he was gone. The ambulance took him to the hospital. Same crew as took Dad Saturday night." Michael added an empty scotch bottle to the redemption container. "That was weird."

"Had you and Silas been drinking?" I asked.

"You sound like those cops. Sure, we'd been drinking. But you don't drown from drinking."

Maybe not, but being drunk could mean you'd lose

your sense of direction and swim out to sea instead of toward the beach. Or you'd pass out and drown. Or you wouldn't be able to swim well, since you couldn't control your limbs. Drinking and swimming didn't mix.

As this family knew too well.

Lily had been drinking when she drowned. But her case hadn't been simple. Maybe Silas's death was.

"So the police questioned you?"

He nodded. "Last night at the hospital, and again this morning. They said Silas was drunk. Sure he was. I was too, but I didn't drown. They sent Silas up to Augusta, to where Dad is."

Augusta. That would be the medical examiner's office.

"How's Abbie doing?"

He shrugged. "She's not talking much."

Well, no.

"Thanks for bringing the food. No place in Haven Harbor delivers pizza or anything. I'd forgotten that."

"Sarah made the food," I reminded him. "When was the last time you visited home, Michael?"

"Here?" He looked around as if looking for an answer. "I don't know. Maybe ten years? I saw Dad a couple of times in the city, though. I'm in school. I can't get away a lot."

"And you're a poet."

"I write poetry." Michael screwed the top off another bottle of scotch and filled his glass again. "And other things. People will see. Everything that's happened this weekend will be good for publicity."

Good for publicity? I didn't question him further.

I hoped Sarah was helping Abbie a little. Neither of them was talking, but at least someone was paying attention to the new widow.

Should I look for Patrick and the other men?

"Where in the city do you live?" I asked Michael. I hoped he could stay upright until Patrick had explained about the will.

"The Village. Greenwich Village."

"I've heard New York's pretty expensive these days," I said. I'd heard enough over the years to know living in Manhattan cost a bundle. And Michael had been complaining about that all weekend.

"Yup." Michael bent down toward me. It was all I could do not to move away. He stunk.

"So do you get paid for your poetry?"

"Not much. But my other project is a moneymaker. And I've got a rich dad." Then he corrected himself. "I *had* a rich dad. When my apartment building went co-op, he bought my apartment."

"And gave it to you?"

"Nah. Stingy bastard. He kept it. Paid the maintenance and all, too. Said when I got my life together I could buy it from him at a fair price. I figure . . . why pay anything if I could live for free?"

"But now he's gone."

"Yup. Gone."

What did that will Patrick had in his pocket say about a co-op apartment in New York City? Ted hadn't supported either of his other children. Why Michael? And did the others know their dad had been helping him out that much?

"I'm an artist, see. Like dear old Dad. And Grampa. Only difference is I write with words instead of brushes. Dad said I could come back here. Help with the business. Write here. Lots of writers and artists live in Maine, you know."

I nodded.

"But I didn't want to come back where everyone knows everyone. I like my privacy." He held his glass close to me, at an angle. Scotch dripped onto my sneaker. "You like your privacy?"

"Sure. But it's nice to have neighbors who care, too."

"Maybe for you. Not for me."

Finally! Patrick, Luke, and Jeremy were heading in our direction.

None of them looked happy.

Chapter Thirty-five

"Eliza Thompson is my name
And with my needle I work the same
That all of you may plainly see
The care my parents took of me."

—Fourteen-year-old Eliza worked this sampler
in silk on linen. It included a brick house,
pine trees, birds, flowers, and the inscription
"Washington City, D.C., September 22, 1823."

The three of them brushed by Michael and me and
settled in the living room.

"Abbie, pay attention. Michael, sit down," Luke ordered. "This is important. Patrick found a copy of
Dad's will in the gallery downtown."

Abbie sat up. Her blank expression disappeared.
"What does it say?"

"How come *he* found it?" Michael muttered from
the chair he'd sunk into.

"He was working, and found it under Dad's blotter."

"Working there on a Monday?" Jeremy sent a spiteful look in Patrick's direction.

"I found it by chance. I explained that already," said Patrick.

"So? Is it legal? What does it say?" Abbie's mood had totally changed.

"It's a copy. Probably the original is with Ted's lawyer, or in his safe deposit box. It's dated about nine months ago, so I'd guess it's the most recent one," Patrick answered.

"That was before he knew about Sarah, right?" said Abbie, ignoring that Sarah was sitting next to her. Was the one who'd been comforting her.

"He didn't know I was related to him until this past July. Two months ago," Sarah said quietly.

"Good," said Abbie.

Sarah flinched.

"What does it say?" asked Jeremy.

Patrick held the papers up. "There's a lot of legalese, of course. But this is what it ends up meaning. Abigail, Michael, and Luke can each select one of their grandfather's paintings to keep. The rest of Robert Lawrence's work, including his sketchbooks and early work and notes, goes to the Portland Museum of Art."

"Shit!" said Abbie, sitting back on the couch.

"What?" asked Michael. "He left everything to a museum? Not to his family? Unbelievable!"

"I'm not finished. The rest of his estate—this house and its contents other than the paintings, and some other real estate holdings and investments—are to be divided between the three of you, with a couple of exceptions. Abbie gets the portrait of her mother that's hanging over the fireplace." Everyone's eyes went to the portrait of Lily and Abbie. "Michael gets the apartment he's been living in on Jane Street in New York City. And Luke gets all of his father's vehicles."

Silence.

Then Luke started laughing. "Dad always said I should have a decent car. I told him I didn't want one in New York City. He thought I had more money than you others, so he left me his tractor and snowplow and ancient sedan. The old guy had a sense of humor after all! I can't believe this. So that's it?"

"Not quite everything." Patrick turned to Jeremy. "To his son Jeremy he left all his own paintings, and his gallery in Haven Harbor, building and contents."

Everyone turned to Jeremy, who looked stunned.

"And his love," Patrick continued, "for his one son who'd inherited the Lawrence art gene. He apologizes for not telling you earlier, Jeremy, and says your mother was sworn to secrecy, but that she'd confirm you are his biological son."

"His son? I'm Ted's son?" Jeremy repeated.

"So his will says."

"Why didn't he tell me?" Jeremy looked around the room. "Did any of you know I was your brother? And Sarah, that means you have another cousin." Jeremy's voice lowered, as though he was talking to himself. "He left me his own paintings, and his gallery. He loved me."

"That's all?" Abbie asked Patrick, curiously ignoring Jeremy.

"That's it. Pretty simple, actually," said Patrick. "Except that you have a new brother."

"How much money will it come to? Dividing everything?" she asked.

"Impossible to say. I don't know what investments he had, or how much this house is worth, or what things in it the three of you would like, or whether you want to sell them. Maybe one of you will want to buy the others out. You'll need a good lawyer," Patrick looked around the room. "Maybe three good lawyers. I suspect the Portland Museum knew it was in the will, so as soon as word gets out that Ted died, they'll be in touch."

"Did he name an executor?" asked Luke.

"In Maine they're called personal representatives. But no. He didn't. I'm pretty sure if no personal representative is named, the court has to do that. Again—you'd better talk to a lawyer."

"How soon will we have our money?" asked Michael.

"In this state nothing's transferred for at least six months after a death. I remember that from when Mama was officially declared dead, last May," I said.

"So what do we live on in the meantime?" Michael leaned forward.

"You could get a job, like the rest of us," Luke said. "Abbie, I assume you'll have Silas's life insurance, so you'll be all right. Insurance usually pays pretty fast."

Abbie shook her head. "Silas didn't have insurance. All he had was his half of the farm and our tractor and pickup. And a rich father-in-law he figured would provide for our futures. Dumb. But unlike Michael, *I do* have a job." Her voice fell almost to a whisper. "Such as it is."

"Spending your day with little people who wet their pants and bite each other," said Michael.

"They're in kindergarten, not preschool," said Abbie. "What I want to know is why I get a picture and you get an apartment in New York City."

"That picture's probably worth a lot," Luke pointed out.

"But what if I want to move to New York? Or Boston? Or London?"

"You'd want to leave scenic Caribou?" asked Michael.

"Tomorrow, if I could," said Abbie.

"Well, you can't leave that soon, even if you had the money," said Luke. "We have to wait for the medical examiner's reports. Both of them."

No one looked at Jeremy, or commented on the biggest revelation in Ted's will.

Chapter Thirty-six

"What tho' in solemn silence all
Move round this dark terrestrial ball.
What tho' not real voice nor sound
And their radiant orbs be found.
In Reason's ear they all rejoice
And utter forth a glorious voice.
For every singing as they shine
The hand that made us is Divine."

—Ten-year-old Julia Ann Crowley stitched this
sampler, dating it "February 10th, 1810:
Washington Navy Yard." She used chenille
and silk threads in cross-, satin, outline,
hem, buttonhole, and Rumanian stitches.

The Lawrence family had a lot to think about.

With only a glance at the kitchen door, Sarah,
Patrick, and I silently agreed to head for her van.
Jeremy followed us.

"Congratulations, Jeremy. Truly. Ted chose wisely for the gallery. And I'm happy to have you for a cousin," said Sarah, giving Jeremy a hug.

"Thank you, thank you. I can't believe it all. My mind is spiraling in all directions. Ted—I mean Father—is dead, and he really cared about me." Jeremy looked at Sarah. "I wish he'd told me before he died, though. And that he could have written that new will, Sarah. He cared about you, too."

She nodded. "I know he did."

There wasn't anything more to say. "Once we know what they decide about funerals we'll probably see each other again," said Jeremy. "Sarah, I'm sorry. I know how hard you worked to make this weekend memorable."

"Well, we won't forget it soon," she answered.

Patrick put his hand on her shoulder. "Hey, lady, you did what Ted wanted. You set the scene. He introduced you to his family, and he told everyone about his cancer. It wasn't your fault, or his, that his children reacted so badly." He looked at Jeremy. "Except for Jeremy."

"Or that he and Silas are now dead?" Sarah said. "Were the stars aligned wrong?"

Jeremy shrugged. "We can mourn Ted. But I'm not sure Silas was a great loss to anyone, except maybe Abbie. And she seems more devastated about losing her father's money than losing her husband."

"Maybe she's in shock," said Sarah. "Right now I don't even know how I feel." She pulled out her car keys. "Let's get going. I need some time away from here to think. I'm going to open my store for the day."

Patrick and I climbed into her van.

"Funny," said Sarah, as she drove toward town. "All

these years I wanted a family. I thought if I had a family, all my problems would be over. That my world would be better. I'd have people around me who cared. I'd have a place. Now, finally, I've met the only family in the world I have left alive, and I wish I were alone again."

Patrick and I looked at each other.

"Families don't always make sense," he said. "I always wanted a brother. I thought if I did I wouldn't miss Mom so much when she was away. I'd have someone to shoot hoops with or play video games with. But who knows? If I'd had a brother he might have been like Michael."

"Or even Silas," I added. "Why did Abbie marry him anyway?"

Sarah shrugged. "Relationships are hard to figure. Maybe she just wanted to get away from home."

I'd wanted to do that, too. But I'd gotten on a bus by myself and headed west when I was eighteen. "I guess."

"Maybe she was scared of being alone," Sarah continued. "And she was pregnant. Maybe she didn't want to be a single parent. Maybe she didn't think she had any choices."

Mama had been a teenaged single parent. Patrick's mother had become a single parent after his father died. Very different people, in very different situations, but they'd both survived being unmarried parents. But everyone was different. I couldn't judge. I hadn't been there. I was twenty-seven now, and I had no desire to have a child. I was still figuring out how to take care of myself. Had Abbie wanted to be a mother? Had she and Silas grieved or celebrated when she lost her baby? I'd never know.

"And why didn't Ted tell Jeremy he had a family before putting it in his will? How could he have announced I was a cousin without mentioning that Jeremy was his son?"

No one answered. Something else we'd probably never know.

"Angie, I'll drop you at your house first." Sarah interrupted my thoughts. "Patrick, since your car is still at the gallery, close to my place, we'll just head down there afterward."

A few minutes later she pulled into my driveway. "Thanks, Sarah. I know you said you were going to open your store, but get some rest, too. You were up most of last night, and the past few days have been incredible."

"I'll try," she answered.

Patrick waved as they headed down to Main Street.

I was tired. But I hadn't worked as physically hard as Sarah had, I hadn't had the dashed hopes Sarah was dealing with, and I'd slept last night, not cooked.

The weekend hadn't left me in shock. It had left me curious.

Two men in one family dead within twenty-four hours.

What were the chances?

I turned my front door key in the lock and headed inside. Trixi greeted me near the sideboard where I'd left my gun. I reached down and scratched between her ears as she rubbed herself on my ankles.

Who would have thought I'd have a use for a gun at a family birthday party?

Sarah was right. Families couldn't always be counted on.

Thank goodness I had Gram.

Chapter Thirty-seven

"Depth of mercy can there be
Mercy still reserved for me
Can my God his wrath forebear
Me the chief of sinners spare."

—Twelve-year-old Ann Lucretia Mayo Scaggs
worked this verse on her sampler, which she
completed March 2, 1831, in Georgetown,
Washington, D.C. Her work included five
alphabets in different styles, a large basket
of fruit and flowers, and a border of hearts,
strawberries, and roses.

Trixi led me to her empty food dish, and sat calmly
beside it. She trusted that I would fill it with something. She was right. A small black cat might not be
everyone's choice of family, but she was mine.

"I'm glad to have you to come home to," I told her
as I filled her dish with dry kitten food. Trixi wasn't

impressed by my words. She found her lunch much more interesting.

"You're probably right," I chattered. "I should eat, too. I don't remember if I had breakfast." I opened the refrigerator. Eggs, milk, cheese. Omelet materials.

I put an English muffin in my toaster, put water on to boil for tea, and started grating Swiss cheese. I wasn't a gourmet cook, but no one was around to judge whether my omelet was perfect.

It tasted fine.

"Okay, Trixi," I said. "We've both eaten. I suspect you'll take a nap. What do you think I should do?"

Trixi jumped up on a shelf below the kitchen window and looked out. Gram had equipped the house with bird feeders in both the front and back of the house. The birds took full advantage, and Gram had made sure her cat, Juno, had inside seating near both feeders. I'd continued Gram's tradition.

"Busy feeder?" I asked Trixi. I looked out at the yard. Two chickadees were devouring sunflower seeds, messily dropping the shells on the ground. I made a mental note to buy hulled sunflower seeds next time I went to the feed store.

Beyond the feeder was the stone wall. And the bright blue tarp Dave and I'd used to cover the bones.

That's what I should do this afternoon. Bury the bones.

I grabbed gardening gloves and a spade in the barn.

The bones were so small. I reached out to touch the skull. *I'm sorry you didn't have a chance to grow up,* I thought. *Didn't have a chance to go to school or fall in love or have children of your own. But I believe Gram was right. You were loved.*

I dug the hole a little deeper. *You've been here a long*

time, and I'm sorry to have disturbed you. I'll make sure you're well covered. I hope no one will bother you again.

As I gently tucked the bones into the soil, I remembered playing in this yard when I was a child. This little boy or girl probably hadn't done that. But maybe two hundred years ago his or her mother had put him out in the yard to lie on a blanket in the warm summer sun while she was hanging damp clothes on bushes to dry. Maybe he'd heard the cooing of mourning doves and screeching of herring gulls. Maybe a chipmunk had run by.

And maybe later on brothers and sisters he'd never met had played tag in the yard near him, or picked apples from the tree in back of the barn. Maybe some days his mother had told him he was loved, and missed.

His family had continued on.

I was a part of that family.

Gently I covered the bones with soil and patted it down.

Then I carefully chose stones with flat tops and placed them side by side over the soil with a few smaller sea stones filling in the spaces between them. The stones would sink when rains and snows came, but the bones of my small ancestor would again be protected.

My back was aching by the time I put a second layer of stones on top of the first. I'd finish another day.

In the meantime I'd taken care of my family.

Would I have children someday who would play in this yard?

If I did, would I tell them about the small bones under the wall?

Probably not.

Bones should lie in peace.

I hoped Ted Lawrence and Silas Reed would rest in peace, too.

And that Sarah and her cousins would, somehow, accept each other. Perhaps not care for each other. But understand each other.

Families weren't simple. They weren't like television show casts where everyone supported everyone else and laughed over dinner.

I sat back on the ground and looked at the wall.

Mama was under the ground now, too. She hadn't been a perfect parent. But she'd loved me as much as she could, and she'd tried to protect me.

Ted Lawrence had sent his children to boarding schools, and rejected Abbie when she'd gotten pregnant and, maybe because of that, he'd let Michael be dependent too long. He'd never told Jeremy he was his father.

But he'd accepted and been kind to Sarah.

She could hold on to that, no matter what happened in the future.

Someone in her family had welcomed her.

Chapter Thirty-eight

"O for an overcoming faith
To cheer my dying hours
To Triumph o'er the monster death
And all his frightful powers."

—Sarah E. Atkinson (1843-1897), known as
Sallie, lived in Alexandria, Virginia. She
stitched her sampler in silk on linen and
made the center of her work a large cat
seated on a cushion or platform—
perhaps its bed.

The end of that Monday called for a hot bath with
bubbles and a glass of wine. I was only twenty-seven,
and my arms and back ached. How did Gram manage
to garden? She was over sixty.

I grinned to myself, imagining her response if I'd
asked her that. "I'm tough, Angel. I do what needs

doing. Keep that up another thirty years or so, and you'll understand."

Trixi tightroped around the top of my deep Victorian footed bathtub, occasionally batting at a nearby bubble.

She kept track of me wherever I was in the house, but I was nervous watching her circle my naked body in the tub. I wasn't embarrassed. I was afraid she'd fall in. Maine Coon cats could swim—some even enjoyed the experience, I'd heard. But Trixi was just an ordinary short-haired cat whose mother had been feral. An uncertain heritage. I didn't want to deal with a panicked, wet cat.

I didn't have to worry for long. She got bored watching the bubbles before I got tired soaking. By nine o'clock we were both curled up on my bed—me under the covers, and Trixi on top. I started to call Sarah, but stopped. She'd probably gone to sleep before I had.

I picked up my file on the embroidery I'd been trying to identify. Maybe a little needlepoint research . . .

My last conscious thought was hoping neither Sarah nor I would have nightmares.

The next thing I felt was Trixi licking my cheek. Time for breakfast.

And, after that, answering my customer's needlepoint question. I'd found what I was looking for the night before. The strange circle surrounding a *D* on the embroidery I'd been asked to identify meant it was stitched by members of the Society of Blue and White Needlework in Deerfield, Massachusetts, an organization founded by Margaret Whiting and Ellen Miller in 1896 to revive country styles of New England needlework. The circle symbolized a spinning wheel. Whiting and Miller employed between twenty and thirty women until the Society ended production in 1925, even overseeing their own spinning and dyeing. At first they only used three or four shades of blue; in later years they added greens and reds. Every summer the Deerfield Society held an exhibition and sale, selling coverlets, curtains, valances, tablecloths, place mats, and napkins. All their designs (strawberries, thistles, clovers, bird, bees, and berries) were based on colonial crewelwork done in wool, but the society used linen threads that were easier to launder.

Beautiful work. I finished my e-mail to the woman who'd asked about her heirloom napkins, and assured her she indeed had a treasure.

Then I focused on getting caught up with Mainely Needlepoint's accounts. I was checking the status of recent orders when my phone rang.

"Is this Angie Curtis?" said a male voice I couldn't immediately identify.

"It is," I answered. Where had I heard that voice before?

"Sorry to bother you. This is Luke Lawrence. From The Point."

"Good morning, Luke." Why would he be calling me?

"Last weekend someone—I think it was Dad—told me you used to be a private investigator."

"I worked for a private investigator," I corrected him. "Yes. When I lived in Arizona."

"Good. I wondered if you'd help me out with something."

"What's that?" How could I help Luke Lawrence? But I was curious enough to listen him out.

"Two policemen were just here," he continued.

"Fact is, they're still here. They're questioning each of us separately. Turns out both Dad and Silas may have been poisoned."

"Red Tide?" That wasn't a new idea.

"For Dad, I think so. But the police won't confirm anything. And Silas drowned. But he had both alcohol and drugs in his system."

"Suicide?"

"I guess all options are possible, but that doesn't make sense to me. Clearly the cops suspect one or probably both Dad and Silas were murdered. You were with us last weekend. You know everyone who was here. And you're the only one who had no connections to Dad or Silas. I'm sure these Maine police will do their best, but I want answers, and I want them quickly. We have to bury my father and brother-in-law, and settle their estates. None of us live here in Haven Harbor. Police investigations can take months. I want to hire you to find out what happened here last weekend. Preferably establish that both deaths were accidental."

I took a deep breath. "I can't promise what I'll find out. Everyone who was there will be a suspect." Including Sarah.

"In the eyes of the police, probably so."

"Who are the investigating officers?"

"A Sergeant Lambert from here in Haven Harbor. Some young guy who keeps looking around the house as though he's never seen a summer cottage before. And a statie—a trooper—Ethan Trask. He looks familiar. Maybe I knew him years ago."

"He's from Haven Harbor," I confirmed. "Now he's a Maine State Trooper. Homicide division."

"Whoever he is, he's spent too much time questioning Abbie. She's a lot more fragile than she looks. And

I have a feeling I'm next. So . . . will you help us? Whatever you charge will be fine."

"I'll have to ask questions, too," I said.

"I understand that."

I took a deep breath. I didn't need or want to get involved with another murder. But I agreed with Luke about one thing. The sooner whoever was guilty (assuming someone was) was found, the sooner Sarah, and everyone else who was innocent, could get on with their lives.

"Call me when Pete and Ethan have left and I'll come over to The Point. I can't promise I'll find anything—or, if I do find something, that it will be anything you'll like. But you have yourself an investigator."

I hung up. Okay. So I wasn't really an investigator. I hadn't put in enough hours to qualify for a license. But I knew these people. I could ask questions and maybe get answers the police couldn't. That had happened before.

And a little extra money would come in handy. Maybe I could hire someone to cut up the rest of that maple lying in large chunks in my backyard, and put some extra insulation in the attic before winter. Gram hadn't added any in years.

But before I did anything else I wanted to warn Sarah about what was happening. It would be logical that Pete and Ethan would begin at The Point. If there had been a murder, that was the crime scene. That's where Ted might have been poisoned, and where Silas died. Soon enough they'd be around to talk with Sarah, and Jeremy, and Patrick. And me.

Sarah should hear what was happening from a friend.

I put on a Fair Isle cardigan Gram had knitted for

me a dozen years ago. All those years it had waited for me in a plastic bag in my bureau drawer.

Gram had always believed I'd leave Arizona and come home. And when I did, I'd need sweaters.

As usual, Gram had been right.

Chapter Thirty-nine

*"May I govern my passions with absolute sway
And grow wiser and better as life wears away."*

—Mary Ann Amanda Fall of Virginia stitched
this verse, plus five alphabets above a line of
closely set houses and trees. She completed
her sampler when she was twelve years old,
in 1839.

Chilly gusts of wind were blowing fallen orange and
yellow leaves from one side of the street to the other
as I headed down toward Main Street and the harbor.
It was a quiet morning. Occasionally a jogger passed
me, or a pickup or car headed out of town. A plastic
pot of orange marigolds caught by the wind rolled
down the sidewalk ahead of me.

I'd forgotten the strength of fall. My cheeks stung,
and I tucked my cold fingers inside the sleeves of my
sweater.

Sarah should be at her store by now. Jeremy would

have opened the gallery. I suspected Pete and Ethan would be out at The Point for a while. They had two possible crime scenes to check and three people to interview at The Point. They'd check the house and grounds too, and were probably cussing out the beach cleanup we'd done Sunday.

They wouldn't disturb Sarah or Jeremy for a while. Patrick and I would be even farther down their priority list.

I reached to open the door of From Here and There before I realized it was locked.

Sarah always opened on time, even in the off season. And this was leaf peeper time. When the "newly wed and nearly dead"—couples with money and without children—visited the coast of Maine to relax, see the colors . . . and spend money. Shops Mainely Needlepoint supplied made sure their Christmas sachets and ornaments and other gifts were in stock well before September. This time of year customers were Christmas shopping as well as buying souvenirs of their visit to Maine.

I peered through Sarah's shop window. No lights; no Sarah.

Maybe she'd overslept?

I took the stairs on the side of the building that led to the outside entrance of her second-floor apartment.

A lot had happened since I'd been here for pizza and revelations of Sarah's past and her hopes for the future.

Hopes that had been dashed during the past few days.

Now I was here to deliver more bad news.

I knocked on her door. Then knocked again.

A few seconds later it opened.

Patrick was standing in front of me, his hair wet. All he was wearing was one of Sarah's purple and pink beach towels.

"Shit. It's Angie," he called back over his shoulder.

Patrick had wanted us to have dinner together this week. He'd kissed me. He'd implied that . . .

I turned to go. To get away. I didn't want to see him, and I certainly didn't want to see Sarah.

"It isn't what you think, Angie," she said as her face appeared over his shoulder.

It seemed pretty obvious what to think. I turned back. "I came to tell you the medical examiner thinks both Ted and Silas were poisoned. Ethan Trask's been called in, from Homicide. He and Pete are questioning Ted's children up at The Point right now. Later today they'll probably be contacting both of you. I wanted to warn you."

I turned and went back down the stairs as quickly as I could.

"Angie . . ." Patrick started, and then I heard Sarah's voice. "Angie, come back."

By that time I was at the bottom of the stairs, heading back up Main Street.

The three of us—Patrick and Sarah and I—had spent the weekend thinking about family. We'd finally agreed that families might be challenging, but you were born to them, so you had no choice about who they were.

Friends, on the other hand, could be trusted.

Except, clearly, my friends.

I hadn't realized I'd cared that much, but the brisk winds were drying tears on my face. I dodged through an alley, taking a shortcut home.

I didn't want to see anyone. Or have anyone see me.

Chapter Forty

"Yet shall thy grave with rising flowers be deft
And the green turf lie lightly on thy breath
There shall the morn her careless tears bestow
There the first roses of the year shall blow."

—Worked by Sally Gorham of New Haven,
   Connecticut, October 20, 1798. She was
   seventeen. Two years later, in December 1800,
   she married Enoch Ives.

Why was I so upset? I didn't have any claims on
Patrick. This past June, when Sarah and I first met
him, Sarah had been the one who was interested.
She'd even good-naturedly told me to stay away: she'd
seen him first.

And I had. Even when I'd sensed chemistry between Patrick and I.

I hadn't even sent him a get well card during the
months he'd been in Massachusetts in the hospital.

Then last month he'd come back. Come back, he said, to stay. And Sarah had told me she wasn't interested.

Of course, that was when she was spending so much time with Ted Lawrence.

But she'd encouraged me to stop in to see Patrick, welcome him back to town.

He and I'd had dinner together a few times. He'd been supportive of the Save the Cormorants campaign.

When Dave's kittens had needed homes Patrick had adopted Bette and I'd adopted Trixi.

I'd thought we might have a chance. To be close friends? A couple? I hadn't allowed myself to think too far ahead.

I wasn't ready for anything serious. I sensed he wasn't either.

And, all right, I didn't want to open my heart to someone and have them turn away. Rejection hurt too much.

It hurt like hell.

Trixi jumped up on my lap and started purring. "Okay, young lady. I'll be all right. We have each other. We didn't really need him anyway." I put her down and covered my face with a cold washcloth. How did my eyes and cheeks get swollen so quickly?

I wasn't an hysterical teenager. I had no claim on Patrick. We were just friends.

But if he didn't want me, why did he have to choose my best friend?

I wanted to pour myself a drink. Something to deaden my feelings.

Instead, I poured a cup of tea and waited for Luke to call.

It didn't take long.

"Angie? The police have left."

"I'll be there in twenty minutes," I promised.

And I was. I had a job to do.

Luke met me in the driveway. "Glad you're here. And that those cops are gone."

Luke looked pale and exhausted. His eyes were puffy, and shadows of light purple were beneath them. It wasn't a fashion statement.

"You said Pete and Ethan questioned each of you; I assume separately," I said.

He nodded.

"What else did they do here?"

"Those two just interviewed us. But after I talked with you a couple of other cops and some crime scene investigators showed up. They had a search warrant for the house and grounds. They took Dad's computer and phone and safe, and those bags of garbage you and the others collected on the beach. They looked through the house, including all the personal stuff in the bedrooms." He hesitated. "They weren't thrilled when I explained why the window was broken in Dad's office and the safe had been shot. Oh, and they took Silas's gun, the one I'd hidden."

"What about your telephones?"

"Only Dad's."

"Did they give you any idea what poisoned your dad or Silas? Was it the same thing?"

Luke looked blank. "I assumed it was the same. I didn't ask."

"And they didn't say," I pointed out, taking a notebook and tape recorder out of my bag. "What about the clams?"

"The Marine Resources people took the clam shells yesterday. When the police took the rest of the garbage, I assumed they were looking for bad clams, too," said Luke. "They told the three of us to stay in the living room while they searched the place. I don't know exactly where they went or what they were looking for."

"I know you've been through this already, but as I said on the phone, I'll need to talk to each of you separately, in private. You understand?"

"I told Michael and Abbie you'd be coming. To be honest, they weren't happy I'd hired you. But they both agreed they wanted this situation over as soon as possible. They want to go home, go back to their lives."

"Do the three of you have any ideas about what happened? About who would have wanted Ted or Silas dead? Or why?"

"Not a clue." His lips tightened. "When Dad said he was going to change his will, all three of us were upset. No secret there. But he hadn't changed his will. The only one who missed out was Sarah Byrne. If she'd expected to inherit, then she was disappointed." He looked at me. "I'd like to think it was Sarah, that maybe she was mad at Dad or something. But why would she kill him before he changed his will? That doesn't make sense. And she had nothing to do with Silas. None of us did, except Abbie. And why would she kill her husband?"

"So no ideas."

"That's why I called you. I suspect the cops don't have any ideas yet, either. But I don't want them dreaming up some plot that implies my sister or brother or I killed my father. Or Silas. We might not be a close family. But we're not murderers."

"Why don't I start with Abbie?" I suggested. "I'd guess she's the one most upset about all this. Silas was her husband. After I talk with her she can have quiet time, or whatever she wants."

In this family, maybe a few drinks. But that was their problem, not mine.

"Come on in. I'll make sure Abbie's ready to see you," said Luke, opening the kitchen door for me.

I glanced into the kitchen. The bottles were gone. "The police took the empties?"

"Empties and partially empty." Luke grimaced. "Michael wasn't happy. They took the last of the Oban."

An empty lasagna pan and the cheesecake plate were on the counter.

"Is Michael sober?" If he was, maybe I should talk with him first, before the day was any longer, and more bottles emptied.

Luke followed my glance at the bar.

"I don't think he's been sober since LaGuardia. But he talked to the cops."

Then it probably wouldn't make a difference. "I'll talk with Abbie first," I decided.

This wasn't going to be a fun job.

Chapter Forty-one

"Life's uncertain—Death is sure.
Sin's the wound—And Christ's the cure."

—Sampler elaborately stitched in silks and
gold on linen by Christian Hutchison
Macduff in 1843 Scotland. She included
delicate floral borders of wildflowers, an
embellished alphabet, and a large basket
of flowers flanked by two peacocks, but, as
was common in Scotland, did not include
the town or city where she lived.

Abbie Lawrence Reed was curled up in the same
corner of the living room couch where she'd been the
last time I'd seen her. Like Luke, her face was pale.
Her hair and makeup had been arranged carefully
when I'd met her Friday afternoon. Now her hair was
uncombed and her face was naked. As I entered the
living room she looked up at me blankly.

"Abbie, I know this is a difficult time. But Luke

hired me to see if I could find out anything more about your father's death. And your husband's."

"Luke told me," she said quietly.

"Can we talk a little, then?"

Abbie nodded, but glanced in back of me. I turned around. Luke was standing in the doorway.

"Luke, I'd like to talk with Abbie alone. If that's a problem, we could go up to her bedroom."

"It's not a problem," he said. "Abbie, can I borrow your truck? Since we're staying a few more days we need groceries. Dad mustn't have cooked, and I can't find the keys to his car."

"My keys are near the toaster," Abbie said. "When you're out, would you get me something for my headache? All Dad had in his medicine cabinet are prescription meds and aspirin, and I can't take those."

"I think the police took everything he had anyway," said Luke. "I'll get you something." A minute later we heard the kitchen door slam.

Abbie looked at me. "I agreed to talk with you, Angie. But only if you interviewed everyone who was here this weekend. Including Sarah."

I felt my stomach tighten. "I've promised Luke I'll do that."

"Dad ate a bad clam. Silas drowned. I don't know why everyone's making such a fuss," she said. "The police were here this morning, and crime scene people were all over the house. And now you're here." She looked up at the portrait of herself and her mother, and then back at me. "No one killed anyone. Maybe it was their fate for the two men in my life to die the same weekend. All I want now is to be left alone to grieve."

"It's possible both deaths were accidents." I acknowledged. "Your father could have eaten a bad

clam. One bad clam would have made you or I very
sick, but in his condition, and at his age, it might have
killed him."

Abbie nodded. "Exactly. That's what I think. I can't
believe anyone here would have killed Dad. We didn't
all get along, but we're not murderers."

Almost Luke's exact words.

"And your husband?"

"Sometimes he drinks too much. This past weekend he did; he was nervous. My father didn't approve
of me, but he disliked Silas even more. When we married he told me I'd made my choice. I'd only seen
Dad a couple of times in the past twenty years. Silas
had met him once before this weekend. So Silas wasn't
looking forward to the weekend. Dad had never
called us all together before." Abbie stared down at
her hands. They weren't as chafed as they'd been
Friday. "We've had a rough time, Silas and me. I
thought maybe if I was nice to Dad, maybe he'd
change his mind. Give me a little money. It would
have made a big difference to us."

"That's why you came."

"He pretty much ordered us all to come. We figured it must be really important for us to be here.
Important enough to miss a few harvest days."

"Did you get a chance to ask your father about the
money?"

Abbie got up and walked to the fireplace. She stood
by the mantel for a moment, and then turned back
toward me. "Friday afternoon, you remember, Silas
and I got here before my brothers. I figured it would
be a good time to talk, before everyone was here. Of
course, I didn't expect you to be here, and a woman
claiming to be our long-lost cousin, and a couple of

guys from the gallery. When Dad invited us he'd said it would be a family weekend."

That's what Sarah had called it. I knew I'd been invited in case Sarah needed a shoulder to lean on. Of course, we now knew Jeremy was family. Patrick had worked at Ted's gallery. I was the only one invited who didn't have a direct connection to Ted.

"I finally had a chance to talk with Dad privately when we took a walk together before dinner," Abbie continued. "I asked him to help us out, and he refused. Said he'd always been clear about how he felt about my marriage, and he hadn't changed his mind."

"Sarah told me you were thinking of leaving Silas," I said.

"Thinking about it? I've thought about it for years. But I have no money, no place to go." Abbie shook her head slightly. "I even told Dad that on Friday. I asked him if it would make a difference to him if Silas and I split. He said it was too late for that."

"You must have been angry."

"Hurt. Sad. Confused. And on top of that, Dad said he wanted my brothers and me to be a family again." She shook her head. "He had no clue. He thought I was asking for a bribe."

"A bribe?"

"To make sure I kept in touch with my brothers and with him." Abbie's laughter verged on hysteria. "A family? We hadn't been a family since Mom died."

I looked up at the portrait. "She was very beautiful. And you looked so much like her."

"I did, didn't I? I was pretty when I was young. Everyone said so."

"How old were you when your mother died?"

"Seven. She died the year after that portrait was painted. Luke was five and Michael was four."

"The portrait's beautiful," I said, staring at Lily's face. She was painted with a Madonna-like smile, not seeming to look at either the daughter sitting next to her or the viewer. "I wonder why your mother didn't have all her children painted."

"She did," said Abbie. "Dad painted a portrait of all of us, about the same time Grandpa did that one."

I glanced around the room. "Where's the other portrait?"

"After Mom drowned, Dad burned it," she said, coming back to sit on the couch. "The boys probably don't remember the painting, or the bonfire. But I was older. I remember. He and Grandpa had a big fight. Dad wanted to burn both paintings, but Grandpa said he couldn't burn that one." Abbie pointed to the oil over the fireplace. "He said that was his painting, and Dad had no right to destroy it. That's when he hung it there."

"Your grandfather hung a painting your father didn't want over the fireplace?"

"He stood on one of the dining room chairs and hung it there himself." Abbie leaned back on the couch. "We lived with him. It was his house. His studio. His gallery." She looked at me. "Why are you asking about the past? I thought you were supposed to find out what happened last weekend."

"Sometimes the past interferes with the present," I said. "Especially in families. Understanding what your family was like in the past may help me understand all of you today."

"There's nothing to understand. We lived here until each of us left. We went to elementary school here in town, then we were sent to different boarding schools in the winter and camps in the summer. We only saw each other on holidays. We really don't know each other. I suspect that was clear to everyone last weekend."

"You haven't kept in touch." I'd already guessed that, but I was glad Abbie's confirmed my assumption.

"I get a Christmas card each December from Luke. I assume he sent them to all of us. I think Dad and Michael met Harold, maybe in New York, but Luke didn't bring him to Caribou, and didn't invite us to New York."

"It must have hurt to have your brother marry someone you'd never met. And not even to have been invited."

"It did. Silas said he wasn't sure he wanted to go to a gay wedding anyway, that it was just as well we weren't invited. But I would have loved to have been there. To see Luke, and meet Harold—he's an actor, did you know? And see New York. I'd hoped Luke would bring Harold this weekend. I was looking forward to meeting him."

"Haven't you ever been to New York?"

"Never. Went to school in New Hampshire, and then got married. Her voice turned bitter. "On a big weekend we sometimes get to an event at UMPI. Or maybe go to Bangor. I haven't been this far south in years."

"You said your dad never gave you money. But he paid for your college, right?"

She nodded. "He made out the checks to the university, and I sent him a copy of my report every semester, to prove I'd been there. He said he was doing that for Mom. That she would have wanted me to go to college."

"She was an educated woman?" I looked again at the portrait.

"She wanted to be. I think she went to college for a year or two, but didn't finish. I don't know all that much about her. By the time I was old enough to ask questions, Grandpa was dead, and Dad said he didn't want to talk about her. The only time he did was when I got pregnant. Then he said I was like her—a beautiful slut. That she'd broken up his family, and I was doing the same thing. That I should leave."

"And you did."

"Silas said he'd take care of me, and he did. I didn't have a choice."

The portrait of Lily was haunting. I kept looking at it. "My mother disappeared when I was ten. I wasn't much older than you. Sarah's mother died when she was two."

"So we were all motherless brats," said Abbie. "Do you have children? Does Sarah?"

"Neither of us," I said, my mind flashing back to the bones I'd buried in my backyard the day before.

"So we're all the end of our lines," said Abbie. "Women are usually the ones who keep families together. None of us had that happen. And none of us are carrying our families further."

Sarah and I had had grandmothers to care for us. Abbie hadn't even had that.

"So far," I said. "Maybe one or more of us will have a family. We're all still young."

"I don't feel young," said Abbie. "Friday afternoon, driving down here, I was excited. Nervous, yes. But excited. I hoped somehow our family would come together, the way we were when we my brothers and I were small. That all the disagreements and problems would disappear."

"That's what your father wanted, too," I said quietly.

She nodded. "Strange, isn't it? Life never turns out the way you want it to."

Chapter Forty-two

"Come read, my little friend,
And learn this for a truth
That learning forms the mind
And manners that of youth."

—From 1836 sampler of Caroline Brice,
"wrought at Mrs. Maunder's Seminary,
Thorverten," in England. Caroline's
sampler is unusual because it includes a
strong outline of St. Paul's Cathedral as
well as three large bouquets of flowers.

Abbie excused herself to go and lie down. I didn't ask
her to stay. I'd heard all I needed to hear right now.

I took a few notes, and went to look for her brother
Michael.

I found him sitting on a granite bench on the lawn
below the house, facing the ocean. He was holding a
tumbler of scotch; any ice in it had long since melted.

He looked up as I walked toward him. "You're here. Luke said you would be."

I nodded. "This is a beautiful place. And it's comfortable in the sun. This morning the winds were piercing for September."

"Winds blow strong between buildings in Manhattan, too," he said. "They're not like Maine winds that churn and swirl and come from all directions. In New York City, winds are single-minded. They tunnel through the streets, penetrating your bones. L.L. Bean should be marketing to people crossing Forty-second Street as well as those camping in Acadia."

"But you like living there."

"In the city you can be free to be whoever you are, or want to be. You're not watched by neighbors or gossiped about at church or expected to live up to your family's reputation." He looked at me. "New York's my home now."

"Your dad must have understood that. He left you your apartment."

"He did. Maybe he understood me, or maybe he didn't know what else to do."

"What do you mean?"

"I'm the youngest. The last great hope for the artistic Lawrences. My grandfather was a great painter. My father's art wasn't bad, but it could never live up to Grandpa's. Both of them kept hoping for another artistic genius. Abbie tried to please them, I suspect, but when she painted she copied. And didn't copy all that well."

"They were disappointed in that?"

Michael shrugged. "Of course. But she was the first, and a girl. I don't think they pressed her that hard. They had two boys to focus on."

"So you and Luke painted?"

"Every Lawrence was expected to paint," said Michael. "No question."

"I didn't realize that," I said. "I've never seen paintings by any of you."

Michael focused on his scotch for a moment and then looked out at the sea. "You're not likely to, either. Luke couldn't draw a straight line. Funny. He's the gay one. You'd think he'd be the artistic one."

"That's a stereotype," I pointed out.

"Maybe. But stereotype or not, he wasn't an artist. Didn't have the expected Lawrence gene. Abbie was better than he was, and she'd already been dismissed."

"Dismissed?"

"Told she wasn't a real Lawrence, told to find something else to do in life that wouldn't disgrace the family too much." He looked at me. "I don't remember much about our mother, but I'm told she was a family embarrassment."

"Your father loved her."

"That was the story, too. That he neglected his art to fall in love with a beautiful woman and have children. Maybe it was true. But then she drank too much, and took lovers, and drowned in a most public and embarrassing manner."

"Who told you that?"

"Grandpa, I think. I don't know. It was common knowledge around town when I was a kid. I heard people talking."

"So Abbie and Luke couldn't paint. Couldn't carry on the tradition."

"Which left it up to me, of course. The sole hope of the family."

"And?"

"I hated art." Michael stopped. "No, I didn't hate

art. I admired it. But in this family, you're expected to do more than admire. You must create."

"You're a poet."

"Right. I 'create with words.' That's what Dad used to say. You're looking at a man who writes very bad poetry and drinks very good scotch whenever he can."

"Your father supported you."

He shrugged. "I told you—I was his forlorn hope. He didn't know anything about poetry. He didn't even care about poetry. That's why I chose to make it my métier. He could tell people his son was a New York City poet, that he found his inspiration in the streets." Michael shook his head. "Pure crap."

"Then you don't write?"

"Oh, I write. I've been working on a memoir. Telling the world what it was like to grow up a Lawrence. The real story. I didn't even get a chance to tell the old man. He would have been furious. It would have reflected poorly on the family name." Michael smiled, looking down at his scotch. "I wasn't sure how to end the book. After this weekend I'll have enough material for a total rewrite." He took a deep drink. "Could be I'll have a best seller on my hands. The truth about the famous Lawrences."

"So that's why you came home this weekend? To tell your family about your book?"

"Partially. To see the place it all started. Luke and I live in the same city and never see each other. Abbie hides out up in the wilderness somewhere. Dad lived with the ghosts of his father . . . canvasses of them. His rebellion was to have his own gallery and represent artists who weren't his father. But his prize possessions were his Robert Lawrences. They were more important to him than his children." Michael looked down at the sea below. "The Point is a beautiful place to live. And die."

What had Michael written in his memoir?

Ted hadn't been close to any of his children, yet he'd accepted Sarah. Or she'd thought he had. Because she hadn't grown up here? Because she was a part of Robert Lawrence? That might explain why he'd acknowledged her relationship to the family and not Jeremy's.

"What do you think happened to your father this past weekend?"

"We all grew up knowing about Red Tide. It's a part of Maine. Kind of ironic, actually. Poetic. He identified with Maine, and then it killed him."

"What happened Sunday night?"

Michael raised his glass toward me. "I was drunk. We all were, a little. But Silas and I had drunk the most. He kept gulping that sludge, that coffee liquor. Said if you mixed it with milk or cream you wouldn't get drunk. Really? Sixty proof plus caffeine and sugar and you wouldn't get drunk?"

"He was the only one drinking that?"

"For sure. No one with any taste would touch it. I wondered why Dad even had it in his bar. I had my scotch, and Abbie was drinking some sort of wine. Luke was carrying around a bottle of vintage cognac he'd found. " He raised his glass again. "You missed a great party. Just like the old days, so I've heard, when Mom was still alive, and she and Dad hosted local artists. Drunks, arguing. Silas kept falling asleep. Abbie was walking around the house making lists of what she wanted when we divided the estate. Luke was on the phone to Harold off and on. I didn't pay attention."

"And then you went swimming."

"Lawrence tradition. Late-night swim. Cold water

was supposed to sober you up. Abbie never did it, even years ago. She always said saltwater messed up her hair. Luke and I just figured she didn't like the cold. Plus, we boys used to strip down to go in. Abbie wouldn't do that, even in the dark."

"So did you and Luke go down to the beach?"

"Nah. He was still jabbering on the phone. He waved me off. But I knew I'd had a bit too much, even for me. You're not supposed to go swimming alone, right? Everyone's mom and dad and swimming instructors tell you that."

I nodded. "So you asked Silas."

"Figured he could use some sobering up. Told him we men were going to brave the currents. He took another swig of that rot he drinks and followed me."

"And then?"

"Then nothing. We got to the beach—took the same path we had Friday night. We left our clothes on the beach. I yelled, 'First one in!' the way Luke and I always did, and ran and jumped in. Brrr, it was cold. I've gotten old and soft."

"And Silas?"

"He went in, too. I heard him splashing. He yelled, 'Cold! I'm heading in,' and I decided to join him on the beach. But he didn't come in. We hadn't taken towels—guess we were too drunk to think of them— but I pulled on my clothes. Took a few minutes. My hands were shaking with the cold, and I was soaked."

"Of course."

"I was almost dressed when I realized Silas was still in the water. I yelled a few times, hoping he'd answer. I figured he'd done what Luke used to do— tell me it was time to get out and then tease me I was too chicken to stay in as long as he could. But Silas didn't answer."

"And?"

"I panicked. I ran up to the house, screaming that Silas had disappeared. Abbie ran down to the beach. Luke called nine-one-one. You've probably heard what happened after that. He'd drowned."

I nodded. "But the ME says Silas was poisoned."

Michael snorted. "No way. Poisoned with that swill he was drinking, maybe. All any of us ate that day was the lasagna Sarah brought over. And her cheesecake. Pretty impressive, that cheesecake. And that's coming from a New Yorker. None of the rest of us were sick. Or died."

"What are you going to do now?"

"Sit on this bench until I finish my scotch. Then go and pour another one," said Michael. "Look out at the place my family ended." He grimaced. "Write a new ending to my book."

I looked down at my phone. **Call me. Please.** It was Sarah.

Chapter Forty-three

"The loss of Time is much
The loss of Grace is more.
The loss of Christ is Such
That no mun can restore."

—This sampler, completed by Mary Howard in
England in 1786, features three trees topped
with different birds above the quotation.
Below is a large castlelike English country
house and a scene of hunting, complete
with riders, dogs, and a fox—a very unusual
subject for a sampler.

I wasn't ready to talk to Sarah, but I'd have to return
her call soon. I'd committed to talking to everyone
who'd been at The Point this past weekend. So far I'd
only spoken with Abbie and Michael.

This wasn't the close-knit, loving family Sarah had
hoped for.

But she and Patrick were both on my list, along with Luke and Jeremy. We'd all been here, family or not.

Had Luke returned from grocery shopping?

I walked back up the hill to the Lawrence house. All was quiet. The truck Luke had borrowed wasn't in the driveway. How much food had he planned to get?

He'd known I wanted to talk with him. Hell, he was the one who'd hired me to talk with everyone.

I shivered. I'd admired The Point Friday afternoon, but after all that had happened here, I wasn't comfortable hanging around the place by myself.

Instead, I headed back to town to talk with Jeremy. The little we'd spoken during the weekend made it clear he knew the Lawrence family well. Like Sarah, he was a member of the family unknown to others. And, in his case, even to himself. He didn't have any reason to kill his benefactor—his father—but maybe he'd have some insights as to what *had* happened.

I parked behind the gallery. It wasn't far from Sarah's home and store. I didn't look forward to facing her after this morning, but I'd have to. I'd stop there after I talked with Jeremy.

A black beribboned wreath was on the gallery's front door. I rang the bell, as a sign directed, and walked in.

I'd always assumed art galleries were for people who were rich, or "interestingly creative," as I'd once heard someone say. Or who were trying to impress others. I'd lived in Haven Harbor most of my life, and most of that time this gallery had been on Main Street.

I'd never been inside.

The first floor was a large space surrounded by white walls, each one hung with ten or twelve large paintings. Large modern sculptures, some made of scraps of wood and some of metal, were in the center of the gallery. Along the front windows, each displaying two paintings, were narrow shelves holding small brass or ceramic sculptures of whales, seals, starfish, sea urchins, and porpoises. A wrought-iron spiral staircase next to a large desk covered with papers and postcards led from this main floor to the second floor. Looking up, I could see smaller paintings hanging upstairs.

Everywhere, the pictures were draped in black.

I almost laughed. It was sad, of course, that Ted Lawrence had died, but to put the gallery in mourning seemed a little overly dramatic for Haven Harbor. Maybe it was an artistic thing.

Jeremy wasn't in sight.

I stared at the wall closest to me. The paintings were grouped by artist.

The first group were traditional Maine scenes: lighthouses, lobstermen, surf, and sailboats. Dramatic seascapes and surreal landscapes too large to fit in my home were on the back wall. I recognized the artist's name: Linda Zaharee. She'd known Patrick's mother, Skye West, years ago, and I'd met her this past June. Had she had anything to do with Patrick's being hired by this gallery?

The art world probably wasn't a large one.

"Angie! How nice of you to stop by!" Jeremy ran down the staircase, clearly happy to see me. "After that dreadful weekend, it's nice to see a friendly face. And, as you can see"—he gestured at the room—"we open Tuesdays, but this time of year we're not overrun by customers."

I nodded. "I like Linda Zaharee's work. Do you sell many of hers?"

"Are you interested in one in particular?" he asked.

"No! I mean, they're wonderful. But they're way

over my budget." The painting I'd been admiring was marked $40,000. It was over the budget of anyone I knew—except maybe Patrick.

"Too bad. Her work is special. We don't sell many, but she and Ted are old friends, so she let us have two or three paintings each year." He leaned over, as though confiding in me. "I suspect they're pieces her New York gallery didn't want. But they're still spectacular." He looked at the paintings with the pride of a young father.

"So this gallery will be yours."

Jeremy sighed. "It's a dream come true. Yes. Ted was kind to remember me."

He hadn't called Ted "Father."

"When did you first meet Ted?"

"When I was at RISD—the Rhode Island School of Design. I was on scholarship, living at home with my mother not far from the school. She'd always encouraged my art, but she clerked at a supermarket. We didn't have much money, although she always managed to have enough for my canvasses and paint."

"You didn't ask about your dad?" I could identify with that. I didn't expect to ever find out who my father was. Jeremy was lucky, even if his luck came late.

"She'd never talk about who my father was. Said it wasn't important. That what was important was my finding my own talents."

"So you did."

"I dreamed," Jeremy said. "I painted, but my first love was the theater. I wanted to be a set designer. That's why I went to RISD. Then, one day when I was a sophomore, Robert Lawrence gave a guest lecture there. Ted was with him. We started chatting at the reception afterward. I wanted to impress him, so even

though I'd never been north of Massachusetts I told
him I loved Maine. He said if I was looking for a job
after I graduated I should contact him, that he was
looking for a bright young man to help in his gallery."
Jeremy blushed. "I mean—a chance to work with
someone in the famous Lawrence family? A dream
come true! And then he called the dean and, to my
amazement, set up a scholarship at RISD and asked
that I be the first recipient. He paid for the rest of my
time in school, and I started coming to Haven Harbor
on my vacations."

"And you had no idea he was your father?"

"Not a clue. Once in a while someone at the gallery
would say we looked alike. He'd joke we'd just worked
together too long."

"So you've known him since you were at RISD."

He nodded. "I called Mom after I heard what Ted
had written in his will. She told me that, yes, he was
my father. That he'd sworn her to secrecy, but had
been sending money over the years. He'd met Mom
when she was young, and worked at a gallery in
Providence. He was married when I was born. He
didn't want his wife to know about me, or the publicity to tarnish the Lawrence family image." The Lawrence family image. What would Michael's memoir do
to that?

"How did that make you feel?"

"I thought Ted valued my ideas and my work. Now
I'm wondering if he was just trying to make up for the
years he wasn't around. The years he wasn't my father.
Maybe he felt guilty; that's why he never told me himself. And then Sarah showed up, and he made this big
announcement and called his family together. . . .
Angie, I'm honestly not sure how I feel about him
right now."

"But you'll stay, and take over the gallery."

"It's a solid, well-known gallery." He gestured at the room. "And will remind me, every day, of the father who didn't have enough courage to acknowledge me."

"Over the years you did meet his—other—children. Did you get to know them well?"

He shook his head. "Abbie was already living up in the County by the time I met Ted, and the boys were in New York. The first few years the boys came for the Fourth of July, and sometimes one of them would come for Christmas. But they just saw me as their dad's employee. I wasn't included in family gatherings." He paused. "And now they're my half brothers and sister. I still can't believe it."

"So," I said as I continued walking through the gallery, "does owning this gallery mean you own all these paintings, along with your father's?"

"Goodness, no!" he said. "Once in a while Ted would buy a painting or two at an auction and hang it here. There are several of those upstairs—would you like to look?"

"Not right now," I said.

"Those belonged to him, to the gallery. I assume they'll soon belong to me, if they haven't sold first. But we hang most of the artists we represent on consignment."

"So the gallery only gets paid when a painting sells," I said, making sure I understood.

"Exactly. The artist creates the work, and we advertise it, and have an opening for each exhibit, and display the work for a contracted period of time. Usually in the summer we hang a new exhibit every month; in the winter, we may leave an exhibit up for two months, or even ten weeks."

"And if you sell a painting?" I asked.

"The gallery gets fifty percent of the sale price," he said.

"The gallery gets as much as the artist?"

"Think of the space we pay for, and the advertising, and food at the openings, and keeping up our mailing lists and having one or two gallerists here at all times. And, most important, the prestigious name of the gallery, and our clients. The artists give their time and creativity. We invest in their work and introduce them to the world."

"And if the paintings don't sell?"

"Then they go back to the artist at the end of the exhibit. Finito, until the next show."

"Interesting. I had no idea how this business was run. I thought galleries owned the art they displayed."

"Not at all," he said. "Happy to have explained it. I'd much rather talk about the business than about what happened last weekend. Have you spoken to the police yet? They seem convinced those two horrible accidents out at Ted's house were murders. Can you believe?"

"I haven't talked with them," I said. "But I heard they were investigating. They've already been here?"

"An hour or so ago," he said.

"What did they ask you?"

"They wanted to know how long I'd known Ted. That's no secret. And they wanted to know about the birthday party, and about his will."

"What did you say?"

"The truth. I told them Ted planned the weekend, and Sarah helped make it happen. Of course, since Ted and Sarah talked here, I knew a lot about it, too. But I had no clue about Ted's wills. His old one or the one he planned to make out." He paused. "I thought I knew everything about myself, and about Ted. But I didn't know the most important thing of all. I'm a Lawrence." Jeremy looked as though he'd just grown another inch or two.

"You didn't think you or Ted had secrets from each other."

"Oh, Angie Curtis, everyone has secrets! But Ted and I trusted each other. I was the only one who knew the worth of the business, and I helped him with his accounts." Jeremy paused. "I was his only employee until he invited Patrick West to work here, too."

"Wasn't it unusual that Patrick started working here at the end of the season? Wouldn't you need extra help earlier in the summer? Not the fall?"

"Some of our biggest sales are this time of year. Leaf peepers and Christmas shoppers, you know. But between us, I think he felt sorry for Patrick. All those horrible burn scars." Jeremy shuddered. "The man has talent, but he'll never be able to paint again. And his uncle's been one of Ted's best customers over the years. Why not offer Patrick a job? He knows art, and his working here would please his uncle. Plus, his mother's a celebrity. That might even lead to more sales. The way I saw it, Patrick was a pity hire."

Ouch. I hoped Patrick never heard that.

"Will you keep him on? When you own the gallery, I mean?"

Jeremy shook his head. "No need. I can run the place by myself, or hire someone younger who wants to learn the business."

And who you could pay less, I thought to myself. "You kept the gallery open last Friday until early afternoon."

"I did. Then I stopped at the patisserie—wonderful, decadent, place!—and picked up the breads and pastries and cake for the weekend. You were in the kitchen at The Point when I brought them in."

"And you were at the party Friday night, and heard Ted's announcement." I leaned over. "Are you sure you didn't know any of that ahead of time? After all, you were so close to Ted."

"I'll admit Ted once hinted that Sarah was a distant relation. I didn't know the details, but I suspected that was one of the reasons for the party. And I knew he'd been tired recently, and taking more time off, and I'd seen doctors' names in his appointment book."

I looked at him.

"Not that I was snooping, you understand. But sometimes I worked at his desk. Checking on customer interests and so forth. Or a doctor's office would call here and leave a message about an appointment. I was as shocked as anyone when Ted said he had cancer. Shocked. Just shocked. And then when Patrick read out that will Sunday! Well, I was just flummoxed. So amazed. So honored."

But hadn't Jeremy been able to give the Haven Harbor Hospital staff the name of Ted's oncologist? I decided not to press the point.

"So the gallery was closed Saturday."

"Ted wanted me to be at The Point Friday afternoon and evening, and all day Saturday, to help out. He knew the lobster bake would take a lot of work, and he wasn't sure how excited his children would be about it."

"Patrick, too. He wanted Patrick at the house."

He nodded. "Patrick too, of course."

"So you and Luke and Michael went clamming together."

"Not exactly together, but yes, we ended up doing

that. Patrick, of course, with his hands? He couldn't have done it. And clamming's too messy for women."

I bit my tongue. I'd been clamming more than a few times in my teens. Muddy, yes. And not always rewarding. Like a scavenger hunt, where the prizes moved. No one who hadn't been clamming could understand how fast a clam could move.

"Where did the three of you go?"

Jeremy counted on his fingers. "First, I drove us to Abenaki Eddy. But diggers were already there."

Diggers with licenses, I guessed. Diggers who wouldn't welcome amateurs.

"Then we went to Conyer's Cove. Luke dug a couple of clams there, but Michael and I had no luck. Then we argued; they wanted to go and buy clams instead of trying to dig them. I told them we'd promised Ted we'd do it ourselves." He paused. "They made some comments about how they could do what needed to be done without me, that I hadn't been around in the old days and they'd managed. We were all angry and frustrated. I dropped Michael at Mackerel Point and Luke at Eagle Rock, as they'd asked. They said they'd get another ride home. As I told the police"—he looked at me as though he knew this wasn't casual conversation—"I don't know how many clams they got. I went back to Conyer's Cove and this time I got a couple dozen. Then I drove back to The Point alone. Michael and Luke called Abbie and she picked them up. When we were back at The Point we threw all our clams in the kitchen sink to clean them, and then took them down to the beach. Ted was the one who ate the bad one. It could have been any of us, you know. Any of us. You or I could be dead right now."

Chapter Forty-four

"*Mrs. Theodore Roosevelt, Jr. recorded family stories and adventures in needlepoint and crewel stitching. She bordered her work with depictions of animals her husband had hunted. Mrs. Roosevelt: 'Each evening, Mr. Roosevelt would examine the animal I had worked upon during the day, offering constructive and anatomical criticism until we arrived at the proper effect for each animal.'*"

—From *American Needlework: The History of Decorative Stitchery and Embroidery from the Late 16th to the 20th Century* by Georgiana Brown Harbeson, New York: Bonanza Books, 1938.

Jeremy's words stayed in my head. *You or I could be dead right now.*

I'd seen the clams. There was no way of knowing which clams had come from which flat, or which digger had brought them home. Clams opened when they were steamed. Opened or closed, they looked the same except for their sizes.

If Ted had died from eating a bad clam, Jeremy was right. Any of us might have gotten that one clam.

But more than one clam at the lobster bake would have been affected. If a flat were covered with Red Tide, all the clams dug there would have the problem. The water, and the algaes in it, would cover the whole flat. From what Jeremy had said, the three clammers had brought back multiple clams from each location.

Anna Winslow had seen postings on Mackerel Point. Michael had been clamming at the Point Saturday. Hadn't he seen the sign?

Maybe the clams weren't meant to poison Ted. Could they have been meant for someone else? No one else had gotten sick, but not all the clams had been eaten. And Ted was the only one of us at the lobster bake who had a fatal illness. He was the most vulnerable. Had he died by chance, as we'd first assumed?

Dave had said other poisons could affect someone the same way Red Tide could.

He'd mentioned botulism. And arsenic. And some kinds of mushrooms . . .

Who would have access to any of those?

And always the question: Why would anyone have wanted Ted Lawrence—or anyone else at the gathering—to die?

I took a deep breath. I had to talk to Sarah. Maybe she'd thought of something I hadn't. And although I didn't want to talk to her about Patrick, I had to.

Sarah'd befriended me since I'd been back in Haven Harbor. We'd worked together on Mainely Needlepoint projects. We shouldn't keep secrets from each other. Especially secrets about the men we were seeing. Or hoped to see.

The sun was going down. It disappeared faster with every September day. By six-thirty tonight it would be dark. The lights in Sarah's store were off. I climbed the stairs to her apartment and knocked on the door.

She opened it cautiously. "Angie? I didn't expect you to come tonight."

"We need to talk. I overreacted this morning. And I need your help. May I come in?"

She opened the door wider and gestured that I should come in. "Beer or wine?"

"Wine," I said, tentatively. Should I ask Sarah about Patrick? Would she say anything? "I should have brought some. But I just came from the gallery."

"How's Jeremy doing?" Sarah picked a bottle of merlot and poured me a glass. I noticed she was drinking soda.

"He's gone a little dramatic. Draped all the paintings with black cloths and hung a black wreath on the door."

"Very nineteenth century," Sarah commented.

"He told me when he was in school he wanted to be a set designer."

"So now all his world is his stage." Sarah and I looked at each other and both laughed.

I raised my glass to hers, and we clinked.

"I'll admit. You and Patrick caught me off guard this morning. I thought you and he were over," I said, as we sat on the couch.

"We never were 'on,' as you would say," said Sarah. "I had some fantasies when we first met early in the summer, But—no—we weren't doing anything."

"Sarah, you can tell me," I said, not smiling. "You weren't doing anything? He just hangs around in your shower early in the morning?"

"He came over last night because he thought I

needed someone to talk with. He was right. We talked, and drank, and finally we ate some crackers and cheese—you know I don't keep a lot of food in the house, and I wasn't thinking about grocery shopping this past weekend. I told him he shouldn't drive home. He slept on the couch." She looked straight at me. "That's all that happened."

Unless she was getting much better at lying, she was telling the truth. Plus, I wanted to believe her. "He slept on this very couch? The one we are currently seated on?"

"This very couch," she answered seriously. "Would you like to move to a chair?"

We both started laughing. True, I hadn't slept with Patrick and had no claim on him. But Haven Harbor was a small town. There wasn't a large selection of eligible men around. And I was attracted to Patrick.

"He's a nice guy," I said.

"Very nice," Sarah agreed. "And remains unclaimed, so far as I'm concerned. Angie, I'm having enough trouble dealing with a family that appears and disappears and then springs up in different places."

"As in . . . the gallery?"

"Jeremy's a dear. A dear cousin, I guess. He's been nicer to me than Abbie or Michael or Luke, for sure."

"That's one of the reasons I'm here, Sarah. Luke called me this morning. Seems the police are investigating."

"You told me this morning before you ran off. They've already been here. They haven't gotten to you yet?"

I shook my head. "Not yet. But I've been talking to everyone, too. Luke was upset about the medical examiner's report—actually, as I think about it, the medical examiner's report was exactly what he was upset about.

Not the fact that his father and brother-in-law might have been murdered by someone." That family reputation again.

"I don't understand those Lawrences," said Sarah, taking a good drink of her soda, "even if I am one."

"Well, you'll appreciate this. Luke hired me to investigate everyone who was at the party this weekend to see if I could come up with something the police missed."

"Does he know you're pretty good at doing that?"

"He knows I worked for a private investigator in Arizona."

"So, are you here to dish, or to question me?"

"A little of both. You knew Ted well. You spent a lot of time with him over the past couple of months. Did he tell you anything about his children that might help us figure out whether one of them killed him?"

"He never said much. Abbie was married to someone he didn't approve of. Michael wasn't talented, but fancied himself a poet, and Ted hoped someday he'd settle into academic life. Luke he hardly mentioned except to say he was doing well and seemed happy." She shrugged. "Which isn't a bad thing to say about your son."

"And Jeremy?"

"Jeremy was almost always around—at the gallery, for sure, and sometimes at The Point. I was certainly surprised to hear he was Ted's son. But maybe I should have guessed. Jeremy does look a little like the other Lawrences, and Ted was clearly fond of him. Son or not, Jeremy was Ted's protégé. It seems right that he inherit the gallery. And Ted's paintings? That was a sentimental gift. They're not worth much, but I like that he left them to Jeremy."

"I'm glad he gave you the two Robert Lawrence

paintings before he died. At least you got something of your father's."

"Now I have to have them insured, I guess." She looked over at the large painting of the lighthouse I'd seen on my previous visit. "I may not have much of a family, but I do have two great paintings."

"And you have friends in Haven Harbor," I told her. "You have me. And Jeremy and Patrick, too. And Gram."

"All the Mainely Needlepointers," she agreed.

"So you're going to stay?" I wondered. "After all, you could sell one of your paintings and go back to Australia in style. Or anywhere else you'd like to go."

"Where else would that be? I'm staying here. Haven Harbor's my home now," Sarah said, gazing at her painting. "I'm not going anywhere."

Chapter Forty-five

> *"Sweet's the scene of recollection*
> *Soft it lulls our cares to rest*
> *When we dwell with fond reflection*
> *On the joys that once had blest."*

—Sampler stitched in Ohio by Elizabeth
Mendenhall, twenty-five years old, in 1832.
Elizabeth was a teacher; she may have made
this sampler (which also pictures a shepherd
and his sheep and dog) as an example for
her students. When she married, at the age
of forty-three, she moved to Randolph
County, Indiana.

"I'd like to think Ted died of an accidental poisoning,
and Silas drowned, probably because he'd had too
much to drink," I said. "But since the police are investigating, and Luke's hired me, I'm trying to figure
out why anyone would have had a reason to kill either
of them."

"That's what you do," said Sarah. "Motive, opportunity, means."

"Exactly. I thought you might have some ideas. You knew everyone better than I did."

Sarah hesitated.

"I only want to brainstorm a little. But there were only nine of us at The Point this past weekend. Two are now dead. I didn't kill anyone. I don't think you did, either."

Sarah looked amazed that I'd even suggested it. "You don't *think* I killed anyone?"

I put up my hand. "I *know* you didn't kill anyone. But I'm trying to put myself in the shoes of the police. To be logical. Ted's death meant you didn't inherit millions of dollars of paintings, and you lost your newly found uncle."

Sarah raised her eyebrows. "And Silas?"

"You had nothing to gain or lose from Silas's death. So that leaves Ted's three—no, four—children, since now we know Jeremy's his son, too. And Patrick."

Sarah shook her head. "Patrick? I can't see that. No motivation—he's already rich and he wouldn't gain anything from either of Ted's wills. Ted's death only meant he'd lose his job at the gallery, which he didn't need, financially. And he didn't know much about lobster bakes. How would he even know how to poison anyone there?"

"I agree. Plus his hands are still clumsy. He couldn't exactly slip a sick clam or a dose of poison onto Ted's plate."

"Poison?"

"I talked with Dave. Other poisons can have symptoms similar to Red Tide's. I'm trying to check out all possibilities."

"Understood. I agree. That gets us to Ted's four

children." Sarah leaned back. "I hate thinking any of them would kill him."

"We don't know that they did," I cautioned her. "His death might still have been accidental. But all of them would benefit if he died before he had a chance to make out another will."

She nodded. "Okay. We'll take them in order. Abbie and Ted didn't get along. He'd cut her off after she got pregnant and then married Silas."

"She said he called her a slut." I hesitated. "Local gossip says Ted's wife was pregnant with a child that wasn't Ted's when she drowned."

"So Abbie reminded him of Lily," said Sarah, not flinching.

Maybe she'd heard the stories about Lily before.

"Abbie told me she asked Ted for money Friday afternoon, before the others arrived. He refused. She was really angry about that. So was Silas."

"You and she talked Friday evening."

"I thought she wanted to find out more about me, be my friend. She told me being the oldest Lawrence child, and a girl, hadn't been easy. She'd been left out of a lot, and since she'd left home she didn't know much about what her father or her brothers were doing. She suspected they stayed closer in touch with each other than they did with her."

"So Abbie wanted money and felt neglected."

"She wasn't the only one of Ted's children who wanted money. What about Michael? Ted's been supporting him."

"Michael told me he's writing a tell-all memoir about growing up in the Lawrence family. Did Ted know that?"

"If he did, he never mentioned it. I suspect a book

Michael wrote about the Lawrence family wouldn't be full of jolly memories and family fun," said Sarah.

"Agreed. Maybe Michael thought a tell-all book would make money. That he wouldn't have to depend on his father as much in the future."

"He was taking notes Friday night while I was talking about how I ended up in Haven Harbor," Sarah said. "I didn't ask him why. I guess they were notes for his book. But no one writes a book overnight."

"True. Michael definitely wasn't happy to hear you were going to inherit the Robert Lawrence paintings. But now he has a lot more to write about: you and Jeremy. And two suspicious deaths. He may be delighted to have new material for his memoir, but I can't see him killing his father to get more to write about."

"No," Sarah agreed.

"The only one who didn't need money was Luke," I added. "That Wall Street job of his sounds like a pretty big deal."

Sarah hesitated. "Have you talked with Luke yet? I mean questioned him, the way you're questioning each of us?"

"No. This morning we only talked briefly about my investigating. While I interviewed Abbie and Michael, Luke went grocery shopping. He hadn't returned when I left."

"Did he pay you up front?" asked Sarah.

"No. I figured he'd be good for it."

"Get cash," Sarah advised. "Luke talks a good story, but Ted once told me he'd trusted Luke to manage some of the family money and Luke lost most of it, along with his own, in the housing crash a few years back. He may have recovered a bit, but I don't think Luke's on easy street."

"So all three of Ted's children needed money."

"And Jeremy . . ."

"Had a regular job, and didn't expect to inherit anything from Ted."

"That's the way it looked. But he's never gotten along with Luke and Michael. He's told me that often enough. He resented them. I can't see him hurting Ted. But why did he go clamming with Luke and Michael Saturday? And which of them brought back the poisoned clams?" Sarah frowned.

"In other words, all four of Ted's children had some motive to kill Ted. We were all together. I guess we all had opportunity."

"And means? We all had access to clams. Although who would have known which clam was the poisonous one?"

"I have no idea," I agreed. "Which means . . . I don't have a clue as to what happened."

Chapter Forty-six

"Religion is the chief concern
Of mortals here below.
May its great importance learn
Its sovereign virtues know."

—Sampler completed by Clementine Russell
in May 1869. Clementine did not include
her location in her stitching.

"It's late," I said, glancing at my phone. "It's been a long day. I'm heading home. If you have any inspirations about what happened this past weekend, let me know."

I walked past the closed gallery and up the hill toward the Green. Crickets were singing, filling the evening's silence with the sound of autumn. The Congregational Church on the far side was lit for Tuesday night choir practice. Lights were also on in most of the houses around the Green. The supper hour was past.

Children and teenagers would be in their bedrooms, working on homework, or pretending to do so, while moms and dads cleaned up the kitchen or watched television. It seemed centuries since Gram and I had lived like that. I had no father, and Mama had left us. But I'd never doubted that I'd been loved. Gram made sure of that.

Sarah, too, had been loved by her grandmother, and Patrick had his mother and his uncle. Jeremy's relationship with his mother sounded close. Children didn't need two loving parents to be valued.

But somehow the Lawrence children had missed out. Lily, whatever kind of mother she'd been, had died when they'd been young. Before they'd really had a chance to get to know her. In her absence, Ted and Robert Lawrence had made sure Abbie, Luke, and Michael were well fed, clothed, housed, and educated. But loved?

What was Michael writing in his memoir?

Especially after this past weekend. He'd been right when he'd said he'd have a new, more dramatic ending for his book.

As I fumbled for my door keys I saw flashes on the Green and heard giggles. Teenagers taking selfies and pictures of their friends in the dark. Not every student was working on homework tonight.

Pictures, I thought, going into my house and greeting Trixi.

Anna Winslow had said that Saturday she'd been on Mackerel Point taking pictures of migrating birds.

I pulled out my phone. "Anna? Angie. Sorry to bother you. But have you looked at the pictures you took on Mackerel Point late Saturday morning?"

"Haven't downloaded them. They're still in my camera," she answered. "Why?"

"I wondered if you'd taken any pictures that included that person you saw digging clams on the beach."

"Not intentionally," she said. "But I suppose maybe in the background. Shall I look?"

"Would you mind sending the pictures to me? I'd like to check them out." If Jeremy was telling the truth, the clammer would be Michael. But it wouldn't hurt to have confirmation.

Was it possible that Michael read the "posted" signs and saw a way to keep what he saw as his rightful inheritance, and make his memoir a best seller?

How many clams—if any—had he dug on Mackerel Point? And what had he done with them?

"No problem," Anna was saying. "Have the police decided Ted was killed by one of those clams?"

"They're still questioning people. But Luke Lawrence asked me to think through the weekend too, and see if I could come up with any possibilities."

"I'll send those pictures right over," said Anna. "I hope they help."

Through the living room window I saw the lights of a car pulling into my driveway.

"Got to go, Anna. Looks like I've got company. Thanks for helping."

Detective Ethan Trask and Sergeant Pete Lambert got out of Ethan's car as I opened my front door. "Hey, Angie," said Ethan. "Got a little time to talk?"

"I wondered when you'd get to me." I reached down to block Trixi, who'd been trying to slip outside. I picked her up and she nestled in my arms, purring. "Wine or coffee?"

"Coffee sounds good," said Pete, closing the door

after them. "It's been a long day. And we're still on the job."

I led the way back to my kitchen, switching on lights as I went. Trixi headed for her food dish, while the men sat at the kitchen table. They'd both been there before.

I put coffee on to brew. "Sorry I don't have anything decent to offer you to eat."

"You haven't exactly had time to cook during the past few days," Ethan said.

"I know you've been talking to everyone who was at The Point last weekend," I said, sitting down as the coffeepot started to drip. "Why didn't you call me?"

"You weren't at the top of our suspect list," said Ethan. "And we knew what you were doing. Luke Lawrence told me he'd asked you to investigate." He shook his head. "You know I can't condone people hiring investigators to compete with the police. Pete and I are working full-time on this case. It's high profile. Lots of pressure from Augusta to get it settled quickly. We've talked to everyone who was at The Point last weekend except you. Some we've talked to twice. And at the same time the crime scene folks have done an initial search and examination of what they found in the Lawrence house and barn, and on their beach."

"Anyone has the right to hire a private investigator," I pointed out. "Luke hired me, but I haven't spoken with him yet, or with Patrick West. I've talked to the others." I looked from Ethan to Pete and back. "You probably know that. And you know me. You know I won't do anything to get in the way of what you're doing."

"Yup," said Ethan. "I know you're being careful. But this is police business. Your asking questions isn't helping us. It's confusing people. And it could be dangerous."

I put my hands up. "I'm just chatting with acquaintances."

"Somehow whenever there's a crime in Haven Harbor you seem to be involved in some way," Pete pointed out.

"Is it my fault people talk with me?" I asked, trying to look innocent.

Ethan sighed. "Okay. Tell us what you've found out."

I got up to pour three cups of coffee. "Not much," I admitted, putting the mugs in front of us. "All of Ted's children needed money. They were upset when he announced Friday night he was changing his will."

Pete nodded. "Basic background. Anything else?"

I looked from one of the men to the other. "I really don't have anything to help you. I don't even know if Ted or Silas died accidentally or were murdered. So far, everyone's stories seem to check out. I haven't had a chance to sit down and analyze what I've heard. I was going to do that tonight."

Ethan sighed. "I was afraid you wouldn't be able to add anything. Angie, I shouldn't be telling you this. But we've worked together in the past."

"You can trust me," I said.

"Good. So this information is just for you. Right now we're not convinced Ted Lawrence was poisoned by Red Tide. Early toxicology reports aren't clear. The crime lab is running more specific tests. Certainly, Ted Lawrence might have been a victim of Red Tide, but he also showed signs that could be arsenic poisoning. Right now we can't say for sure what killed him."

"Arsenic!" I said, sitting back. "But isn't that hard to get today? Hasn't it been banned?"

"It has. But you can still get it—or find it—here in Maine, especially in old barns where it was used to kill rats and mice."

"We've even had people report finding arsenic residue in old bottles in antique shops," Pete put in.

"What about Silas?" I asked. "Was he poisoned with arsenic, too?"

"Not Silas. We have other questions about his death, but the cause is pretty clear. His alcohol level was way above the legal limit."

"Wicked high," Pete agreed.

"But he also had a lethal level of Percocet in his system," Ethan added.

"How could that happen?" I asked. "Who had Percocet?"

"Ted Lawrence. We found a bottle of Percocet in his medicine cabinet. The prescription was legal. His oncologist had written it, and Lawrence had filled it in Portland last Wednesday. Only three pills were left in the bottle."

"So either Ted was in horrible pain at the end of last week," I said, thinking it through, "which wasn't evident. Or someone else took the pills and gave them to Silas."

"Exactly. We also found several kinds of poison, including arsenic, in Ted's barn," added Pete. "They weren't hidden. They were labeled clearly in a cabinet holding garden supplies."

"So everyone who was at his birthday weekend had access to both poisons," I said. "Not even counting the Red Tide clams."

"You've got it," said Ethan. "We're beginning to think it's lucky only two people died last weekend. The whole lot of you could have been wiped out."

I sat quietly, my mind whirring. Who could have done such a thing?

"We've gone through the list of people there, and we've talked to everyone. We saved you for last because we figured you had the least reason to kill either Ted or Silas."

"I hardly knew them," I said quietly.

"Exactly. Plus, since Luke told us he was going to ask you to investigate, we hoped you'd hear something we didn't."

"Not everyone talks to the police," Pete pointed out.

"Who else knows arsenic and Percocet may have killed Ted and Silas?" I asked.

"Other than the medical examiner's office, just the three of us," said Ethan. "We're trusting you won't tell anyone else. And that you'll help us find out which of those Lawrences killed their father."

Chapter Forty-seven

"Though lost to sight,
To memory dear."

—Needlepointed words from about 1890
  surrounding a framed postmortem
  photograph of a woman.

"I'll do my best. But I haven't even talked with Luke yet." Or Patrick. But he wasn't one of the Lawrences. "Have you found anything else?"

"You're right when you said money seemed to be the issue. All three of Ted Lawrence's kids—all four, if you count Jeremy—were having financial issues. They've all admitted they were upset when their father told them he was going to rewrite his will and leave Robert Lawrence's paintings to Sarah Byrne, a cousin they'd never heard of."

"That's right," I agreed. "Sarah's my friend, but I don't think their reactions were unexpected. Ted sprung it on them—Sarah's relationship to the family, his own cancer diagnosis, and rewriting his will—all at once. That's a lot to absorb."

"How close are the three of them?"

"Not at all, so far as I could tell. Abbie hadn't seen her brothers in years, and although Michael and Luke may have occasionally crossed paths in Manhattan, they were living separate private lives. Abbie didn't know her father had been supporting Michael for years. I don't think Abbie or Michael knew Luke was having financial difficulties, and Luke and Michael didn't know she was in an unhappy marriage."

"So in your opinion, whoever murdered Ted or Silas did it alone."

"Did Ted's children work together to plan to murder their father? They hardly knew each other, and there was only about twenty-four hours between Ted's revelations Friday night and his death Saturday night." I paused. "On the other hand, all three of his children believed they'd benefit if their dad didn't rewrite his will." I looked from Pete to Ethan. "Everyone had a motive and, from what you've said, everyone had access to whatever killed Ted. Those of us at The Point last weekend were together, but we weren't watching each other every moment. We were busy getting the supplies and equipment and food for the lobster bake, and then were down at the Lawrences' beach pulling it together."

"That's what we've been thinking," said Ethan. "We agree it doesn't seem to be a conspiracy. We think someone acted alone to kill Ted. And unless someone at that Saturday gathering saw something that would prove what happened, the only way we can figure this out is to compare everyone's stories."

"Silas's death, though," I said. "That's a whole other

situation. He and Abbie weren't a happy couple. But murder? No one else in the group would benefit one way or the other if Silas died."

Pete nodded. "We've been focusing on Abbie as the primary suspect for Silas's murder. Would she have killed her father, too?"

I shook my head. "She still hoped to reestablish a relationship with him. He was dying. She was angry with him, but I can't see Abbie as his killer."

"Okay," said Ethan standing. "We're stuck. Ideas?" He looked from Pete to me and back again."

I frowned. "If we're going to find out what really happened at The Point last weekend we'll have to bring everyone who was there together, and go through the time line. See if anyone remembers a detail they didn't tell you or me. See if any stories contradict each other."

"Are you sure that would be a good idea?" asked Pete.

"Luke, Abbie, and Michael know they're all suspects. They're exhausted and angry and in shock. But I don't think they'd cover for each other. They don't seem to have established any loyalties or alliances."

"It's worth a try," said Ethan. "We need to find out what happened to Ted Lawrence before the press finds out he's dead and a media circus begins. And that could happen any time. Plus, all three of Ted's children are making noises about having to leave Haven Harbor." He paused. "Jeremy is another situation. But I suppose we have to consider him a suspect, too.

"Bringing them together will only help if it happens soon. Every hour makes a difference. They could be building a defensive wall right now."

Ethan looked at me and then at his phone. "How fast can you pick up Sarah and Patrick and meet us at The Point?"

"They may be asleep," I pointed out.

"Then wake them up." Ethan looked at Pete. "We'll get Jeremy. I want everyone together who was at The Point last weekend. Angie's right. Reconvening Ted Lawrence's birthday guests may be the only way to get the whole story out."

"I'll get Patrick and Sarah to The Point in thirty minutes," I promised.

I called both Patrick and Sarah, put on a clean sweater, and picked up my gun.

I probably wouldn't need it. After all—Ethan and Pete would be there. Real detectives, with real guns.

But I didn't want to take any chances. Maybe tonight would be when the fireworks Ted had planned for his birthday would explode.

Chapter Forty-eight

*"Promise Little.
Do much."*

— Needlepointed motto, c. 1880. Framed, but
   not signed or dated.

Fifteen minutes later I picked Sarah up at her apartment.

"I hope the police don't expect us to look our best," she grumbled, combing her short streaked hair with her fingers as we headed out of town to pick up Patrick.

"I don't think they'll be paying attention to how we look."

Patrick was waiting for us outside his carriage house on his mother's estate. He climbed into the backseat. "I know law enforcement is a twenty-four/seven operation, but couldn't this have waited for the morning? And what about Jeremy? He was at The Point last weekend."

"Ethan and Pete are picking up Jeremy. The sooner this gets solved the better for everyone. Glad I was able to get through to both of you." I hadn't seen Patrick since that morning, when he'd been wearing only a towel. This was awkward.

"What would you have done otherwise?" asked Sarah, bringing me back to our mission. "Pounded on our doors?"

"Possibly," I said. "Or thrown stones at your windows or . . ."

"Got it," said Patrick. "Hope this doesn't take too long, though. I'm exhausted."

We all were.

Ethan's cruiser was at The Point when I pulled my car in next to it. Thank goodness, I thought, they arrived before we did. They were in charge. I didn't want the challenge of waking one of the Lawrences to interview them again.

We knocked on the back kitchen door we'd been using all weekend. I heard Ethan yell, "Com'on in!"

Sarah went in. She held the door for Patrick and me.

"We'll be there in a minute," I said, touching Patrick's arm.

The door closed behind Sarah. I took a deep breath. "This morning. Sarah told me what happened, why you were . . . dressed . . . the way you were. I was an ass to jump to conclusions."

Patrick shook his head. "A very pretty ass, then."

"I was jealous," I admitted. "I thought you and I. . . ."

Patrick bent down and kissed me, soundly and sweetly. "You and I. Yes. I'm sorry about this morning. I should have run after you."

I grinned. "Not such a good idea in what you were wearing. But we're okay, then?"

He kissed me again, lightly. "Very okay."

"Then I guess we'd better go help solve a murder."

Dinner must have been sandwiches; bread and cold-cut wrappers littered the kitchen table. I was relieved to see at least a couple of bottles of soda. Not everyone had been drinking alcohol.

We joined an unhappy-looking crew in the living room. Abbie and Luke were sitting on the couch; Jeremy and Michael had claimed armchairs. Patrick and Sarah sat in straight chairs near a mahogany card table that seemed permanently set up for a never-occurring game of chess. Pete and Ethan had pulled in chairs from the kitchen. I did the same, staying close to the door.

I might have suggested the idea, but Ethan, with Pete as backup, was in charge. I didn't want to get in the line of fire—verbal or physical. This was a police operation.

"Okay. Everyone's here," said Ethan. "I want to go over exactly what happened this weekend. Who talked to whom, where everyone was, and when."

Michael slumped down in his chair. "We've already answered your questions. And Angie's. How's this going to help?"

"Each of you remembered last weekend slightly differently; you saw and heard different things. We're hoping getting all that out on the table will help explain what happened to your father Saturday afternoon. And to Silas Reed on Sunday."

Michael shrugged. "Do your thing. I can't see it'll be any use, but the sooner we get this over, the sooner we can get some sleep."

Ethan turned to Abbie. "You and Silas drove here Friday afternoon. You were the first of his children to arrive."

"I'd been here earlier," Jeremy put in. "But I was picking Luke and Michael up at the airport."

"Right," said Ethan, gesturing to Pete, who'd taken out both a tape recorder and a notebook. "You and Sarah and Angie and Patrick were all here by early in the afternoon."

"Technically," Patrick pointed out, "Angie and Sarah and I'd been here since first thing in the morning. Jeremy picked up orders at the patisserie after he closed the gallery at noon."

Ethan turned to Abbie. "Late Friday afternoon you and your father went for a walk, Abbie. Am I right?"

"We walked to the barn, and then down the drive. I wanted to talk to Dad in private."

"You asked him for money."

"We needed a new tractor," she said. "Yes, I asked him for money. He hadn't helped us in years. I thought he might have mellowed."

"But he hadn't," said Pete.

Abbie shook her head. "No way. He was as stubborn as always."

"Was the money you asked for really for a tractor?" asked Pete, looking at his notes. "Because later that evening you told Sarah you'd leave Aroostook County in a heartbeat if you had money."

Abbie looked at Sarah. "Someone's got a big mouth. I might have said something like that. We talked about a lot of things."

"So," Ethan continued, "Friday afternoon your father told you he wouldn't give you any money. And, of course, later that evening he told all of you he was planning to leave the Robert Lawrence paintings to Sarah Byrne. I'd guess you were pretty angry about that. After all, even if Sarah was a relative, she was only his niece. You were his daughter."

"I wasn't thrilled," said Abbie. "Sure, I was angry. We all were." She looked at her brothers. They didn't look back.

"You took his rejection personally," said Pete.

"Wouldn't you have?" she spat back.

"Abbie, you live on a farm, right?"

She sighed. "You know I do."

"So you know about poisons. The kind of poisons used to get rid of mice and rats."

"We have an *organic* farm. We don't use poisons."

"But you know what they are, and what they're used for," said Ethan.

"I suppose so. But what has that to do with anything? Dad ate a bad clam. I don't understand why you're grilling me about my life!"

"Your father had poisons in his barn," said Ethan. "Poisons similar to those people use on farms. You were in that barn several times Friday afternoon and Saturday."

"I was," Abbie agreed. "So was everyone else. The clamming rakes and boots were in the barn; so were the wagons we used to cart food down to the beach, the tarps and garbage bags, and the shovels used to dig the pit."

Ethan nodded. "Noted. When we talked with you this morning, Abbie, you had a headache."

"We all were hung over to some degree," Luke interrupted. "Why are you drilling Abbie? She lost her husband as well as her father."

"I suggested to Abbie that she take something for her headache before she talked with us," Ethan continued. "She said she didn't have any painkillers, and there weren't any in her dad's medicine cabinet that she could take."

Right. She'd said the same thing to me later that

morning. Ethan was really focusing in on Abbie. Her back was getting straighter and she was clutching the arm of the couch.

"So, Abbie. You'd checked out your father's medicine cabinet," Ethan said. "The cabinet where he kept his Percocet. The Percocet we found remnants of in a bottle of Bradley's Coffee Brandy. And in your husband."

Michael sat up. Everyone looked at Abbie. We all knew who'd been drinking Bradley's all weekend.

"Why, Abbie?" asked Luke. "Why? We all could use some money. But killing Silas would just leave you with a farm to work. You told us he didn't even have life insurance."

"Why? Because that bastard thought I killed Dad," Abbie blurted.

Sarah gasped.

"I hated Dad. I hated his paying more attention to you boys than he ever did to me. I hated looking so much like our mother than he didn't want to look at me. I hated being sent away to school and I hated his throwing me out of the house. For years I didn't ask him for anything. But Silas and I've had our problems, and this time I was desperate. I needed to get out. To find a man who could give me children. To be something more than a farm wife drudge who wiped the noses of other moms' kids. Sarah was right. Friday afternoon I didn't ask Dad for money for a tractor. That's what Silas wanted me to do. I asked Dad for enough money to start over. I told him I wouldn't bother him. I just needed to get out. Get away."

Michael looked at her. "I didn't know your life was that awful. I thought you were living the way you wanted to live."

She sniffed. "No one ever asked. I figured no one

cared. And when I finally got up enough courage to ask Dad for help, he refused. Said I wasn't a little girl anymore. I was grown up, and would have to figure out my own life. Silas knew I'd asked for money and that I was hurt when Dad refused to give me any. And then Dad announced he was leaving all Grandpa's paintings to someone we didn't even know!"

"So you were upset." Luke looked at Michael. "We were all upset. That was understandable."

"Friday night, before he passed out, Silas said we should leave. Go home. We hadn't gotten what we'd come to Haven Harbor for, and we should get out. I convinced him we should stay until Sunday." Abbie looked around the room. "I wanted to talk with you guys. Talk to people who remembered the same things from our childhood. Maybe I was a little like Dad. I wanted our lobster bake—the bake we all knew by then would be our last together—to be perfect."

"You were a big help in organizing it," Sarah assured her quietly.

"We worked well together, didn't we?" said Abbie, her eyes filling with tears. "I made sure I sat next to Dad at the bake. I kept thinking this was probably the last time I'd sit next to him." She started crying. "And, of course, it was."

Luke picked up a box of tissues from the table next to him and handed it to Abbie.

"Anyway, after we got back from the hospital Saturday night Silas accused me of poisoning Dad. He said he didn't believe Dad had been poisoned by any sick clam, the way Angie's friend said. He said he didn't know what I'd done, but he was sure I'd added something to Dad's dinner."

Abbie blew her nose, loudly. "I told him I'd never do such a thing. Never! Dad and I weren't close, and

I was angry—but I'd swallowed that. Dad was going to
die. Why would I poison him? But Silas kept saying he
was sure it was me. That I had a mean streak, and I was
jealous of Sarah, and if Dad died before he made out
a new will we'd inherit, the way we'd hoped. I kept
telling him he was crazy. He'd had too much to drink.
He didn't know what he was saying." She looked over
at Luke. "You heard him, Luke. You told him I'd
never hurt Dad. I really appreciated your standing up
for me. I hoped Silas would forget his crazy idea by
the next morning."

"But he didn't?" Michael asked.

"He said if I didn't call the police he was going to
call them Monday morning. Tell them his wife was a
murderer." Abbie looked around the room. "He
thought I'd killed Dad, and now you all think I killed
Silas. How can you think that? I didn't know what to
do. But I didn't kill my husband or my father!"

No one answered at first.

Then Luke spoke. "I overheard him talking to you,
Abbie. I couldn't let him turn you in, whether or not
you'd killed Dad. You're still my sister." He turned to
Pete and Ethan. "I thought it would be easy. He was
the only one drinking Bradley's. Everyone knows
you're not supposed to mix alcohol with painkillers. I
figured Silas would just go to sleep, and it would be
the end of his crazy idea that Abbie'd killed Dad.
But then, Michael, you asked him to go swimming,
and the idiot decided to go."

"He did," said Michael, slowly. "He even had a final
drink of Bradley's before we went down to the beach."

"Luke?" said Abbie, the truth dawning.

"At first I thought it would be all right. People
drown, especially if they drink. Everyone knew Silas

was drinking. But then you police got involved, and started asking questions. I didn't kill Dad. I don't know who or what did. But yes. I put the Percocet in Silas's brandy."

Abbie put her head in her hands.

"Someone had to stand up for my sister."

Chapter Forty-nine

*"'Tis true twas long ere I began to seek to live
   forever
But now I run as fast as I can, 'tis better late
   than never."*

—Verse on 1814 sampler stitched by Mary
   Burden (born February 25, 1801), which
   included a queen and a cat in stem and
   cross-stitch with a strawberry border,
   an inn, and a three-storied house.

The living room was silent, except for Abbie's sobs.
   Then my phone vibrated. Who could be calling now?
I pulled it out of my pocket and glanced down.
   Anna Winslow had sent me the photographs she'd
taken at Mackerel Point Saturday. With all that was
happening, I'd almost forgotten she'd said she'd do
that.
   While Ethan was reading Luke his rights, I scrolled
through the pictures. One after another showed birds,

or water, or sky, or mud. Perhaps places a bird had been seconds before. Then I saw something else.

"Pete," I said quietly, "Anna Winslow just sent me a group of photographs she took out at Mackerel Point Saturday morning."

Pete looked at me. "And?"

"They're time stamped. I assumed they might show Michael Lawrence trying, or failing, to dig for clams. But there's more."

He glanced over at Ethan and Luke. Abbie was still sobbing. "Kitchen?" he mouthed toward me.

I nodded.

At the kitchen table I handed him my phone. "Anna's not a professional wildlife photographer. But look at the mud flat."

Pete held the phone close to his face so he could see the details. "I see the time and date stamp on each photo."

"All the pictures were taken Saturday morning, within the time period we know Michael, Jeremy, and Luke were clamming. "Jeremy said he'd dropped Michael at Mackerel Point."

Pete nodded, clicking through quickly. Then, "Wait! Let me go back a shot." He paused and looked even closer. "This picture's focused on the water, but some-one's been digging there," Pete pointed out.

"Whoever was digging wasn't a professional, for sure," I said, looking over his shoulder. "They dig in lines; that clammer was wandering."

"No professional would have been at Mackerel Point," Pete agreed. "It's been posted for the past two weeks. All the local clammers know that."

He clicked to the next photo. And the next, focus-ing in on the mud flat.

We both peered at the screen.

Finally . . . "There!" I pointed. "There's a man with a rake and bucket." The figure was standing up, not digging. I enlarged him as much as my phone would allow.

"Didn't you say Jeremy dropped Michael off at Mackerel Point?" asked Pete.

I nodded. "He said he went on to Eagle Rock." I peered at the time stamp on the photo—"11:50."

"By that time," said Pete, skimming through his notebook, "Abbie had picked Michael and Luke up and taken them home."

"Leaving Jeremy free to go back to Mackerel Point and dig more clams."

Neither of us had any doubt. The clammer in the photo wasn't Michael. It was Jeremy.

Chapter Fifty

"While you, my dear,
Your needlework attend,
Observe the command of a faithful friend
Silence the inward arguments to stain
Or all your needlework will be in vain."

—Dated September 22, 1803. English sampler
 by Armison, age ten. She also stitched a
 heart, an apple tree, and a mounted hunter
 chasing a rabbit.

Pete and I walked back into the living room. "Jeremy,"
I said, looking at him. "Jeremy, you killed Ted."

Everyone turned toward the corner where Jeremy
was sitting.

Jeremy got up and ran. But with Pete and Ethan
after him, he didn't even get as far as the kitchen door.

Each of them held one of Jeremy's arms. They
pulled him back to the living room and sat him in the
chair where he'd been sitting.

"Why do you think that, Angie?" asked Ethan, looking from Jeremy to me.

"I have pictures," I said. "Photographs that show Jeremy digging clams at Mackerel Point—a mud flat closed because of Red Tide—after Abbie drove Michael and Luke back to The Point."

"So—I was digging clams. So were the others. How does that prove I murdered Ted?" asked Jeremy. "Ted was my father just as much as he was Abbie's and Luke's and Michael's, and I knew him better than any of his other children did." He glanced from side to side. "Besides, even if I dug some bad clams, how could I have made sure Ted ate one?"

I thought back to the lobster bake. "You helped set up the bake. We all did. Luke served the food. I remember: he fixed Ted's plate first."

"I didn't have anything to do with serving the food," Jeremy sputtered. "You just said so yourself. Luke did that!"

"You were sitting on the beach, like the rest of us." I thought back. "You sat on Ted's left side; Abbie was on Ted's right." Then I remembered. "Wait!"

Everyone looked at me. "Ted was having trouble cracking his lobster's claws. He handed you his plate and you did that for him."

Ethan focused on me. "Did he add anything to Ted's plate?"

"I don't know. We were all focusing on our lobster and mussels and clams. Not on each other."

"Somehow he must have added one or two bad clams to Ted's plate," said Pete.

"He must have cooked them earlier, then," I pointed out. "If they'd been in with the rest of the clams at the bake, Luke could have served them to anyone."

"You have no proof of anything like that," said Jeremy. "Why would I have killed Ted? He was my mentor, my father. I was closer to him than anyone else in this room."

"You were very upset Friday night," I said. "You were so agitated after Ted announced that Sarah was his niece and he was dying and changing his will that you stomped off and didn't come back until Saturday morning."

"So I was upset. Ted and I were close. That doesn't make me a killer!"

"But Ted was your father," I said.

"I didn't . . ." Jeremy began.

"I know. This afternoon you told me that when they'd been planning the weekend, Ted had implied Sarah was a distant relative of some sort. And you knew Ted hadn't been feeling well recently and had been visiting doctors. You were even able to give Haven Harbor Hospital the name of Ted's oncologist. You knew he'd invited his children to The Point for a special reason. I think you suspected, or maybe even knew, that you were Ted's son. You expected Ted to announce that when he introduced Sarah. Instead, Ted didn't even say what he planned to do with the gallery he'd promised would someday be yours."

"I didn't know I was his son!"

"Sunday, after Ted's original will was discovered, you were most excited about inheriting the gallery. You brushed off the major news: that you were Ted's son. Another illegitimate child recognized. You didn't focus on that part of the will because you already knew you were his son."

"All right! I knew I was Ted's son," Jeremy said. "Patrick made a big deal of finding that will down at the gallery. Well, I'd seen it there, too. I knew what it said. And yes, I expected Ted to acknowledge both Sarah and me Friday night. Instead, Ted ignored me. He made a fuss over Sarah, and he didn't even promise me his gallery."

"Your patron, and father, betrayed you."

Jeremy looked around the room. "All you selfish brats, only wanting what your father would leave you after he died. After I'd worked with him almost every day for nearly fifteen years. He'd trusted me. He'd called me his 'only real son.' And then Sarah shows up and he decides to leave the only things he cared about . . . his father's paintings . . . to her. She'd never heard of Robert Lawrence until a couple of years ago. I'd spent my life admiring his work, and caring for it. Just as Ted did. He owed me."

"And you made sure he ate one or more bad clams."

"I didn't really plan to kill him," said Jeremy, tears beginning to slide down his face. "I was just so angry. Here I was, driving his other sons around. Picking them up at the airport Friday, and them acting like I was their personal driver. Taking them out the next morning to clam. It was Michael's idea to go to Mackerel Point. I just did what he asked me to do. I knew Mackerel Point was posted. He saw it was too, as soon as we got there. But he told me to leave him there anyway, that he didn't need me. Abbie would pick him up. That's when I got the idea to go clamming by myself. I waited until Michael left. Then I went back and dug a half dozen clams. I took them home with me, and steamed them." He looked at me. "You were right, Angie. I had the clams in the pocket of my fishing jacket. I didn't have a plan. I didn't know what I was going to do with them. But then Ted had trouble cracking his lobster's claws—his hands weren't strong anymore—and I added the clams to his plate when he was talking with Abbie."

Chapter Fifty-one

> "*Education*
> *Youth like softened wax with ease will take*
> *Those images that first impressions make*
> *If those are fair their actions will be bright*
> *If foul they'll clouded be with shades of night.*"
>
> —Quotation from English sampler stitched
>   in 1797 by Margaret Hilditch.

It was a week later. Sarah's living room was quiet.

She'd invited Patrick and I to join her for dinner, and we'd finished every scrap of her shrimp and mushroom casserole and made a sizable dent in her maple cheesecake.

We hadn't talked a lot. The weight of everything that had happened was still heavy. Despite her vow to watch her drinking, Sarah had brought three Victorian brandy snifters up from her shop for us to use while sipping the aged cognac Patrick had contributed to our evening, and her coffee table was covered with a needlepoint tablecloth she'd made that incorporated Maine symbols—lobsters, lighthouses, sailboats, skiers, Mount Katahdin, and Mount Washington (which balanced Katahdin, even though it was technically in New Hampshire), Adirondack chairs, lobster pots and traps, and herring gulls, chickadees, and great cormorants.

We were all thinking about what had happened.

Luke and Jeremy were in jail; they'd both confessed and were working with lawyers.

"What's going to happen now?" I finally asked.

"Ted's estate will have to be settled, of course," said Patrick. "The Portland Museum of Art will get the Robert Lawrence paintings. The Point will be sold to someone, and the resulting money should pay for Luke's lawyers, with some put in trust for him until he's served his sentence. The rest will be divided between Michael and Abbie." He paused. "I've told the lawyer handling the estate I'd be interested in buying the Lawrence gallery in town when the estate is free. It looks as though Jeremy will agree with that, and my lawyer is working to arrange for me to rent the gallery until I can buy it, so it won't have to be closed for months. Jeremy can't run it from prison, of course, and I think being a gallerist as well as an artist would suit me."

I raised my glass to Patrick. "To new lives."

"I'm glad the museum is getting the paintings," said Sarah. "They'll know how to care for them and display them, and other museums can borrow them for special exhibits. They'll be available to the public, not hidden away in private homes or galleries."

"I'm glad you have your two, though," I said,

glancing up at the Robert Lawrence painting of Haven Harbor Lighthouse that dominated the room. "And that you found your family."

Sarah nodded. "Biologically, I know who I am. I'm glad I got to know my grandmother in England, even for a short period of time, and to have been part of Uncle Ted's life for a few months."

"Has knowing those people made a difference in the way you look at yourself?" asked Patrick.

"A little," Sarah said. "For years I've been focusing on where I came from. 'Not knowing when the Dawn will come, I open every Door.' Now I can concentrate on who I am, and where I'm going. And on the friends who'll go with me."

I raised my glass to her, and Patrick followed my lead.

"To Sarah."

Sarah's Maple Cheesecake

1¼ cups finely ground graham cracker crumbs
  (about 1 package)
5 Tablespoons granulated sugar
5 Tablespoons of softened butter
1¼ cups pure maple syrup
¼ cup cold heavy cream
3 8-ounce packages of softened cream cheese
3 large eggs at room temperature
1½ cups sour cream at room temperature
2 teaspoons pure vanilla extract

Thoroughly mix cracker crumbs and 1 Tablespoon sugar with soft butter. Press into bottom of nine-inch spring form pan and place in freezer.

Preheat oven to 350 degrees.

Boil maple syrup for three minutes, remove from heat, and stir in cream. Refrigerate.

With mixer, cream the cream cheese until light and fluffy. Add four Tablespoons sugar and the eggs, one at a time. When maple syrup is room temperature, beat it in. Then add sour cream and vanilla.

Pour filling into chilled pan of cracker crumbs and bake for one hour. Cool on wire rack. Cover. Chill at least six hours before serving.

Acknowledgments

With thanks to . . .

My wonderful agent, John Talbot, and editor, John Scognamiglio, without whom Angie and Haven Harbor wouldn't exist.

To all those who found space and time to help me complete this book despite difficult days: JD and Barbara Neeson, for their support and their quiet home by the sea, where half this book was written. My sister, Nancy, who listened. My friends with whom I share the www.MaineCrimeWriters.com blog—especially Kate Flora, Kathy Emerson and Barbara Ross—my "kitchen cabinet" in good times and bad.

To Henry Lyons, who gently nudged me when my website needed updating.

To all my wonderful readers who write reviews, tell their friends about my books, and friend me on Goodreads or Facebook. Their enthusiasm and encouragement makes me smile every day—and keeps me writing.

And, most of all, as always, to my husband, Bob Thomas, the love of my life, for whom the past months have been difficult, but who tells me he loves me every night and every morning, despite his pain. Love you, too, Bob. As always, for always.

Books by Lea Wait

Mainely Needlepoint Mysteries
1 – *Twisted Threads*
2 – *Threads of Evidence*
3 – *Thread and Gone*
4 – *Dangling By a Thread*
5 – *Tightening the Threads*
6 – *Thread the Walls* (coming in November 2017)

Shadows Antique Print Mysteries
1 – *Shadows at the Fair*
2 – *Shadows on the Coast of Maine*
3 – *Shadows on the Ivy*
4 – *Shadows at the Spring Show*
5 – *Shadows of a Down East Summer*
6 – *Shadows on a Cape Cod Wedding*
7 – *Shadows on a Maine Christmas*
8 – *Shadows on a Morning in Maine*

Historical Novels for ages eight and up
Stopping to Home
Seaward Born
Wintering Well
Finest Kind
Uncertain Glory

Nonfiction
Living and Writing on the Coast of Maine

**Please turn the page for an exciting sneak peek of
Lea Wait's newest Mainely Needlepoint mystery**

THREAD THE HALLS

coming soon wherever print and e-books are sold!

Chapter One

"As some fair violet, loveliest of the glade
Sheds its mild fragrance on the lovely shade
Withdraws its modest head from public sight
Covets not the sun nor seeks the glare of light,
So woman born to dignify, retreat, and be unseen,
Fearful of fame, unwilling to be known,
Should seek but Heaven's applause, and her own."

—Stitched by Eliza Ely in 1881, somewhere
   in New England.

"Gram, where's my star?" I called to her. "It has to go on the tree first."

"It's in a gold box. Probably in the same carton as the lights," Gram answered from the dining room, where she and Reverend Tom (I still had trouble thinking of him as just "Tom," no matter how often he told me to drop the Reverend) were adding to the bowl of eggnog.

I'm twenty-seven. Old enough to admit it was silly. But I wanted this Christmas to be the way I remembered it as a child. The way it had always been. After all. Christmas meant tradition.

Tradition at home in Haven Harbor, Maine, meant Santas on the mantel and a tree that touched the ceiling and filled the bay window overlooking our porch and the town Green beyond. I secretly believed one of my Victorian ancestors had added that window just to frame their Christmas tree. Patrick, the new man in my life, and I had cut this year's tree and he'd helped me balance it in the Christmas tree stand Mama and Gram had used before me.

Now Gram was married to Reverend Tom, and had new ways of celebrating the holiday, many of them involving his ministerial duties and the rest of his church family. She was taking their first Christmas as a married couple in stride. They'd also started establishing their own traditions, like hanging only silver and blue balls on their tree.

My tree would be mostly gold and red, plus ornaments I'd made with Mama and in elementary school and Girl Scouts, and a few new ones (some needle-pointed) that I'd added this year. It wouldn't be as color-coordinated as Gram's tree, but it would be beautiful. It would be mine. My first as a grownup, on my own. I hadn't thought to have a tree in my Arizona apartment. Life there had been temporary.

As usual, Gram was right. The gold box was under a string of colored lights Patrick and Dave hadn't used when they'd covered the tree with tiny white lights. I opened the box carefully, hoping the ornament would be as I remembered it.

It was a large, lopsided star I'd made out of wire from a coat hanger covered with aluminum foil. I'd proudly brought it home from kindergarten and given it to Mama to top our tree. After that, it was always the first ornament on the tree. I remembered Mama's perfume mixing with the pine smell of the tree each year as she lifted me high enough so I could put my star on the very top branch.

When I was a teenager I'd talked about replacing my star with something more elegant. But secretly I loved it and the years it represented: Christmases with Mama.

Now back in Haven Harbor after ten years working for a private investigator in Phoenix, that star meant "home," despite how much I'd changed since I'd last seen it. In the six—almost seven—months I'd been back in Maine not only had Gram married Reverend Tom, but she'd given me our family home and decided I should be the one to run Mainely Needlepoint, her custom needlepoint business. And, of course, I'd met Patrick.

I climbed the paint-spattered stepladder I'd brought in from the barn and carefully wound a wire around the base of the star, attaching it to the top of the tree.

Now I was ready for Christmas.

Through the wide windows in back of the tree I could see the brightly lit Green. Members of the Chamber of Commerce had set small potted pine trees around the edges of the square, their branches wound with hundreds of tiny white lights. The town Christmas tree towered above them. Across the Green electric candles shone inside the wreaths hung on every window and door of the homes there.

Christmas in Haven Harbor was as it had always been.

This one would be the best ever.

Tonight my home was full of friends I'd invited to

my tree-trimming party. Patrick West, the guy who wasn't perfect, but who made me smile. Sarah Byrne, who'd had a rocky few months but had become my closest friend. Dave Percy, who taught high school biology and whose poison garden intrigued me. Captain Ob and his wife, Anna, who'd had a difficult summer, but were now ready to ring in a new year. Ruth Hopkins, who did needlepoint when her arthritis allowed, and wrote books when it didn't. Katie Titicomb and Dr. Gus, parents of one of my high school friends. Clem Walker, a high school friend who lived in Portland and worked for Channel 7, but was now home for the holidays with her family. And, of course, Gram and Reverend Tom.

And Trixi. As the tree began to shake in its stand, I realized I hadn't seen her in a few minutes.

I reached through the wide branches and caught her: one small black kitten, on her way to the top. She jumped from my arms and skittered to her favorite hiding spot in back of the couch.

Last Christmas had meant white lights twinkling on Saguaro cactuses and dinner with my boss in a Mexican food diner. I hadn't even hung a wreath on my apartment door. In Arizona pine wreaths cost a small fortune.

Here in Maine making wreaths was a cottage industry. People sold them on the side of the road, out of their trucks, the way they sold blueberries in late July. For the cost of one wreath in Phoenix you could buy eight here. Mainers hung them on every door and window, and sometimes left them up until spring.

As I climbed down from the ladder, Patrick's arm went around me. "Penny for your thoughts? You look as though you left us for a while."

"I'm here." I smiled, turning around into his arms.

"Very happy to be right here." I stood on my toes and kissed his cheek. Who needed a kissing ball or mistletoe when Patrick was around?

He looked around the room, took a deep breath, and announced, "This is probably a good time for me to invite all of you to Aurora for a Christmas Eve party."

For a moment no one said anything.

"Skye will be back for Christmas?" I asked. Patrick's mother had spent the fall on a movie set in Scotland.

"Mom's been saying the cast and crew would work through Christmas, but then there were rain delays in Glasgow and script problems. She called last night to say they'd decided to close the set for the holidays, and she was coming here. And she's bringing with her some of the others working on the film."

"Really?" Clem asked. "Anyone famous?"

Clem was the only one of us who'd never met Patrick's mother, Skye West, a stage and screen actress who'd bought Aurora as a retreat, far from the pressures of Hollywood. We'd all made it an unwritten rule that she should have the privacy she valued.

Patrick looked at Clem. I suspected he'd just realized my old friend was also a member of the media. By issuing a general invitation, he'd included her. "Her co-star, Paul Carmichael, is coming, and an actress I don't know, Blaze Buchanan. And Thomas and Marie O'Day, the screenwriters, will be here reworking the end of the script with Marv Mason, who's directing."

"Wow!" Clem breathed. "I'm a real Paul Carmichael fan. He's gorgeous. And Marv Mason has won two Oscars!"

"Sounds like a working holiday," Ruth Hopkins pointed out.

"Exactly. Mom said there've been problems on the set they hope to work out while they're here. She sounded distracted. Plus, she wants me to decorate the house in what she termed 'Maine Christmas fashion,' so all is 'as she dreamed' when she arrives." Patrick smiled, but looked tense. "Her plane gets in December twentieth."

"She wants you to decorate the whole house in two days?" I gasped. Skye's house was enormous.

Reverend Tom shook his head. "Sounds as though she's been watching old Christmas movies and thinking about Currier and Ives prints. This is Haven Harbor. Not a movie set."

"Exactly," Patrick said glumly. "She even rattled off a list of what she wants—garlands everywhere, and an enormous tree, of course. And that's just the beginning. She wants a horse-drawn sleigh and carolers. And an elegant lobster dinner for Christmas Eve. Which you're all invited to."

Silence.

Ob was the first to speak. "I'll help you with the tree, Patrick. What are neighbors for? But Anna and I've planned a quiet Christmas this year, just the two of us. I'm afraid we'll have to pass on the invite to your fancy party."

"Gus and I will be heading to Blue Hill for Christmas with the grandkids," said Katie. "We won't be in town Christmas Eve."

"I'd be happy to come," Sarah said quickly. "And you'll be here then, right, Dave?"

"I'd thought of spending the holidays in Boston, But sure. I can come Christmas Eve." Dave looked cornered.

"I'll come," said Ruth, quietly.

"I'll be there for sure," Clem put in.

"And I'll help you decorate," I put in. Like Ob and Anna, I'd looked forward to a quiet Christmas, mine with Gram and Tom. And Patrick, of course. But now Patrick had other obligations.

"I'd really appreciate that," he said, squeezing my hand. "I know most of Mom's friends in the movie business. I'm afraid there may be more drama at Aurora than Haven Harbor is used to."

"Just as long as any dramas stay there," said Reverend Tom quietly. "Here in town we're pretty set in our ways of celebrating the holidays. After all, Christmas is a religious holiday and a time for families to celebrate together. Not a spectacle."

"I understand," Patrick nodded. "I do."

His hand tightened on mine.

He might understand. But did his mom and her Hollywood friends? My dream of a quiet, perfect Maine Christmas was fading fast.

Connect with Us

Visit us online at
KensingtonBooks.com
to read more from your favorite authors, see books
by series, view reading group guides, and more.

for sneak peeks, chances to win books and prize packs,
and to share your thoughts with other readers.

facebook.com/kensingtonpublishing
twitter.com/kensingtonbooks

Tell us what you think!

To share your thoughts, submit a review,
or sign up for our eNewsletters, please visit:
KensingtonBooks.com/TellUs.